BY YOUR SIDE

A FRIENDS TO LOVERS ROMANCE

Southern Charms Book Two

Kat Long

Cover Design: Kris Guiao
Editing: Rebecca Colvin of Just Ask Her Production, LLC

For Clarie Kingsley.
Your resilience is breathtakingly beautiful.
#AlphasForDavid #LoveForClaire

1 - JENNA

Oh, my God. That feels so freaking good.

"Right there," I hissed as his strong, warm hands caressed my back, pinching and kneading the tight muscles.

Grasping the edges of the table, I struggled to keep still and not moan any louder as waves of pleasure rolled through my naked body. This man was turning me into mush. The room smelled like lavender, and I focused on the soft music coming from the speaker in the corner as he moved lower, down past my shoulders to a tender spot right above my butt.

"A little to the right." The breathy voice squeaking through my lips was so unlike my usual bravado, but I could have cared less as the thin white sheet slipped further down my exposed back.

Don't stop.

A soft moan escaped my lips, and my toes curled when his hands hit that one particular area that needed all of his concentration. I gripped the table harder and closed my eyes as he dug his thumbs in deeper, dimpling the skin.

What was his name again? Fred? George? Ron? Honestly, it didn't matter, as long as he kept touching me. I moaned again, but it must have sounded like a grunt because he stopped his caresses. Sitting up, I tried blowing my hair out of my face but somehow only managed to make him back up further.

"Um, are you okay?" he said.

Propping my elbows up and ensuring my boobs were covered, I turned to glare at Mr. Muscles. There he stood in all his tall, Norwegian glory. He tilted his head and raised his eyebrows, waiting for me to tap-out, or at least speak.

"Yes. I'm more than okay, Mr. Muscles. No safe word here. Do your worst."

Oh. My. God. Backtrack!

"I mean. I'm sorry, Sir. Please continue." Mumbling and mortified, I hiked the sheet up higher before face-planting back on the massage table. It was the only way to save myself the embarrassment of looking into his ice-blue eyes.

After another second and some serious telepathic communication, his hands began their firm caresses again, moving down my legs and to the balls of my feet.

Thank goodness I remembered to shave.

The last thing I needed was to damage his perfect hands with my prickly leg hair.

Just once, I'd like to not worry about shaving, pedicures, and the thousand other little things we, women, do to look presentable. There was nothing wrong with a bit of makeup and self-care, but most days, I came home covered in dog hair and cat scratches—the life of a vet and all that. I mean, a ferret peed on me yesterday, but at least my manicure was on point.

My nameless guy with the magic hands pressed down hard on the arch of my foot, and another moan slipped out. This time, I didn't hide the sound. I whimpered and shuddered, making him press down harder.

"Is this too much for you, Miss Crews?" he said, using those magic hands to caress the pressure point he'd agitated.

"No," was all I managed to whisper before he continued to mold and reshape my body into one that wasn't overflowing with stress and indecision. I breathed deep and closed my eyes, focusing on his hands, the music, and how good I felt.

Either I dozed off or passed out with pleasure because all too soon, he closed the door with a click and told me quietly to get up and dressed when I was ready, and there'd be cucumber water with strawberries waiting for me up front. I swear I heard him say it was a pleasure serving me today, but my body still had to be high on endorphins from the last hour spent under his spell.

"Cucumber water? Count me in," I said to myself as I groaned and stood up. The promise of fruit and hydration was the only thing keeping me from pulling the thin sheet higher and falling back asleep.

My muscles felt looser than they had in years, and I stumbled around for my clothes, trying to regain the feeling in my legs that Mr. Magic Hands had turned into jelly. Dragging on my green scrub pants and a matching top with tiny porcupines wearing pink bows, I turned on my phone only to be rewarded with several text messages, all from the same person—the bane of my existence—Dr. Duvall.

He hadn't always been an ass, and I didn't understand what was with the sudden mood swings.

When we first met, he took a chance on me, right out of vet school, and welcomed me into his practice, *Animal Medical Clinic, AMC* for short, but the vet techs and I had noticed a change within the last year. He'd become short-tempered and more concerned with making money instead of the animals under our care.

Peering at my phone, I sighed and shook my head at what he'd sent—an itemized list of the treatment plan I used on a sweet, stray dog before a young couple adopted him. Of course, I'd pay the cost like always, but this time he ended the message with a snarky comment about prohibiting stray animals into the clinic.

I started working with him four years ago when he said he was looking to partner with someone straight out of vet school, someone for him to take under his wing. At twenty-eight, it wasn't like I was a teenager, but that was how he treated me most days.

All the work Mr. Magic Hands had done was gone. A tension headache started as I made my way to the front of the spa. The receptionist handed me a tall glass of cucumber water and motioned me to one of the lounge chairs, where a small plate of fruit was waiting. My phone beeped again, reminding me that my responsibilities came first, no matter how frustrated I was with Dr. Duvall and what he was doing to *AMC*.

Annaleigh: Hope you enjoyed your day. It only took you three months to use your present, lol. Thank you again for always taking care of my boy. Love you!
Me: Anytime. Drinking delicious cucumber water before heading back to the clinic.
Annaleigh: Hate that you have to go back to work, but you are killing it on the job front! Lunch this week?
Me: Absolutely. I'll text you later.
Annaleigh: Sounds like a plan. Don't let Dr. Dumbass get you

down.

Me: Thank you, I won't.

Annaleigh: I hope not. You're too damn talented to get hung up on what one old fart thinks.

Smiling now, I slipped my phone back in my scrub pants and made my way to the front desk, stopping to glance at the aromatherapy lotions.

"Miss Crews, I hope you found your treatment today to your liking. Your certificate includes three, so I took the liberty of booking your next appointment, with Charlie, of course."

My inner lioness did a little growl of approval. "Thank you, it was. I look forward to using Charlie again."

Geezus, I sounded like a perve.

But knowing I'd see Mr. Muscles again released a smidge of my ever-present stress. The massages had been a gift—a sweet but unnecessary gesture from my friend Annaleigh and her boyfriend Max to say thank you for saving their fur baby. It was nothing but a lucky coincidence. One evening, I was walking Baxter, Annaleigh's boxer, when he ate something toxic. Activated charcoal was in my truck, and Baxter had no lasting issues. Nonetheless, I was grateful to have access to Mr. Muscles.

On the way back to the clinic, I rolled down the windows in my red SUV, enjoying the balmy seventy-degree weather and making a quick detour to a plant nursery, staying long enough to grab a little cactus in a small ceramic pot for my desk.

Upon finally arriving at *AMC*, the lights were off, and relief washed through me.

No humans to deal with...

Opening the door as quietly as possible, I took my clogs off and tiptoed to my office, not wanting to wake the animals tuckered out for the night.

"Meow. Meow. Meow."

Dang-it!

Peeking around my door was Chick, a petite calico cat with her ears back and hackles raised.

"How's my girl?" She stared at me for a moment before hopping closer on three legs. Picking her up, she settled on my lap while I completed the unfinished charts from the day.

"I tried to be quiet, Chick. I know you were sleeping. Did you get enough snuggles today?"

The sweet furball looked at me and meowed again, attracting another stowaway that brushed against my leg. Reaching down, I scooped up Duck, our white and gray short-hair cat, and laid him next to Chick. They booped noses before settling contently on my lap.

We adopted Chick and Duck as our office cats after one of our oldest clients passed away. They were a bonded pair, and the vet techs and I couldn't bear the thought of separating them. We shared their responsibility, but I had a particular soft spot for these two because they were the only cats that liked me.

Several hours later, my eyes felt like sandpaper, and I had finished the last of my charting and checked the appointment book. Stella, the bulldog, was due for a C-section, and Herman, the Great Dane, was having a hip replaced. I stuck a note on my computer with those reminders and shut everything down before standing up to stretch, feeling the good ache Mr. Magic Hand's muscular touch left.

As I made my way to the exit, I slung my backpack over my shoulder and slipped my clogs back on, pulling out my short brown ponytail and running my hands through my hair. Then I completed my initial lock-up routine of the office, set the alarm, and took one step outside when bright headlights turned into the parking lot.

It took a minute for me to register the light bar on top of the vehicle and the push-bumper. By the time I figured out it was a police officer, I had one hand lifted in greeting and the other one shading my eyes from his headlights.

Had I accidentally set off the alarm? Was there something wrong?

I waited for the officer to pull beside my car, and when he did, the door opened and out stepped a man as tall as a sequoia. No, a cypress. Was there anything taller than a cypress? *Yep.* This guy.

I looked up, then kept looking as he stepped out and walked my way. His hair was light blonde, cropped close to his scalp, and in the dim light, I could see tattoos peeking out of his shirt collar and down both arms. He looked solid and hard, with broad shoulders that stretched his uniform shirt across his upper body.

He was holding his hands close to his chest, whispering to something as he came closer. Moving quieter than someone his size should, he lifted a hand in greeting.

More tattoos. Nice.

He didn't smile, and he didn't grin, only cradled his other hand next to his body, like he was protecting something tiny.

When our eyes met, I was suddenly facing the most beautiful set of dark eyes I'd ever seen. They were brilliant and fierce and appeared to be glowing in the moonlight. A million thoughts were bouncing around in my head, but I was speechless.

I couldn't think.

I couldn't move.

He stepped closer and reached out, touching my arm.

"Miss? Are you okay?"

I shook my head and nodded, tearing my eyes away from his to answer.

"Yes, thank you. We're closed for the day, but is there something I can help you with?" I said, trying to sound as professional as possible and not relay the awkwardness I felt.

I squared my shoulders and reached out to shake his hand. He grasped mine and shook firmly. His hand was rough and warm, but I managed to nod at where his hand rested protectively.

"Yes, ma'am. My name is Officer Mark Hansen, and I apologize for the late hour, but I have a tiny problem and need assistance."

2 - MARK

My Ford Interceptor Utility SUV cruised down the highway, and I ran my hand over the familiar leather. It had been an uneventful day—a few speeding tickets, a minor fender bender with no injuries, and paperwork, but even after an easy twelve-hour shift, I was ready for a shower, food, and bed. Even gaming couldn't hold my attention.

I hadn't been shopping lately, but there had to be peanut butter in the pantry or something in the freezer I could microwave. My phone flashed with a message, but I waited until I pulled up to a red light to check, shaking my head when I saw it was a group text from my brothers.

Mil: You off work yet? Want to grab a beer?
Me: Not tonight. Maybe this weekend
Mag: Told you he'd say no
Mav: He always says no
Me: No I don't

Mil: Whatever bro. What ominous sign did you see today?

Mav: You walked underneath a ladder?

Mag: You broke a mirror?

Mav: You saw a black cat break a mirror into thirteen pieces?

Me: Assholes

Mav: GIF of a middle finger

Mil: Tell Us! Don't make us add mom to this thread. You know you're her favorite.

Me: Ugh. Fine. No signs. Yet.

Mag: Oooohhhh. Mr. Big Bad Police Officer getting nervous? Better rub that rabbit's foot!

Me: Assholes

Mil: Temper, temper.

Me: I'm driving

Mag: And setting a bad example for all of us regular folks that know you're not supposed to text and drive. Update us on the house tomorrow. Later, Bark E. Mark.

Ugh, I hated that stupid nickname. I dropped my phone on the seat, muttering about my dumbass brother. My five o'clock shadow was rough on my palm as I scrubbed my hand over my face, but I was off for the next week, so a shave could wait until I got a good night's sleep—nothing like a forced vacation to do absolutely nothing. I smoothed down my mustache and put my hands back in the ten-and-two position, waiting for the light to turn green.

If I'd taken them up on that beer, it would have gotten me out of my head for the night, but then I'd have to listen to them razz me and end up driving one of their drunk asses home.

Nope.

I had plenty of things to occupy my time without worrying about them. The front porch steps desperately needed replacing, and the bathroom on the second floor had a leaky faucet. The whole point of buying my childhood home was so I could restore it to its original glory, and this vacation was my time to do exactly that.

My radio squawked, and I reached forward, listening to dispatch.

"Officer Hansen, come in."

"Hansen here, go ahead."

"We got a call about an older lady in a bathrobe dragging a ladder down the road."

Oh great.

Dispatch didn't have to say another word. I knew who it was. On the off chance I was wrong, I reached under my shirt and rubbed the horseshoe pendant my dad gave me before joining the force. There was only one reason dispatch would call me on a non-traffic violation at the end of my shift.

Mrs. Lovejoy.

We jokingly called her Loony because that's exactly what she was. Her husband died something like twenty years ago, and with each passing decade, she went further off the deep end.

We got a call about her once a month, and I was the lucky fuck that was usually asked to reign her in because she lived two streets over from me. It was never anything serious, mostly nosy neighbors afraid she'd hurt herself doing something dumb.

I hit my head against the headrest, not in the mood for her brand of crazy tonight. This past week had been a doozy. I helped my neighbor Jake out with a crazy stalker situation involving his assistant. My gut told me it was far from over, but I passed it up to my superior and hoped I was wrong.

"Hansen. Older female was last seen on Spinner's End. Do you require another officer to investigate?"

"Negative. I'll check it out."

I put the radio down harder than I should have, pushing my speed higher to get to my neighborhood.

Sure enough, Loony was dragging a ladder down the street in a flowered bathrobe with matching slippers. I gave my siren one quick blast, but she raised her arm and shoed me away like I was interrupting some big important mission. I blew out a deep breath and pulled my cruiser to the side of the road, jogging to catch up with her and that damn ladder.

I swear, somewhere, there was a big guy in white with a tranquilizer gun and a huge butterfly net looking for her.

Loony was struggling and breathing heavily. Her curlers were coming out of her long white hair and sticking out of her hairnet. She stopped for a second, letting the ladder drop on the road, and reached into her robe pocket, pulling out something and scattering it on the ground. I got closer and lifted my hand in greeting, but she ignored me and picked the ladder back up.

Damnit!

"Mrs. Lovejoy? What's going on here? Why are you dragging a ladder down the road?" I said, coming up right behind her and reaching for the ladder. She pulled it from my grip and shoed me away.

"Oh, you hush now, Mark Hansen, and go on about your business. Rhonda, down the road, said she saw a baby kitten around here. I'm too short and too old to be tramping about the woods, so I'm going to climb up the ladder to find the little rascal."

She continued to drag the ladder, leaving indents in the dirt, so

I walked in front of her and grabbed it. That got her attention. She straightened her barely five-foot frame, put a hand on her hip, and hit me with a mom glare that used to scare the hell out of me.

"I mean it! Don't make me call your mama. I will not leave a poor defenseless kitten in these woods all night."

She waved her hands around like the shrubbery, and surrounding bushes were a national forest instead of a patch of land separating two neighborhoods.

Loony grabbed the ladder back and set it up right there on the side of the road. She stepped on the first rung, then the second. Her foot slipped when she got to the third, and she tipped backward.

Oh shit!

I darted through the ladder, grabbing her by the waist and steadying her. As soon as she was safely on the ground, I stumbled backward, reaching for my rabbits' foot and horseshoe.

It wasn't bad luck. I didn't just walk under the ladder.

Mrs. Lovejoy shook her head and tried to push past me, but I stopped her.

"I'll find the kitten and bring your ladder back. You head on home."

She leveled me with that mom glare again but nodded, making her white hair bounce and another curler drop to the ground. I picked it up and handed it to her, and she reached into her robe pocket, pulling out a handful of something squishy.

"You're a good boy, Mark. Here. Use this. I'll be checking up on you tomorrow."

She held out her hand and passed me the slimy mess she had in her robe.

Gross.

It was ground hamburger meat, and I looked behind her and saw the globs she had dropped, hoping to attract the kitten.

Great.

The only thing I'd attract with a handful of raw meat was a rogue raccoon, I thought, as I watched her totter off muttering about buying more ground beef.

At least her intentions were good. It was bad enough she had two little sugar gliders and a pot-bellied pig named Pepper that constantly escaped her backyard.

The neighborhood started a Facebook Group called *Where's Pepper* so we would at least know where that damn pig was. Pepper was particularly fond of Ms. Petunia's cucumbers down the street and usually ended up there. Maybe I should start a petition to have a Hawaiian Luau complete with a pig-on-a-spit if Pepper ever reached a hundred pounds.

Nah. The pig was a menace, but I wasn't that heartless. I couldn't imagine her with a kitten, a pig, and those sugar gliders. I laid the ladder on the side of the road and moved through the brush, looking for the kitten. I thought about leaving, but what if Mrs. Lovejoy was right? If there was a kitten somewhere around here, it wouldn't last long. Briarwood had fox sightings at least once a week.

The prickly bushes scratched my arms and got caught on my pants as I pushed and trudged along. After ten minutes, I had to turn on my Mag-lite, and after twenty, my hands were bleeding. I hated giving up, but my eyes were gritty, and I was dead on my feet.

What sane person would go stumbling through the brush smelling like raw meat when there was a perfectly comfortable bed one street over?

I put my Mag-lite back in my utility belt and made my way back to my SUV. I slammed the door and grabbed sanitizer, slathering it over my hands to get rid of the meat smell. The Ford started with a growl, and I radioed back that all was well with Loony before pulling back on the road.

I'd barely made it thirty feet before a black flash ran in front of the vehicle. Slamming on the breaks, I lurched forward and hit the steering wheel with the palm of my hand.

What the hell?

I'd seen enough car accidents to get nervous when anything ran out in front of me, even if this thing was the size of a freaking tangerine. I mashed the button to turn on my flashers, and my hand went back to my pendant before I stepped out, keeping my headlights on to see what I'd almost hit.

There wasn't anything in front of my car, so I did a full circle around before getting on my hands and knees and shining my light underneath. On my second sweep, the light caught tiny blue eyes and jet-black fur. This little pipsqueak of a kitten was pressed against my left rear tire, its eyes tracking my movements.

Laying down on my stomach and scooting under my vehicle as best I could—the baby let out a pathetic squeak. Scooping it up and sliding out, I cradled it against my stomach.

I found the kitten, but what the hell do I do with it?

My palm opened, and my eyes found the kitten's. It stared back, unblinking. It was small and dirty, with big blue eyes and one bent ear. I couldn't take it home, and no shelters were open past five. It didn't look like it would make it overnight without help, but there was no way this devil was going to Loony either. She'd try to dress it in a tutu and make it ride Pepper before feeding it raw meat.

I wracked my brain for what to do when I remembered my buddy's vet clinic where he took his daughter's guinea pig. Deciding to start there, I grabbed a hoodie from the back seat and set the kitten in the hoodie. It made a squeak and burrowed deeper, wobbling around in a circle on skinny legs before falling to its side.

I pulled back on the highway and drove five under the speed limit while glancing at the cargo. This vet better still be open. There was no way I knew what to do with a kitten, especially a freaking black kitten. First, almost walking underneath a ladder, and now a black kitten most definitely crossing my path—it was too much.

I'd been superstitious since first hearing the rhyme about stepping on cracks. Even if I wasn't, having all those omens in one day would make me believe. My hoodie wasn't moving, so I nudged it with my finger at the next red light. It wiggled, and those two blue eyes peered back at me. Thank goodness. I couldn't imagine the number of amulets I'd have to wear to get rid of that bad juju.

I cracked my neck and gripped the steering wheel, fighting the urge to swerve around the cars that were all doing the speed limit. My body felt itchy, like for every moment I had this thing in my squad car, the longer my bad luck would last. I stole a glance over again, and it was still staring at me, unblinking.

AMC was coming up on my left, so I slowed down and automatically put my hand out to protect the demon spawn. It followed my hand without moving its head, and I swear the eyes changed from blue to red for a split second.

Creepy.

The lights were off at the clinic, but I pulled in, driving around to the back on the off chance someone was still inside.

There was a lone SUV in the lot, and I pulled in beside it, seeing a tall woman with short brown hair walking out of the back door. I reached over to grab the kitten, listening to its one meek little squeak and holding it close to my chest as I opened the door.

My boots crunched on the gravel as I stepped closer to the lady, shushing the kitten. She had beautiful dark eyes that were opened wide. I didn't mean to alarm her, but it wasn't like my tires squealed as I pulled in the lot with my light and sirens blazing. I lifted my hand in greeting, taking in her green scrubs and slender legs.

"Miss?"

In the parking lot lights, her features were clearer. Those big brown eyes were bright with flecks of hazel and got larger the longer I stood, and her brown hair was closer to auburn, barely touching her shoulders. Her narrow waist that tapered to curvy hips made my mouth water.

Touching her shoulder, she shook her head, coming back from wherever her mind had gone.

"Miss..." I stepped toward her. "Are you okay?"

After what felt like an eternity, she smiled.

"Yes, thank you. We're closed for the day, but is there something I can help you with?"

Her voice sounded sweet and assuring, like sticky salt-water taffy after a day at the beach. She offered me her hand to shake, and I took it, shaking firmly. Her hand was soft, but her grip was firm. She held my eyes confidently and tilted her head, waiting for me to respond.

"Yes, ma'am. My name is Officer Mark Hansen, and I apologize for the late hour, but I have a tiny problem and need assistance."

The kitten chose that moment to peek its head out from my hand and hiss, showing a row of tiny teeth. The woman shook her head and let go of my hand, looking down where it was rested in my hoodie.

I prided myself on being aloof, but I didn't want to be that way with her for some weird reason. I felt something deep in my chest when

I looked at her, something that made my blood heat and my palms sweat. Something that I forced myself to ignore as she leaned closer to the kitten.

"I'm Doctor Jenna Crews. Oh, and what do we have here, Officer Handsome? Er, um. Officer Hansen, I mean."

Even in the dim light, I couldn't miss the pink that crept up her neck. My inner caveman beat his chest at her accidental admission, and I puffed out said chest as I stretched my hand out. The kitten demon-spawn hissed again, and she pushed her purple framed glasses up with a grin.

Doctor Jenna Crews? More like Doctor Cutie-Pie.

"Yes. Dr. Cutie, I mean Crews." Teasing her, unable to keep the smile from my face. "I found this kitten and was hoping you'd take it off my hands since the shelters are closed."

"Yes, I see. Unfortunately, we are not in a position to take in stray animals, but I'm glad you didn't take it to a shelter."

My face fell as she reached out and picked up the kitten by the scruff of its neck, silencing another hiss. It tried to bat at her with weak paws, but she put her other hand on her hip and brought the kitten to her face, turning it this way and that.

"You hush. Quit acting like you have a pair."

"Why are you glad I didn't take the hell-spawn to a shelter?"

She turned around, still focused on the hissing spitfire, and reached into her backpack.

"Because black cats have one of the lowest adoption rates of all felines. People have the preconceived notion they are bad luck, so nobody wants them. It's horrible."

Well shit.

"I'll check her over." She lifted the kitten higher. "Yep, it's a girl, but she's tiny, Officer Hansen, and looks weak. She can't stay here. We don't have anyone on staff overnight tonight."

Damnit.

"She doesn't seem weak with the way she's hissing at you. Shouldn't vets have animal skills?"

That kitten was doing everything in its power to scramble away from her, but she didn't seem to be taken back by my abruptness. It lit a fire under her, and she narrowed her eyes and glared.

"Ugh, it's just cats. Freaking cats hate me. And shouldn't cops be a little less cliché? You're a walking advertisement for a bad seventies' porno with that mustache. What do you really use your big flashlight for?" She gestured to the light strapped to my utility belt.

I unclipped the light and held it up for her to see before flipping it in the air and catching it. I hit it against my palm, making her jump, then leaned down and met her eyes.

"Trust me. There is nothing cliché about any of my equipment."

She rolled her eyes and smiled. "Touché Officer Hansen. Let's see what we can do for her tonight."

I followed her through the back door watching her hips sway as she carried the kitten to an exam room. The room was small and bright, with several corkboards covered with pet pictures hanging on the walls, along with children's drawings and large posters of animals.

She sat the kitten in the middle of the exam table and wrapped it in the hoodie before turning and brushing past me. She smelled like something fruity, mixed with lavender and wet dog. Well, mostly like wet dog, but it wasn't as off-putting as I thought it would be. It kind of suited her.

"What are you doing?" I asked, right on her heels as she flitted around the back room, opening drawers and whispering to herself. I turned around and crossed my arms, leaning up against a metal counter while she worked.

"I'm going to give her a de-wormer and see if I can entice her to eat. She looks about three weeks old and will need extra care when you get home. You'll also need to pick up a litter box, more food, and formula."

"All that for something so tiny? Can you make me a list or something?"

"Sure, I can do that. Where do you live?"

"Briarwood," I said, rolling my shoulders, resigned this was going to be my responsibility until I could come up with a better option.

Dr. Crews stopped and tapped her chin before opening a small refrigerator and taking out a vial of yellow medicine. She shook it, then drew a small amount into a syringe.

"You're close to *Pet World*, and that's on my way home. I think they're open until nine. Look up the hours, and once I'm done checking her over, we can swing by."

"Oh, um, sure. Thanks," I said.

Was it weird she offered to go shopping with me? Did she do that often?

She looked at me again, and her eyes got wide. "Um. Making a list is just as easy. I didn't mean to impose or assume you needed help."

She looked at the floor, then the syringe, anywhere but me.

Sighing, I leaned back on the counter. "I'll check the hours. Thanks for offering. I wouldn't know where to begin."

"No problem."

The kitten was sleeping but opened her eyes and peered at Dr. Crews, hissing as she moved closer. She gave her the syringe with yellow medicine, then laid her back on the exam table with the food. The kitten stumbled forward and sniffed before hissing again and face planting into the bowl. Its face was covered with food as it ate, and after a minute, it started purring.

I hated to admit it, but that was pretty fucking cute. This little black nothing was scarfing down food like a boss and purring like a freight train.

Dr. Crews ignored the hissing and watched, whispering words of encouragement and praise. She stroked its fur, and when it finished, she wiped its mouth and put drops in its ears, earning another hiss.

"Alright, Officer Hansen," she said, taking the food away and putting the kitten back in the hoodie.

"Mark, please call me Mark."

"Okay, Mark, and you can call me Jenna. Your little girl looks pretty healthy. Let's set her up for success."

She turned to me and smiled, picking up the kitten and handing her over. The kitten turned to Jenna and hissed, then turned those blue eyes to me and slowly blinked. Once. Twice, before purring again.

Great.

BY YOUR SIDE

3 - JENNA

You can't keep this kitten at the clinic—Doctor Dumbass would freak out. Officer Handsome will be perfectly capable of finding her a home. *Plus, nine out of ten cats hate you,* I mumbled, shaking out my shoulder and wondering who the hell I ticked off in a past life. Maybe some sort of pet shaman, or a crazy cat lady, because Handsome was right. What kind of vet couldn't calm a one-pound kitten?

Me.

I peaked in on Chick and Duck before I locked the clinic door and walked to my SUV, trying to squash the nervousness brewing in my belly. The ridiculously good-looking cop was right behind me. His heavy footfalls echoed on the gravel while he whispered to the kitten like a gentle giant. My ovaries did a little somersault listening to him.

Somersault or not, his comment irritated me. I could have turned him away, could have brushed him off, but I didn't, regardless of how many times the black kitten hissed.

"They close at nine, right?" I said, pulling my hair back in a ponytail and unlocking the car door.

"Yeah. We have just over an hour. I'll meet you there, Dr. Cutie."

I rolled my eyes at the nickname but smiled as he brushed past me to his cruiser, opening the passenger door and arranging the kitten in the seat. Checking her over and nodding with satisfaction, he walked around to the driver's side and gave me a wave before getting in.

Waving back, I didn't wait for him to pull out first. Getting on the highway, I tried to use the easy drive to clear my head and think about the nonprofit I was volunteering with this weekend, not the sharp jawline and miles of muscles that was Officer Handsome when my check engine light blinked on.

That wasn't good.

I'd just replaced the water pump, and no regular maintenance was due. I hit the power button on the stereo and listened for any weird noises. Thank goodness whatever was wrong wasn't obvious. Maybe it was a malfunction. My SUV was close to ten years old. Odd stuff was bound to happen.

Pulling into *Pet World,* it was hard to worry about any potential car trouble when I spotted him walking closer. He'd changed out of his uniform shirt and was wearing a dark T-shirt that did nothing to take away from his thick, corded forearms.

In his hands was the hoodie, and two tiny ears were peeking over the hood.

Holy hotness.

His black boots were polished to a shine. You could see your reflection in them, and his eyes were darting this way and that, completely aware of his surroundings. He looked like a force to be reckoned with, and kitten or not, it was intimidating as hell.

He strode past me, then looked over his shoulder and raised his eyebrows like I was putting him behind schedule.

"Thank you for taking what I said about caring for her to heart," I said, taking several steps to catch up with him. Mark nodded and looked left and right, clearly unsure of where he was going.

"Alright, Dr. Cutie," he said. "Lead the way."

He swept one arm in front of him, then brought it to the top of the kitten's head, giving her a little scratch. Tugging on his arm, I grabbed a buggy and pulled him toward the cat section. I noticed a large compass tattoo covering his forearm and sweeping down his hand as we walked. The intriguing design had me staring as we headed down the first aisle, gathering items.

He picked out a pink cat bed, and I bit my lip to keep from smiling when I watched him pick up a tiny purple collar with sparkles and a bell. He hid it under the cat bed and cleared his throat, piling cat toys on top.

"No, Mark. Get this one," I said as he picked up the biggest litter box on the shelf. "She's too small to use that." I picked up a shallow box and a small bag of litter, putting them in the cart.

"But if I get the bigger one, I won't have to scoop cat turds as often," he said, running his hands through his hair.

"Yeah, and when she can't get into the box, she'll leave a nice little present for you somewhere in your house."

"Damnit. Okay," he said, putting his choice back and grabbing the buggy from me. "So, how many pets do you have?"

"None. Just plants." I tossed a feathered rattler in the buggy for Chick and Duck. He stopped pushing and looked at me with his eyebrows pinched. I raised mine in confusion. "What?"

"Nothing. I just don't get it. You're a vet, but you don't have any pets, and cats hate you," he said like I was some great mystery to be solved.

"Um. I have a ton of plants and a pregnant possum that lives underneath my back porch. But those wouldn't count as pets in the traditional sense. I feel like I'm too busy to take care of a pet."

"The way you took care of this spitfire, I just figured you had a whole herd of animals."

Mark shrugged his shoulders and patted the kitten's head, picking up a container of treats. I took it from him and replaced it with a better brand before smiling. I was figuring him out. He was gruff and to the point, but not an asshole in any way. More like he wasn't going to waste his time saying fifty words when fifteen would do.

I tossed a squeaky toy in the buggy and looked at him. "Nope. Just a vet who loves plants and is a treasure-trove of useless facts."

"Tell me one then, Dr. Cutie."

"Did you know there are volcanic snails?" I said, not missing a beat. "They're called Scaly-Foot Snails, live by hydrothermal vents, and are the only known living creature that incorporates iron into its skeleton."

"Seriously? That's wicked. Where did you learn that?"

"I wish I could tell you it was when I was interning with volcanic researchers in Hawaii, but really, I just read it in a book."

"Wow. You and I read vastly different books."

"Hmm, let me guess," I said, making a big deal of stopping and putting my hand on my hip like I was thinking hard. "You're into spy novels and espionage."

"Bingo." He smiled, showing off straight, white teeth. "Tell me about volcanic snail books." He glanced at our haul before picking up one last toy and motioning to the checkout. I nodded and took my items from the cart, but he took them right back and shook his head.

"Oh. Thank you, Mark."

He nodded his head and raised his eyebrows, waiting for me to answer the question.

"Right, well, I read a bit of everything. Romance, Science Fiction, Marine Terror, even Blue Aliens."

"Marine Terror? What the hell is that?"

"Oh. It's about prehistoric giant sharks and ocean animals, showing up in present day."

"Seriously?"

"Totally," I said. "There are some awesome authors out there."

I pretended not to notice that the cashier was ringing him up with the biggest, gooiest smile on her face. Mark took it all in stride, barely acknowledging her and answering with grunts and nods.

Letting out a barely audible, "Thanks," he gathered up the bags in one hand, held the kitten in the other, and strode out the automatic door like he owned the place.

"So listen, thank you for this." He followed me to my SUV and stood there like all the bags were filled with feathers and not a ton of supplies.

"Sure." I took a business card from my wallet, scribbled my cell on the back, and tucked it in his front pocket. "Call or text if anything comes up. I can usually answer quicker at this number than if you call the clinic."

"Yeah, I'll do that."

"Bye, Officer Handsome."

"Bye, Dr. Cutie."

I shut the door with a smile, putting my key in the ignition. Mark opened the back door of his cruiser to put in the bags but made no move to leave. I guess he was waiting for me to go, so I cranked my SUV.

Nothing happened.

I tried again. And again.

On the third try, I laid my head back, trying to remember if I had renewed my Triple-A membership when Mark opened my door, startling me.

"What happened?"

"I don't know. The check engine light came on earlier. I was just going to look for my Triple-A card now."

"Don't worry about that. Come on. I'll drive you home. Where do you live?" He motioned with his head because his hands were full.

"Oh, no. You don't have to do that."

"Truly, it's the least I could do, Jenna."

Having him give me a lift would be easier than waiting for a tow in the humid night air, but I didn't want to put him out. Scrunching my eyebrows, I stared at him.

"I don't mind," he said as if he knew what I was thinking. "Where do you live?"

"Magnolia Crescent, but I don't want to impose."

"Jenna," he rumbled, his voice sounding like smooth whiskey over ice. "It's my pleasure. Now, come on."

Sighing, I reached over to grab my bag before getting out of the SUV and locking the door.

He plucked the keys from my hand. "We'll leave the ignition key under the wheel well. I'll call a friend of mine to come and check it out."

"No, seriously. That's too much," I said, shaking my head and trying to grab the keys back.

"If I minded, I wouldn't have offered. I'm happy to give you a ride."

Reaching his cruiser, he carefully passed me the sleeping kitten and took the key from the keyring. He ran back and tucked the key under the wheel well.

I bit my lip, willing my cheeks not to blush as he came back to open the door for me.

"At least let me come over and help you set all this up as thanks," I said, sliding into the seat.

Oh my God, Jenna. You offered to go shopping with him, and now you've invited yourself to his house? How hard is it to throw litter in a box and food in a bowl?

He gave me a look I couldn't read, then walked around to the driver's side and pulled out his phone, talking low, probably to his friend about my SUV. I tried to be casual, taking my phone out of my pocket and answering a text from my friend Addison about grabbing dinner next week. I was tapping my foot on the floorboard when he opened the door and got behind the wheel with a smile.

"Thanks for the offer, Jenna. That would be helpful. I'd love for you to come..." And he winked.

BY YOUR SIDE

4 - MARK

*O*ver. I'd love for you to come over.

I shook my head and cracked my neck. Leaving out that one word was messing with my mind, filling it with images that would make a stripper blush. I started the cruiser and touched the Evil-Eye pendant hanging from the turn-signal lever, looking both ways and heading past Magnolia Crescent to my neighborhood.

Jenna took in all the gears and gadgets on the dashboard while her foot tapped out a steady beat on the floor.

"I didn't mean to invite myself over. I'm sure you're more than capable of setting up shop, and you must be tired," she said, staring out the window. She looked calm, but that foot-tapping said otherwise, so I cleared my throat and tried to put her mind at ease.

"Well, you invited yourself shopping with us," I said, making a right-hand turn. "I figured you'd be tagging along tonight."

"What? Really?"

I had to smile, and it took her a second to return it, but when she did, her entire face lit up, and I had a hard time focusing on the road.

I wasn't prepared for what that smile did to me, almost as if Jenna was giving me some rare gift by letting me see the light in her eyes. Gripping the steering wheel, I felt vulnerable and out of my element, hoping we could ride the rest of the way in silence so I could push whatever this was back down from where it came.

"Are you superstitious?" Jenna asked a few minutes later, pointing to where I was absentmindedly rubbing the pendant.

"Um, yeah, I am." I forced myself not to elaborate, waiting for her to laugh.

"Did you know that psychologists have proven people who believe in superstitions have less stress?"

What? Was this chick for real?

"Less stress?" I repeated, turning into Briarwood.

"Yeah, and if you have any superstitious rituals before playing a sport, you perform better. It's science." She shrugged her shoulders as if she calmed a man's nerves every day when he admitted a part of himself most people thought was ridiculous.

Jenna leaned forward as I turned down my cul-de-sac and wound around the driveway.

"Wow, Mark. Your house is beautiful," she said, taking in the wrap-around porch and red shutters. Pausing to look for a moment, she was right. I had finished the landscaping before the southern weather became scorching and noticed the gardenias had bloomed.

"Thanks," I replied, pushing the garage door button and pulling in. "I grew up here."

"You did? That's amazing you moved in."

"Yeah?" I said, turning off the cruiser.

This house needed work, but it wasn't done making memories.

"Yeah. You can feel the love this house has. I'd love to live in my

42

childhood home. It's a two-story blue house with a gigantic oak tree in the back and a witch window in the attic. I remember my dad spending a summer sanding down the floors and building me a nook where I could read and watch the birds."

I was speechless. I'd always been a man of few words, but this pretty girl, with her bright smile and useless facts, made my skin tingle. Not in a bad way, but unfamiliar. The second I saw her walking out of the clinic, I felt my stomach flip-flop like I'd just pummeled down a thousand-foot roller-coaster without being strapped in.

I had to get myself together, make a comfortable place for the kitten, rub a four-leaf clover, and go the hell to sleep.

Walking in the kitchen, I put the bags on the granite island. She did the same as if she was waiting for me to talk. Deep hazel eyes, almost as dark as chocolate, stared back at me. They were beautiful, mysterious, eyes any sane man could get lost in—I should say something, anything. I should ask her if she wants something to drink or order a pizza. I should thank her again or ask her on a date.

Date? Where did that come from…Pffft date. What?

That was the last thing I needed. I was better alone, happier. I'd seen too many guys on the force get divorced because their wife couldn't handle the job, the hours, the commitments. I remembered my dad's words, *'if I could do it all over again, I wouldn't.'*

When I decided to become a cop, I chose to be a lifelong bachelor. I was going to be the cool uncle with the big house. Nothing more.

"Okay, right," she said, tapping her foot on the floor and probably assuming my silence was something other than my world being slightly tilted on its axis. "Let's get her set up in the master bathroom. You'll want her in an enclosed space with a tile floor for the first week or two. Lead the way."

I mumbled my thanks, grabbing all the bags and breezing through the kitchen and living room, then walking up the stairs and down the hallway. Stopping in front of my closed door, I took a breath and faced Jenna, rubbing the back of my neck.

"You'll have to excuse the room. I wasn't exactly expecting company," I said before stepping in to turn on the light.

Aside from a pair of gray sweatpants laying haphazardly on the bed, the room was clutter-free, but I still felt the need to apologize. Who knew why? The blue curtains were closed over the large bay windows that overlooked the backyard, and my black chest of drawers and matching nightstands were practically empty. I laid the bags on the gray comforter as she walked in behind me and laughed.

"Are you serious, Mark? Are you apologizing for dust-bunnies under the bed? This room is immaculate. I'll bet the bed even has hospital corners."

"What? It does not," I answered.

Yes, it does.

"Hmm. Not only am I fairly certain you're lying, but there is nothing wrong with a neat room. It says a lot about your personality. Me, on the other hand, I can't remember if I made my bed this morning."

"My personality? You're not going to try to guess my sign next, are you?"

I scratched my stubble and blew out a breath as she walked by me to the bed, running her hand down the comforter before giving me a sly grin.

"No, but I'll bet I could. Tell you what, if your bed doesn't have hospital corners, I'll tell you an embarrassing thing about me. And if it does, you'll tell me an embarrassing thing about you."

"Why?" I said before I could stop myself.

For once, I wished my room wasn't neat and organized because learning something embarrassing about this mystery in front of me sounded better than anything else I'd do tonight. Maybe the kitten purring in Jenna's arms was really a good luck charm meant to bring Jenna into my life.

Nope. Don't start thinking like that.

Maybe I needed to get laid. This love affair with my hand was getting old. My exhausted mind had to be grasping at straws.

"I knew it," Jenna said, flipping the comforter up to reveal neat, hospital corners.

"But I never agreed to anything," I countered, grabbing the sweatpants and throwing them in the closet.

"Well, it was worth a try, Mr. Grumpy."

Before walking to the bathroom, she handed me the kitten and got to work, smoothing down the comforter and picking up the cat bed. Flipping on the light, I watched as she set up the bed and eyed the giant clawfoot tub. She swept her eyes over the large walk-in shower, black and white tile floor, and dual sinks before turning back to me.

"Grab the bowls, mix some food, and give her water," she said, snapping me out of my trance.

I blinked, shaking my head again as I dumped kitten food in a bowl and set a water dish beside it before taking the kitten and putting her in front of the food.

"Is this normal?" I gestured to the way she had face-planted into the food again, eating louder than an old man slurping soup at a deli.

Jenna laughed and crouched down beside me, low enough for me to get a tempting peek at her cleavage. My eyes were drawn to her creamy skin, making me lose all rational thought when her tits swelled

45

as she laughed.

"Oh yes," she said as I dragged my eyes away. "We don't know how long she's been on her own. She needs to eat small meals every few hours. She'll calm down after a few days."

Her shoulders shook as she laughed, a strand of hair falling across her face. I found my hand moving before I did. My fingers caressed the soft skin of her cheek as I brushed it behind her ear. I heard the hitch in her breath, and the tension rode up my arm, my body itching to get closer to her.

She turned her head to face me, my hand staying dangerously close to the back of her neck. It would take nothing to bring her closer.

"Meow," came a cock blocking squeak, pulling us both out of whatever the fuck was happening.

"I could use that embarrassing moment now," she said, standing up and smoothing back that same strand of hair.

"The last date I went on asked me if I was a traffic cop because I failed at being a regular cop."

I froze and pursed my lips, standing up to let the kitten slurp her food in peace.

Where the hell had that come from?

That was beyond embarrassing and straight into uncomfortably awkward. I freaking talk to people for a living, and here I was, tongue-tied by a beautiful doctor who was taking time out of her night to help me.

"I can't believe someone would say that to you."

Great. Sympathy.

I didn't need sympathy. I only agreed to that stupid date to get my idiot brothers off my back, and all it left me with was a comment that stuck with me. It festered, appearing when I least expected it to ruin my day.

"It's not a big deal," I said, walking back to the bedroom and turning on the television. A rerun of *Friends* was on, and I adjusted the volume then leaned against the bathroom door.

"Oh," she said, glancing behind me at the television with her arms crossed. "Can I tell you a story?"

"Sure." I rubbed the back of my neck and picked up the kitten, cleaning her like Jenna did earlier and getting up the purple collar from the bed to fit around her neck before setting her back down.

"About five years ago, I got into a car accident. I was coming through an intersection, and a truck ran a red light, T-boning me. I remember every detail. The screech of tires, the crunch of metal. My pounding heart. The smell of burning rubber, of blood. It was one of the scariest moments of my life. My airbag deployed, but I hit my head and fractured my leg."

She pointed to a thin line across her forehead, and I reached out to run my fingers along the pale line. Her body language changed, and she leaned in, but I stopped with my hand inches away and shoved them in my pockets with a sigh.

"It was a traffic cop that was first on the scene, Mark. A traffic cop held my hand and pressed gauze to my forehead. He told me silly, stupid stories to calm me down and comforted me when I cried. He rode with me to the hospital and stayed until my parents came. So, yeah. I know I've only known you for all of five minutes, but good riddance to anyone that would say something that shitty to you."

Jenna.

My heart was roaring in my ears to thank her and touch her, but I was frozen like my subconscious knew everything would change if I did.

47

Fuck it.

I reached out and took her hand, pulling her to me to crush her against my chest. She stiffened, but I didn't let go. She felt too good. I rested my chin on her head and wrapped my arms around her back. I felt it the moment she hugged me back. She took a breath and leaned into me, lifting her arms to my waist.

She molded to my body, and the roaring in my ears stopped, leaving only our steady breaths. My mouth was dry as she clutched my shirt, holding on to me as hard as I was her. In the silence, enveloped in her warmth, my senses came alive like the Fourth of July. Every nerve ending was on fire, and each time I breathed, her hair moved, filling my nose with the scent of peaches. She nuzzled against my shirt like she was breathing me in, and the thought made my cock twitch in my slacks.

Her cheeks were flushed, and I swallowed as her eyes followed my movements. It was almost cruel when her pink tongue darted out to wet the seam of her lips. Tantalizing. Daring me to bring my mouth closer to her, daring me to find out if her whole body tasted like peaches.

I wanted to cup her jaw, kiss her scar, and tangle my fingers in her hair. Instead, I slowly released my grip, resting my hands on her hips.

"Jenna," I rumbled, trying to convey my thanks for everything and trying to put more in the hug than I could in a hundred useless words. I wanted nothing more than to show her my gratitude.

"Thank you for earlier this evening, for that story, and for now."

The air in the bedroom was stifling and too thick while Jenna's eyes burned into mine, turning me to ash and making me question things that used to be set in stone.

A small squeak roused us both, and we looked at the kitten, who was gazing at us from the bathroom door. Jenna's phone made a noise, and she took it out of her pocket, frowning at the screen.

"My friend Addison will be here in about ten minutes," she said, taking another step back.

What?

"I would have gladly taken you home."

She slid her phone back in her pocket and shook her head, reaching for the kitten that batted at Jenna, looking healthier than earlier.

"No. I couldn't ask you to do that. You need to stay here."

"Are you sure?" I said, my body betraying me, as I stifled a yawn and shook out my shoulders, reaching for the kitten and putting her on the bed. She turned in a circle and climbed on my pillow, kneading the space before settling in.

"Thank you, Mark," she said, glancing at the television, then back at me.

Her voice was raw and husky, like she was affected by me as much as I was by her. "Text me tomorrow, and I can always swing by with high-calorie supplemental formula if she's not eating well." Her voice sounded more confident than her body language. She clenched and released her fists, proving my point.

"Will do, Dr. Cutie. And I should have an update on your car later on."

"My car, right. Yes, thank you," she said, wringing her hands together.

"I love this episode," I said, trying to ease the tension by pointing to the television. Some part of me shamelessly hoped she would stay and watch the show. She looked at the screen again, and her face lit up like she had a brilliant idea.

"That's what you should name her, Mark—Princess Consuela Banana-Hammock." She let out a giggle, then shrugged her shoulders.

"There is no way I'm naming her that. Are you crazy?"

But honestly, if it made Jenna giggle like that again, I'd almost consider giving her that ridiculous name.

"Not today," she said with a wink. "But she needs a name. And not a cliché one like Midnight or Lucky. A good, strong, feisty name."

"Let's focus on making sure she's healthy before we go giving her a ten-syllable name," I said, digging a knuckle in my eye to stave off exhaustion.

She just smiled, like my body and mind weren't at war with one another, and picked up the kitten, taking her back to the bathroom and shutting the door with a soft click.

"Remember, I'm just a text away if you need anything, Mark."

"Right, thanks."

I nodded and motioned for her to head downstairs. She brushed by me, and I followed her down, the warm air hitting me like a slap in the face when I opened the front door.

There was a red convertible in the driveway, and Jenna stood beside me, lingering on the porch. Then turned and looked at the car, waving her hand in greeting to a girl with flaming red hair.

"Jenna," I said, touching her elbow, so she looked at me. "Thank you for taking time out of your day to help."

"Anytime, Mark. And thank you for taking her in. You're going to be a good Cat Dad."

She put her hand on my arm and gave it a tight squeeze, then let go and swiftly walked down the steps and got in the car. The driver gave me a curt nod, and I returned it before lifting my hand to Jenna. She returned the wave, and I watched the taillights disappear until it was nothing but a spark in the dark. I pulled out my cell phone, wanting to text her one more time, but thought better of it and put the phone back.

Cat Dad.

The second she said those words, I knew it was true. I couldn't take her to a shelter. As soon as I bought that purple sparkle collar, she was mine. The front door clicked shut, and I took the stairs two at a time, going to my bedroom and pulling off my shirt and shoes. I shucked off my pants and quietly opened the bathroom door.

Two bright blue eyes were staring at me as I closed the door and turned on the shower.

"I'm not naming you Princess Consuela Banana-Hammock," I said, turning the water as hot as it would go. She stretched and trotted over to the bathmat, tilting her head as if saying, "We'll see about that, Dad."

I stepped in and let out a sigh as the hot water hit my back. Bracing my hands on the wall, I groaned, letting the water soothe my muscles and trying to get the scent of peaches out of my head.

BY YOUR SIDE

5 - JENNA

"**G**retchen, I don't have time for this today. I have to go," I said as if the wild, pregnant opossum living under my porch gave a damn.

She needed to know there was food before I left, but all I could see with my phone's flashlight were two beady eyes in the corner of the dark space.

Whatever.

It wasn't like I expected her to eat from my hand.

Shaking my head, I put the overripe fruit on the step and walked to my driveway. I still couldn't believe Mark had my car towed here and the battery replaced.

What a guy.

The parking lot was all but empty when I got to *AMC*, so I parked beside Dr. Duvall's lone sedan, balancing donuts and coffee in one hand and unlocking the back door with the other. The clinic was quiet, and the only sounds were Chick's and Duck's meows as they circled my legs demanding treats and attention. I'd barely booted up my computer and gotten one powered donut hole in my mouth before there was a sharp knock on my door.

Looking up, Dr. Duvall was frowning at me, glasses perched on his head and arm crossed across his chest. He was good-looking for an older guy, reminding me a little of a Martin Sheen. That was if Martin Sheen had a permanent scowl on his face that made his forehead lines stand out against his white hair. He pursed his lips, the twinkle in his blue eyes gone. It was like with each day that passed, he was more miserable with his job and had lost whatever drove him to become a vet in the first place.

"Good morning, Larry," I mumbled around a mouthful of sugary goodness. "I brought you a black coffee, and there are donuts in the..."

He held up a hand and cut me off, already ruining my mood before I could reach for his coffee.

"Dr. Crews. We need to discuss the raises you suggested. I was curious if you were going to take a salary reduction to cover the costs?"

"What?" I swallowed the donut that had turned into a cement block in my mouth.

"A five percent increase is unreasonable," he said, squaring his stance like he expected me to put up a fuss. "The most I'm willing to do is two."

"Two percent?" Clenching my fists, I stood up and sent my chair into the wall behind me. "Our vet techs haven't had a raise in two years. Five percent was the minimum amount I suggested. Anything else is unacceptable."

"That's not your decision to make."

"It is, actually." I crossed my arms, ready for this fight. A pushover, I was not. "I own fifty percent of this clinic and have an equal say in the decisions. Our employees deserve this, and you know that. Why are you pushing back so hard? I've worked through the budget, and this is something we can more than afford to do."

He hung his head, and for a second, his stern features softened, and he looked like he did when I joined the practice. He looked like a man that carried a burden and not one that went out of his way to make my work life miserable.

"Fine." He sounded exhausted, and his fingers trembled slightly as he ran them through his hair.

He kept his eyes on the floor as he walked out, throwing his hand over his shoulder in a half-hearted wave.

I mulled over his words and wondered if I'd been unreasonable these last months. But that couldn't be right. I'd crunched the numbers... something had changed. My phone beeped, and a warm feeling spread across my belly, erasing the tension creeping up my shoulders.

Officer Handsome: Morning, Dr. Cutie. Got a useless fact for me?
Me: Good Morning. Did you know that some species of cicadas can lie dormant for up to seventeen years underground?
Officer Handsome: I did not. Do you know what's brown and sticky?
Me: Brown and sticky? Do tell.
Officer Handsome: A stick.
Me: OMG!
Officer Handsome: Well, you said I'm a Cat Dad, might as well tell Dad Jokes.
Me: All you need is New Balances and Cargo Shorts.
Officer Handsome: I prefer the term Utility Pants.
Me: Well, I hope you and your Utility Pants have a good day. How's your girl?
Officer Handsome: Not eating as well as she did yesterday.
Me: Bring her in tomorrow. I can fit you in the late afternoon.
Officer Handsome: Thank you. That works. Later, Cutie

Me: Later, Handsome

"I don't remember the last time I've seen you smile that big," Melissa said, taking a bite of a bagel and waggling her eyebrows from my open door. Her jet-black hair bounced like the puppy ears on her vet tech uniform as she winked and pulled a donut out from behind her back.

"Mmm, thanks," I mumbled, taking a big bite. "Love that scrub top."

"So it's a guy?" she said, not at all taking my casual attempt to change the subject.

"Is what a guy?"

"The reason you have this ooey-gooey look on your face."

Did I?

I thought back to the way I felt in Mark's arms. He probably hugged me to shut me up, but the hopeful part of my mind whispered, *"You know that was more than a hug. The way he held you, the way he caressed you."*

"What, no..." I said, shaking my head hard enough for tendrils of my ponytails to come loose and fall around my face. Just because some enormous, tattooed, delicious guy held me like I was the most important thing in his life did not mean I was going to develop feelings and live happily ever after.

"You're such a liar," she said with a smile. "But stay in denial if you want. Mrs. Daniels is here with her dog, hoping to squeeze in for an early appointment. First surgery isn't until nine. Would you prefer we made an appointment this afternoon?

I stood up and stretched before finishing the last sip of my coffee.

"No, that's okay. Bring her to exam room two, and I'll be there in a few minutes."

"Will do," Melissa said, taking my lab coat from the back of my door and handing it to me. "And I found that butter pecan creamer you like so much. Can I make you another cup of coffee?"

"Thank you, that would be amazing. Is she the one with the Beagle?"

"No, Yorkie."

"Got it, thanks."

I straightened my lab coat and fixed my ponytail before walking out the door and down the hall, stopping at exam room two. Taking a peek at the chart, I nodded then knocked gently on the door. Mrs. Daniels was pacing the small space, cradling her Yorkie. She wore a bright purple tracksuit with matching shoes, and her white hair was coiffed eloquently to the side.

"I'm so glad you could squeeze me in, Doctor," she said, passing her Yorkie to me. "Sugar has been struggling to go potty, and her acorn is swollen and red. I don't know what to do."

Her acorn?

Sugar looked at me and whined, and I stroked her soft brown fur, murmuring soothing words and setting her on the exam table. Her eyes and ears were clear, but her bladder was full. I checked her vitals, then turned back to Mrs. Daniels.

"We need to get a urine sample and do an x-ray to check for blockages. How long has this been going on?"

"Since last night, Dr. Crews. Her poor acorn is so swollen, and I'm worried."

"Okay, we'll figure out what the issue is. What do you mean by acorn?"

I put my stethoscope around my neck and kept one hand on Sugar, waiting for Mrs. Daniel to explain. Melissa knocked on the door, and I passed Sugar over, running through the needed tests while I waited for an explanation.

Mrs. Daniels paused until Melissa left, then rolled her eyes and threw up her hands. "You know, her *acorn.*" She started pacing again with her eyes on the ground, muttering to herself about vulgarity. "Sugar has been licking her area obsessively, and now, it's red and swollen."

When she said area, her hand traveled down to the waistband of her pants, and she looked like she was in physical pain from the effort of this conversation.

Oh. Her acorn.

I tried to hold in a laugh, but it threatened to bubble up, so I bit the inside of my cheek and schooled my features.

"You mean her vagina, right Mrs. Daniels?"

"Tsk, we do not use such language, but yes."

"Okay, thank you for telling me. Please wait here, and I'll be back shortly to let you know our game plan."

Mrs. Daniels nodded and slumped down in the chair as if saying the words *area* and *acorn* had taken every drop of energy she had. I patted her shoulder and let myself out, leaning against the door before a giggle escaped. Clapping my hand over my mouth, I walked over to Lacy, who had just taken a urine sample from Sugar.

"What's so funny?" Lacy handed the sample over to Melissa to test for infection.

"Oh, you know, Mrs. Daniels just called Sugar's vagina an acorn."

I put my hand on my stomach and took a deep breath to keep from laughing harder.

"An acorn? That's a new one," Melissa said, picking up Sugar and scratching her head. "More like a hairy acorn."

With that, the three of us couldn't control our laughter, and I put my hands on my knees then wiped my eyes. Melissa and Lacy kept laughing after I stopped and only let up when Sugar gave a sharp bark like she knew we were laughing at her mama.

"Sorry, little one," I said, rubbing her belly.

One of our medical students, Kim, walked back from the x-ray room with a somber look on her face. "Everyone," she said. "Sugar has bladder stones."

"Shit," I said, pulling my hair out and retying it in a bun. "Prep the OR. I'll talk to Mrs. Daniels. Page Dr. Duvall so he can cover my first two surgeries. If he can't, push everything up an hour. Kim, scrub in with me."

"Yes, Doctor," came a chorus of voices as each tech set off to prep.

I walked back to the exam room with the news that Sugar and her acorn would be fine, but she needed surgery immediately to remove the stones.

So much for an easy day.

BY YOUR SIDE

6 - MARK

Do you know the difference between a newborn baby and a kitten? Yeah, me neither.

I was lying in bed less than a week later, rubbing a spot behind her ears and thinking of a name. She meowed in the bathroom for all of ten minutes that first night before I opened the door and bundled her up, laying her on my chest. She sniffed my chest hair like it personally offended her I had so much, then curled up in a ball and fell asleep.

I slept like shit, hardly able to move for fear of waking her up. Was she too cold? Too warm? Hungry? Thirsty?

I needed a nap.

Groaning, I stretched and reached above my head, only to be rewarded with tiny needle claws digging into my pec. I bit my lip and plucked her off, setting her on the bed and swinging my legs to the side. I rubbed my chest and stumbled to the bathroom, lifting the lid to do my business. As I finished, a stench hit my nose. It smelled like someone ripped ass after eating Mexican mixed with Thai.

Holy shit.

I turned around with my dick in hand and saw the kitten staring at me as she did her business. Then she covered it up and hopped out of the box and back to the bedroom like she owned the place. I rolled my eyes and finished up, washing my hands and holding my breath before grabbing the scooper and doing some damage control on that litter box. I wondered if I should text Jenna about that smell.

Jenna.

I always thought it was stupid when I heard people talk about feeling that elusive electric spark. It was a crazy exaggeration made up by the sappy romantics who loved love. It was wild theories, like taking a dumb social media test to see what flavor ice cream you were, but now, my perspective had shifted, and I had no clue what to do about it.

When I wrapped my arms around her and felt her tight up against me, something felt right. I forgot to breathe. Forgot everything except how her body molded to mine. It had to be a fluke. Things like that didn't happen from a damn hug. I'd just been alone too long, but a quiet voice in the back of my head whispered it was time to stop making assumptions and time to take what I wanted.

"Meow. Meow."

The kitten was sitting by my foot, staring up at me with those big blue eyes as if she hadn't left the bathroom smelling like, well, shit.

"Come on, let's get you breakfast," I said, lifting her up as I walked downstairs.

I opened the pantry and stared. Oatmeal sounded as appealing as the cardboard box it came in, but I spied a jar of apple butter and grabbed it, deciding on that with toast and eggs.

"What should we name you?" I set the kitten on the couch. She sat down and looked at me like she was about to answer. "I am down for anything but Princess Consuela Banana-Hammock."

"Meow. Meow."

"That better be agreement, Little Lady."

I turned on the television in the living room before going to the kitchen and taking out the ingredients. The eggs were cooking up perfectly, and I sliced some gruyere to melt on top. All the while, the kitten stared at me from the couch. She turned her head slowly to the television, then back to me. My eyes flicked to the screen, and a laugh spilled from my lips. The same episode of *Friends* as the other night was on, and the kitten slowly blinked before focusing her eyes back on the screen.

Nope. Not happening.

But she needed a name. A badass name like Jenna said. Maybe I should text her to see what she thinks.

"What about Shadow?" She doesn't look my way. "Gray? Midnight? Twilight?" Nothing. Not even a flick of her ear. "I know," I said, plating everything and walking to the living room.

Setting breakfast on the coffee table, I picked up the kitten. Ignoring her squeak of protest, I held her with both hands above my head and lowered my voice. "I have no problem taking your skinny ass upstairs to the balcony and showing you off to the neighborhood."

I swear to all the gods—she rolled her eyes before leaning forward to sniff the eggs on my plate. "Buzzkill." I scoffed as she turned up her nose and looked back to the television.

"I didn't offer you any, Princess. *No!* How about Phoebe? You look like a Phoebe, baby girl. Still nothing?" I shook my head and picked up my plate. The termite guy was coming at ten, so I shoveled down the rest of my food before I thought of any more ridiculous names.

At five minutes to ten, a neon orange van with a cartoon bug on the side pulled in front of the house. I was ripping up the front porch steps and stopped, wiping the sweat from my face. The van looked ridiculous, but my brothers recommended them.

"Mark?" he asked, stretching his hand out to shake mine. I gripped his firmly and nodded. He had a good, solid handshake and hard features—he looked like a no-nonsense and competent guy.

"Yes, sir. Good morning."

"The name's Bill. When's the last time your house was inspected?"

Straight to the point and no chit-chat—I liked this guy already.

"I'm not sure. I recently bought the place and couldn't find the most recent termite inspection."

"Okay. That's a little worrisome, but I'll get you checked out. You replacing the porch steps?" he asked, pointing to the pile of boards. I grunted acknowledgment and turned to the porch, seeing two little black ears peeking through the screen door. "Mind if I take a look?"

"Not at all," I said, scratching my scruff. I hadn't gotten around to shaving, and it was prickly as fuck.

Bill bent down and picked up one of the rotten boards, making a hissing noise that made my stomach clench. I rubbed my pendant and crossed my fingers while he picked up another board and snapped it like a matchstick.

Fuck.

"Looks like you have bad news for me," I said, stepping up beside him and crossing my arms. My fingers itched to grab the rabbit's foot in my pocket, but it looked like it wouldn't do me any good.

"I'm not going to sugar-coat it for you. This looks like an infestation. I'd contact the old owner right away and possibly a lawyer. Mind if I grab my bag and get started?"

"Yeah, man. Thank you."

He turned away when I remembered my pint-sized pip-squeak in the house.

"Hey Bill, do you use any chemicals that will harm cats?"

"Not at all," he said, giving me a curt nod and glancing at the door.

"Good," I said, rubbing the back of my neck. "I'll leave you to it then."

Sighing, I sat down beside the rotten porch steps, taking my phone out of my back pocket and dialing mom. She picked up after the first ring, greeting me how she always does.

"Well, hello, my favorite son. How are you doing?"

"Fine. I guess," I said, stumbling over how to ask her if she kept up with inspections.

"Hmm. Would you like to hear how my feud is going with old Cam Winston down the street, or would you like to tell me why you called?"

"As much as I'd like to hear how much better your hydrangeas are blooming compared to his..."

"It's not hydrangeas, and you know it. I just finished trimming a six-foot topiary dick and put it directly in front of that awful dogwood tree he insisted on planting in his backyard. Honestly, my backyard will be nothing but genitalia by the time I'm done with him. Next, I think I'm...."

"Mom," I said, interrupting what would have been a ten-minute conversation about if a middle finger was better than an ass for her next topiary design.

"Oh, right. What's up?" Mom said with a laugh.

She knew I was straight to the point, just like my dad. I could imagine her in the kitchen, having a second cup of coffee and a blueberry muffin while glancing out the window above her sink to check her zucchini plants and obscene topiary creations.

"Two things, mom. First, do you remember the last time the house was inspected for termites?"

"Oh, I can't say for sure. The last time I remember was when you boys were in High School. Why?"

"High School?" I said, louder than I should have. I ran my hands through my hair and paced, wearing down the grass. I could feel my blood pressure rising as Bill walked around the corner with a sour look on his face. I took off in the other direction, putting space between the man that was going to ruin my day.

Freaking bad luck.

I put my hand in my pocket and rubbed my rabbit's foot, hoping to salvage some part of the morning.

"Yes. Those things are good for like twenty years, aren't they?"

"No, mom. Definitely not twenty years."

"Is there an issue with the house?" Her voice was getting high with worry.

"Nothing I can't handle, mom. The termite guy is here, and it looks like the house might have a little damage."

"Damage? What kind of damage, Marcus?"

Oops, backtrack.

"I don't know, but it doesn't seem serious—don't worry. But I need your help with something else. Are you free tomorrow?"

"You aren't changing the subject without a promise to let me know what the verdict is, young man."

"No, ma'am."

"Good—now, what's happening tomorrow. My rage-knitting class was rescheduled, so I'm free."

"I have to work and was hoping you could come over and house-sit for me."

"House-sit? What for?"

"I, um—got a pet."

"What? A pet? You? House-sit for a pet?"

Great, me getting a pet was so far out there. She was repeating everything I said.

"Yeah. I got a kitten, and I don't want to leave her alone all day."

"Oh, wonderful, honey. I'm so glad you adopted. Of course, I thought you'd eventually get a Mastiff or German Shepard, but I've always had a soft spot for kittens. I'll be glad to cat-sit for my little grand kitten. You are my favorite, after all. I'll see you in the morning, and I'll bring breakfast."

I almost reminded her I was close to thirty and perfectly capable of cooking my own breakfast, but I'd be an idiot to turn down her cooking.

"Sounds good. Thank you, Mom. See you in the morning."

"Anytime. Bye, Marcus."

I hung up and looked around. Bill must have moved inside, so I stomped back up the porch and through the front door. The kitten was lying in the cat bed but hopped out as I got closer.

"Hey, Phoebe. Let's go find the bug guy."

I walked down the hall to the kitchen, then stopped in my tracks, looking down at the black ball of fluff. *Phoebe worked.* She looked like a Phoebe.

She was a Phoebe. *My Phoebe.*

"Alright, Mark. I'm all done," Bill said, breaking my train of thought.

"Is it bad?"

"Yes and no. There's damage to several of the support beams underneath the house. It's fairly easy to get rid of the infestation, but the repairs will take time and a construction crew trained to handle this type of situation. I can give you a recommendation or two if needed."

Bill wrote out his report and waited for me to process the information. I shook my head and closed my eyes. I was probably going to have to move out for who knew how long.

Where would I stay?

I could bunk with Miller and Magnum, but Phoebe would get lost under the mounds of dirty laundry, and my oldest brother, Maverick, was more of a recluse than me.

"Thanks for your help, Bill. I'll get someone started on the repairs right away."

"Glad to hear it. We'll make sure the wood's been treated properly so this doesn't happen again."

"I appreciate it. Thanks for coming out."

Of all the crazy shit that had gone wrong with the house, that was the last thing I expected. My salary was decent, and I had some money saved, but this would take a big chunk. I was planning to upgrade the house, and most of what I had would go toward rebuilding it.

It could be worse, I grumbled, kicking a stone on the pavement. The roof could have collapsed while I was sleeping.

At least I was going to see Jenna later. That should get me out of this shitty mood and this dumpster fire of a morning.

By the afternoon, I needed another shower before taking Phoebe to *AMC*. I'd thrown myself into ripping up the rest of the steps. It was a pretty stupid thing to do because now I had to jump from the porch to the sidewalk, making the house look like one gigantic eyesore.

After showering and getting dressed, I picked up my phone and stared at the screen. I should text my brothers and see who they'd recommend. Groaning, I pulled up the group text and quickly scrolled through the dozens of messages I missed. My brothers mostly talked in GIFs and sarcastic comments, so it was easy enough to skim through everything I missed.

Me: I need a construction company recommendation that won't rip me off.

Mil: Well, hello, younger brother. How are you on this glorious day?

Mag: We are doing fine, bro. Thanks for asking. And could you please stop texting us so much? It's annoying.

Mav: Why do you need a recommendation?

Me: The house has termite damage.

Mil: WTF?

Mag: GIF of bomb exploding

Mav: What's the extent of the damage?

Me: I don't know, but it looks like the porch will have to be replaced and a good portion of the downstairs and roof.

Mil: Holy shit. How did we not know?

Me: Because we took mom's word all was well with the house and didn't check for ourselves.

Mav: Ouch.

Mil: We suck.

Mag: I was at the townhouse yesterday and changed the batteries in her smoke detectors.

Mil: Kiss-ass. You just wanted to raid her fridge.

Mag: I would never! How dare you, sir?

Me: We all could have done better to help with the upkeep after dad died, and we won't let it happen again. Now, recommendations?

Mav: Right. I'll text you the number of a few trustworthy guys.

Me: Thanks, man. Later.

I slid the phone into my pocket when it felt like fire ants were biting my left ankle. Dancing back a step, I looked down to see Phoebe scampering up my pant leg, just as impatient to see Jenna. Fumbling to untangle her claws from my jeans, I managed to grab my wallet and keys, making it to my Tahoe before realizing I didn't have a carrier. I was going to have to stop at the pet store again on the way home.

The drive to the clinic was uneventful, with Phoebe sleeping in the seat and me glancing over every five minutes to make sure she was okay. The clinic parking lot was pretty full, but I found a spot close to the entrance. When I opened the door, a dog barked, and it took me a minute to figure out it was a chime over the door.

Cute.

I checked in, cradling Phoebe as best as I could. She kept squirming and trying to burrow deeper into my shirt. Her little needle-claws were digging into my chest, letting me know she was pissed, so when a tall woman with jet black hair called my name, I was more than happy to leave the busy lobby for a quieter exam room with purple walls.

The vet tech introduced herself as Melissa and entered her vitals, laughing when Phoebe bared her teeny tiny teeth and hissed before saying she was taking her to the back for tests. I nodded as she left, keeping my eye out for any sign of Jenna.

I paced for a minute, taking the time to smooth down my shirt and run my hand over my short beard. Ugh, I should have taken more time to check myself in the mirror before I left, but I was too pissed at the whole termite situation.

Jenna didn't keep me waiting long, and when she walked in, the subtle scent of peaches followed her, making my mouth water. She was holding Phoebe, dressed in scrubs that matched the walls and smiling. Those scrubs hugged every sweet curve, showing off her sexy-as-sin hourglass figure. Her purple framed glasses paired with strawberry-colored lips made her look like a sinfully delicious dessert. It made me want to savor every morsel, then lick the spoon clean.

The harsh light of the exam room only accentuated her features, showing off one dimple and making me realize I'd missed her. Her smile and her eyes had left an impression, and seeing them again released some of the knotted tension brewing in my body.

"...worms," Jenna said.

I hadn't heard a word. I was too enthralled with her and the way her hips filled those purple scrubs—hips I wanted to grab and dimple as I kissed her lips to see if she tasted as sweet as she smelled.

"Hmm?"

"Worms, Mark. She has intestinal parasites. The dose I gave her last week didn't do the trick. It's probably making her belly hurt, and that's why she's not eating. I want you to mix a bit of baby food with her kitten formula. She's too young for any vaccinations, but we ran an in-house blood test to check for anemia. Her bloodwork's fine, so we're going to treat the parasites, and she should be back to normal in a day or two."

"Worms?"

"Um, everything okay up there, Mark," she asked, passing Phoebe over and squeezing my arm.

"Yes. Fine. Sorry, I'm distracted."

"Distracted? Why? Are you both not settling in together well?"

She leaned closer and put one hand on her hip, waiting for my answer. The scent of peaches was distracting. She was distracting.

Oh shit. Well, I can't say, "Sorry, Jenna, your hips distracted me."

I wracked my brain for an excuse, any excuse, while she raised her eyebrows and squeezed my arm again, almost kneading my aching muscles. The soft fingertips of her hands short-circuited my brain until there was nothing but her touch. Not the buzz of the industrial lights or the hum of the air conditioner. Her short nails dug into my skin, the mild pain enough to leave me desperate for more.

Fuck, that feels good. I'll give you an hour to stop, Dr. Cutie.

I was putty in her hand as I imagined the desperate, breathy sounds I would draw from her body.

"Woah," Jenna whispered, stepping away and grabbing her clipboard from beside the computer to fan her face.

"Hmm?" I reached forward, grasping at the air, searching for her elusive hand that disappeared long before I was done with it.

"Mark. You. Umm. You said that out loud. And you kinda growled at me."

"I did what?"

"Growled. Low. Deep. Sexy. Shit. I'm sorry," she said, backing up and hitting the computer station with her hip.

The clipboard fell, startling Phoebe, who hissed and attempted to climb underneath my shirt, digging her claws in and breaking my fantasy. She rubbed the spot, spinning out of the way of the computer station to stand beside me.

Wow—as she moved in front of me, I leaned in, smelling her hair and almost getting a broken nose for my trouble. But I was under her spell, tangled in her web, and needing one more hit to make it through the rest of my day.

"No, I'm sorry," I replied, picking up the clipboard and handing it back to her. I gave up on prying Phoebe off of me to face Jenna and squeeze her arm. I wasn't going to pass up the chance to reciprocate touching her after hearing the sounds she made—sounds I thought were a figment of my imagination.

"My house has termite damage, and I need to move out for who knows how long. I don't know where I'm going to go, especially with Phoebe. I don't even have a carrier, for fuck's sake."

The words spilled out of my mouth, and I regretted them as soon as they did. I wanted anything but her sympathy.

"Did you know that termite queens have the longest lifespan of any insect in the world? Some live between thirty and fifty years, and they reproduce annually."

I let go of her arm and furrowed my brows. She listened and spouted off a useless fact without judgment, looking at me with an adorable smattering of freckles across her nose and a quirky fact on her lips. Lips I couldn't stop staring at...

"Why do you do that?" I asked before I could stop myself.

"What?"

Jenna pretended to look over the clipboard retrieved from the floor, but it was easy to see the way her eyes tracked my hands as I adjusted my collar and tried to contain Phoebe's squirms.

"You're upset about the house, even though it was something out of your control. There's no point in apologizing or telling you it will be fine, so I told you a useless animal fact."

She shrugged her shoulders and reached out to pet Phoebe. "I gave her more medicine. Text me if she still isn't eating after adding the baby food."

"Sure. Sorry about, umm, growling. I hate not being in control. This situation is frustrating."

"I'm not. I've never heard anyone make that noise before. It'll work out—Phoebe's attached to you. As long as you're with her, she'll be fine. I mean, as long as you're staying in a safe place, where she has space. And there shouldn't be any other animals in the house. It would be best if it was with someone she already knew—that might help. Someone who was used to kittens and wouldn't mind giving her the extra attention. In fact, why don't you both just stay with me."

As soon as she said those words, her posture got stiff, and her cheeks turned red as if she hadn't realized what words just tumbled out of her cherry-red lips, but I heard her loud and clear. So did my dick, who decided he wanted in on the action.

"I mean, I'm sure a guy like you has a ton of friends and plenty of options. You don't need to stay with me and my hundred plants. That was a stupid thing to say. Plus, my house is older and not very big, and you look like you need a lot of space. I mean, your beard, muscles, tattoos, and strong, rugged features. Your beard looks a hundred times better than a mustache, and it brings out your dark, soulful eyes…"

Her eyes got wide, looking like a deer in headlights, and she glanced at her feet, then back at me, fanning herself again with that damned clipboard again. I wanted to yank it out of her hands and see if I could make her whole body as pink as her cheeks. "Another fun fact, I ramble when I'm nervous."

She swore under her breath, and damn if it wasn't as cute as she was.

"Thank you for the offer," I said, rubbing the back of my neck and trying to ignore the needle-claws ruining my shirt and digging into my chest.

Truthfully, she was probably my best option, but this had fucking complicated written all over it.

"Oh, it's no trouble. And you don't have to give me some random excuse for why you can't. It was weird of me to ask you. I think we have some baby food around here. I'll check and send Melissa in. It was good to see you, Mark. Really good. I'm glad you grew your mustache out."

She hurried out of the room before I could pry my foot out of my ass to respond.

Melissa came in a few minutes later with several jars of chicken and turkey baby food and a spare carrier, but I kept glancing at the door, hoping Jenna would come back in. I wanted to say goodbye and tell her how good it was to see her and to thank her for the carrier and the offer.

"She's already seeing the next patient," Melissa said, not looking up from the computer.

"Am I that obvious?" I answered, chuckling to myself and safely stowing Phoebe away.

"Just a little."

Melissa reached out to shake my hand and walked me to the receptionist's desk to check out. As the front desk ran my card, I looked at the receipt and realized they didn't charge me for the extras. I opened my mouth to say something when the receptionist read my mind.

"We keep extra supplies on hand in case they're needed."

"Are you sure I can't pay for these?"

"I'm sure, but you can grab some supplies and drop them off the next time you're at the pet store. We can always use them here."

"I'll be sure to do that. Thank you."

"You're welcome. I've scheduled her vaccine appointment in three weeks. Make sure you call if there are any changes."

"I will."

I secured Phoebe in the front seat and cranked the engine, sitting in the parking lot, unable to drive away. Rolling my eyes, I grabbed my aviator's and slammed them on my face, wishing I had kept Jenna in the exam room long enough to accept.

BY YOUR SIDE

7 - JENNA

"And then, I freaking said he could move in with me. What the hell was I thinking? He looked at me like I was a three-headed dog named Fluffy. I ran out of there as fast as I could."

I loudly slurped my sangria and groaned, looking at my three best friends and waiting for them to tell me what an epic mistake I'd made. They all had matching expressions on their faces like they weren't buying into my sob story. Annaleigh looked at me and pursed her lips, shaking her head and causing her blonde hair to swish across her shoulders.

We were sitting in Olivia's living room, devouring the last of her homemade cookies.

I laid my head back on her gray suede couch. It was so comfortable, and I sunk further into the cushions, waiting for someone to break the silence. Knowing my carb-crutch, Olivia passed me another, and I shoved the whole thing in my mouth without chewing. Her eyes got wide, but she smiled, putting the plate back on the table closest to me.

Owning her own bakery, she always had homemade cookies and pastries, and they were always delicious. Except for that time, she tried to do a spicy and sweet cookie, mixing jalapenos with peaches—Yummy, in theory—horrible execution.

"Seriously? You asked him to move in with you?" Olivia said as I shivered at the thought of that cookie and reached for another delicious white chocolate raspberry one. "I don't care if he's a cop, or a firefighter, or a priest. You don't invite a stranger to live with you. How do you know if he was even telling the truth?"

"I know. I don't know what happened. One minute we were talking about Phoebe, and the next, I was inviting him to move in."

Addison made a harrumph and crossed her arms over her chest. She was still wearing a purple power suit from earlier today but had taken off her jacket, revealing a cream shell underneath. She ran a hand through her red hair and raised her eyebrows, staring at me.

"What?" I said, between a mouthful of cookies, but she harrumphed again and rolled her eyes. "I'm not a mind reader, you know, Addi."

"Listen, Jenna. That's bullshit, and you know it. I'm calling a Southern Charms intervention. We're helping Annaleigh work through her stuff with Max. We helped Olivia when she and Edward started dating, and you all helped me when Tommy cheated on me and when I went through, um, my thing. It's time the tables were turned."

She stood up, stuck one hand out, and put the other on her hip, waiting.

Ugh. Whenever something big was going on in our lives, the four of us would work through it. We affectionally called our group, *Southern Charms* and got together as often as possible.

"I one hundred percent agree with Liv, but I'll second your decision, Addison." Annaleigh put her hand on top of Addison's and looked at Olivia.

"Motion passed," Olivia said, adding her hand. I reluctantly did the same, and Olivia nodded. "Addison, you have the floor."

"Thank you," Addison said, removing her hand and standing up to her full five-foot-eight frame and glaring at me with fire in her eyes that matched her hair.

"First off, yes! Inviting him to stay with you was a completely crazy thing to do, and I sort of want to slap you upside your head and then take you to buy a stun-gun. As long as we've known you, you've been the practical one. The one who calls us on our bullshit with a random fact and no-nonsense attitude."

"I don't think I need a full-on *Southern Charms* intervention for a guy I've known for all of twenty seconds," I said, reaching for another cookie. Annaleigh popped my hand and tilted her head to Addison, silently letting me know I needed to pay the hell attention. "Y'all know I ramble when I'm nervous. I cannot be held accountable for my actions when I ramble."

"It's not just for that nutzo invitation, and you know it," Addison said, putting one hand on her hip and lifting the other like she was going to tic points off on her fingers. "You are always the first to support us, but you brush us off and handle it yourself when we try to return the favor. You were on what, five, ten dates with Jason and then randomly stopped seeing him? And you think because you're a workaholic, no one will see you for the beautiful badass you are."

Addison breathed and took a swig of sangria while Annaleigh had a smile on her face, and Olivia watched in awe.

"You think there's no way Mark would want to stay with you, but I guarantee that if you had given him a chance to respond, he might have said yes. I think this might be exactly what you need because you, Jenna, are a freaking catch. You have the kindest heart of anyone I know, and you sure as shit are the smartest. Don't second guess or be ashamed that you took what you wanted. You wanted Mark, so you asked him to move in. Granted, I know y'all just met, but who the hell cares? It was a crazy thing to do, but maybe crazy is what you need."

"Here, here," Olivia said, raising her glass. Everyone followed suit and looked at me, waiting. I took a minute to process her words, closed my eyes, and took calming breaths. She was right. Maybe running out of the room was taking the easy way out of admitting what I wanted.

"I, um, don't know what to say."

"You don't have to say anything," Annaleigh said, standing up to refill our drinks. "You're an amazing fucking person. Has anyone commented on the fact he named his kitten Phoebe? Because if that isn't the cutest damn thing ever, I don't know what is."

"That was sort of my suggestion."

"Are you serious? How did that happen?"

"When we got to his house, that episode of *Friends* was on—"

"Omg, that's hilarious."

"Totally, I'm just glad he kept her. You should see them together. He's this big, silent, tattooed adonis who cuddles and coos over a kitten."

"As if he could say no to you and your purple glasses, making you look like a sexy librarian. What was his name again? I wonder if the cop that helped me knows him. I have his card at my house and could call him if you like."

"Um. Yeah, I guess. His name's Mark Hansen."

"Are you serious?" Annaleigh said, grabbing my hand and staring at me. "That's the same officer that helped me. Covered with tattoos, mustache, but seems like a nice guy?"

"Oh, wow, but Mark's a traffic cop. How did he help you with the stalker?"

"He's my boss's neighbor." Annaleigh grinned. "Jake called him as soon as he got wind of what was going on. Jake's a fantastic boss."

"I'd say so," I said, taking a moment to let it all sink in.

If Mark was the same officer that helped Annaleigh deal with her stalker, this would be the perfect way to thank him. It was the least I could do for him helping to protect my best friend.

"So Annaleigh, how are you and broody Max doing?" I asked, reaching for one last cookie. I needed to change the subject, and thankfully, no one called me out.

"Oh, good. Thanks. I told you, Benjamin, that jackass stalker harassing me at the bank was fired, but it feels like the drama with him isn't over. Max is amazing, though. I'm crazy about him. I think this is it—he's it for me."

"Oh, honey," Olivia said, standing up to hug her and almost spilling her sangria. "I'm so happy for you."

Annaleigh hugged her back, and before I knew it, all of us were on our feet, embraced in one giant hug.

I loved these girls.

"Jason said I was too loud in bed." The words tumbled out of my mouth, and I stared at the floor. "And when I asked him to do something different or said something like move lower or higher, he told me he didn't need a roadmap, and that something was wrong with me if I couldn't finish."

They broke the hug to stare at me. I could feel the heat of their gazes as Olivia spoke.

"I will snap him like a butterbean. He still sells insurance, right?" She threw her arms up in the air and reached for her phone, probably about to creep his social media to find out if he changed jobs.

"Oh, stop, Olivia. I broke up with him not long after. I know he's an asshole, but he got in my head." I got up and walked to the kitchen, taking a few water bottles from the fridge.

I should never have gone out with him after that first date. There was never a spark, never a connection, and I haven't dated since.

"A dickless asshole who wouldn't know where a G-spot was if it bit him on the ass," Addison yelled from the living room as I walked back and put the waters on the table. I cracked one and took a sip, pulling my hair out from its ponytail and blowing out a breath.

"The type to give your tits a squeeze, two pumps in your pussy, and expect you to thank him and make him a sandwich after?" Annaleigh said, taking one water and another cookie.

"Yes, I mean, no. He just thought he was God's gift to women, and I should sit back and enjoy the ride."

"Well, that's a load of crap," Annaleigh said. "Listen, I'm the last person who should tell you this because god knows how long I lived in the past, but you can't let one thing determine your future."

I couldn't help but glance at Addison as Annaleigh spoke, and I noticed we all were looking at her, but she was focused on her wine glass like it was diamond-encrusted.

"So, yeah," Annaleigh finished. "You want to be loud, scream. You want to give directions, freaking draw him a color-coded map. Do you want to invite Mark to stay with you? Do it. Just be smart. Don't let one comment keep you from dating or from what you want."

She shrugged and stood up, stretching and glancing at her watch. I checked mine and saw it was almost eleven. Even though my weekend was nothing more than volunteering at a local rescue, I still needed sleep. Addison followed suit, and with one more cookie, we said our goodbyes, making plans to go to *B's Bar* one evening next week.

Olivia grabbed my arm as I was walking out the door and pulled me into a tight hug.

"I don't think inviting him to stay with you is the way to get over the way that jackass treated you, but I also know you and know you trust your gut. Just be careful, okay?"

I nodded and hugged her back, and she handed over a ziplock bag with the rest of the cookies. I followed the girls out the door and down Olivia's driveway before turning around and waving to her as I climbed in my truck and cranked the ignition.

Maybe they were right. It was stupid of me to let one foul, evil little cockroach under my skin. Tomorrow, I'd text Mark and tell him the offer was there if he needed it. A part of me hoped he'd say yes, but even if he didn't, I wouldn't be embarrassed. I'd own it. *Probably.*

BY YOUR SIDE

8 - MARK

I was scrambling to clean before Mom got here. If there was one dish in the sink or shirt in the laundry basket, she'd take care of it. She was already doing me a favor today by watching Phoebe while I was at work. I didn't need to leave her a mess. So the dirty laundry went in the closet with the door shut, and the dishes went in the dishwasher. I straightened the pantry, replaced the hand towels in the bathroom, and threw away all the takeout containers in the fridge. She'd still find something to do, but I felt better giving the house a quick once over.

I was tying off the trash when she opened the back door with two casserole dishes in her hand and a frown on her face. The kitchen floor creaked as she came closer, reminding me the house was a ticking time bomb, and I had to find a place to stay. *Soon.*

Mom had on jean capris, a green button-down shirt, and white keds, like she was ready for a game of bridge or to gossip on her porch with a white wine spritzer. Her short blonde hair matched mine, came down to her chin, and was white at the temples. I quickly walked over and kissed her cheek before taking the casseroles and laying them on the stove-top while she sighed and looked me up and down.

"What happened to the porch steps, Marcus? I had to maneuver these dishes all the way around the house, but the landscaping is beautiful."

She patted my shoulder and took an apron off the pantry door, tying it around her waist and pulling two coffee cups and sugar out of the cabinet.

"Hi, Mom. I took my frustration with the termites out on the steps."

"Well, better the steps than the drywall. Grab my knitting bag and purse from the front seat, please."

I nodded and headed out the back door, jogging to her car and grabbing her things. The missing steps looked awful, but I would meet with the crew on Wednesday to come up with a game plan. Maverick came through with a recommendation, and Bill sent me his full write-up to pass along to the construction guys. They could work me into their schedule and looked to get the work done in about a month.

I shook my head and locked her car door, bringing the purse, knitting bag, and two sacks of groceries. The back door made an ominous squeak as I opened it, but in the quick minute or two, I was gone—she'd filled the kitchen with the smells of sweet French toast and crispy bacon.

"Put the groceries on the counter, hand me the syrup, and go get my grand kitten."

She reached behind her as I opened the fridge and passed over the syrup, then shooed me away. Phoebe was waiting for me at the top of the stairs, pacing back and forth like a little lioness, and meowed at me as I climbed the stairs. I cooed an apology, picking her up and carrying her down.

Mom was waiting with outstretched hands, and I passed Phoebe over, hoping I could steal a bite of whatever she was cooking while she was distracted. The groceries were on the counter, and I snatched the loaf of bread she brought and turned it right side up. An upside-down loaf of bread was bad luck, and I didn't want to spend the day worrying something was going to happen with the house.

"Marcus, it's so tiny. Whatever made you adopt?"

"She, Mom, it's a girl. Named Phoebe. Loony was freaking out about a stray kitten wandering around the neighborhood. I took her to the vet, and, um, she's grown on me."

"Loony. If I never hear her name again, it will be too soon. I would never have thought you'd get a black kitten. Not as superstitious as you are. You picked that up from me, you know."

She baby-talked to Phoebe, who started purring as soon as Mom hit the sweet spot behind her ears. I snatched a piece of bacon from the stove before she could stop me and broke off a little for Phoebe. She ate it out of my hand, then snuggled up to Mom like I wasn't even there.

"What? No, I didn't. That was all Dad."

"You were too young to remember, but I chased him out of the house so many times to give him that lucky rabbit's foot keychain he always forgot that he eventually tattooed it on his shoulder."

"Huh," I said, reaching in my pocket to rub my own rabbit's foot, my mind whirling until Mom pushed a plate in my hand. I sat down at the round table in the kitchen, and she joined me a minute later with two cups of coffee. Phoebe stayed curled up on her lap, and I glanced at her before digging into my French toast casserole.

The toast melted in my mouth, and I couldn't stop the moan I made around my second mouthful of food.

"This is amazing," I said, offering Phoebe another tiny piece of bacon.

"I know." Mom sipped her coffee. "I was thinking about your predicament."

"It's an easy fix, and I'll be back in the house in no time."

"Yes, but I have a feeling you aren't telling me how serious the damage is. You bought the house from me, not knowing about the termites. So I'm going to pay for it, and I don't want to hear any excuses. You pay for any upgrades you want to do, and I'll handle the rest. Now drink your coffee and say thank you."

Mom crossed her arms and gave me the same look she did when I was a kid. A look that was ball-shrinking, unyielding, and not up for discussion. I'd talk with the construction crew and make sure they lowballed the structural damage. This was my fault. I should have had the house inspected as soon as I moved in.

"And don't you dare think about talking with the construction company. Maverick already told me who you're using."

Damnit. The woman was a mind reader.

"I want you to stay with me, Marcus."

"Mom, your place isn't pet friendly, and I'm working the night shift for two weeks starting Monday. I won't disrupt your life like that."

"Yes, well, one little kitten will be fine. It's not like we have to walk her. I've started cleaning the spare bedroom, you'll have your own bathroom, and we can even go to a knitting class together. The ladies would love to meet my youngest, and on your days off, you can help me in the garden and with my bonsai plants."

She took a breath to take a sip of coffee, smiling at me and nodding like she had already decided what was going to happen. If a leaf fell outside, she'd wake up, and my crazy hours would put her out more than she'd admit.

Phoebe stared at me. "Mom, I appreciate the offer, but I'm staying with a friend. I've already accepted her offer."

Shit.

"*Her?*" Mom said, setting Phoebe on the floor and crossing her arms. She gave me that look again, and I felt a drop of sweat drip down my neck.

I still didn't know if Jenna meant it, but it was the first thing that popped into my head. I should have said I was bunking with a guy from work, but it was too late.

"Yes, a friend. Her name's Jenna, and she offered me her spare bedroom."

I tried to act casual, but my hand drifted to my pendant, and my smile strained my face.

"She's the vet that helped me with Phoebe."

"A doctor, Marcus? Is she pretty?"

I could deny it to Mom, tell her I didn't notice, but she'd see right through me.

"Yeah, she's pretty and spouts off random facts like she's a trivia champion."

Mom gave me an all-knowing smirk but stayed quiet, sipping her coffee. Phoebe squeaked and made it halfway up my pant leg before I pried her loose and sat her on my lap with a piece of bacon. "Well, I'm just glad you're not staying with your brothers. Not that they wouldn't welcome you with open arms, but those boys are going to stay wild until they find good women to settle them down."

I grunted in response and scarfed down the rest of my food. By the time I cuffed my sleeves and straightened my tie, Mom was waiting by the back door with a thermos. I gave her another kiss and took the offered goodies, hightailing it to my cruiser.

I cranked the engine and pulled out of the garage, glancing in the mirror at my house with no front steps. I flipped on my radio and called dispatch, letting them know I was headed in. I dreaded even thinking it would be a calm day, but the thought flitted across my mind. Maybe I'd have time to swing by the vet clinic after my shift.

My beard itched, and I rubbed my cheek, scanning the area around me as I pulled up to a four-way stop. Not many cars were on the road, but I still took an extra few seconds to look around. It was clear to my right and left, but I had to do a double-take when I looked straight. Something was wrong with my eyes. I pushed up my aviators and stared at the red mini cooper coming my way.

A giant white...something obscured the passenger window. It had a long neck, like a giraffe, and was wearing sunglasses. How long had it been since I'd been to the optometrist?

I kept staring as the white thing moved closer. The mini cooper stopped at the stop sign, and the driver raised his hand in greeting as I continued to squint at whatever the hell was in the front seat. It was partially covering the driver's side window, so I sighed and flashed my sirens and lights, motioning for him to pull over. He held both his hands up and nodded, turning left into a gas station. My eyes couldn't be that bad if I saw him nod, but I had no freaking clue what he had beside him.

I pulled my cruiser behind him and kept the lights flashing, picking up the radio to call in the license plate. While I waited, I looked for any telltale signs of nervousness from the driver. He sat calmly, didn't fidget, and didn't glance in his side or rear mirror obsessively. Regardless of whether or not he looked harmless, I didn't let my guard down.

"Officer Hansen. Vehicle's registered to a Anthony Goldstein, nineteen, of North Charleston. No outstanding warrants or violations. Proceed."

"Copy that," I said, opening the car door and making sure I switched my body camera on.

As I approached, the driver looked in the side mirror and gave me a tight smile, keeping his hands on the steering wheel. I touched his back panel and kept one hand loosely on my holster, my eyes darting between the giant white thing and the driver.

"Good morning, sir. My name is Officer Hansen with the North

Charleston Police Force. May I see your license and registration, please?"

"Yes, Officer," he said, passing over his information.

I looked over everything and checked the dates before realizing what was in the passenger seat. It was a giant swan float. Not a little child's float for a backyard pool, but one that looked like it could fit several large adults. He had the passenger seat as low as it would go, and the swan spilled into the tiny backseat, taking up all the room and pushing against the back window. I couldn't help but crack a smile when I realized that's what had me so stumped.

My eyesight was fine.

"I guess you know why I stopped you. Your passenger is obstructing your field of vision."

I gestured to the swan, and the guy leaned his head back and nodded.

"I knew it was a mistake to blow it up before I got to Edisto Beach. But my air pump broke, and I couldn't make myself let the air out after I finally finished."

"You blew this up yourself?"

That was impressive. The guy was young, but it took some serious lung capacity to blow that whole thing up.

"Yes. I guess I'll have to let it out now."

I wracked my brain and glanced at his backseat. My eyes roamed over several heavy textbooks, and I got an idea.

"Not necessarily, but we have to adjust the float so its neck doesn't touch the front window."

"Seriously, Officer? You'll help?"

"Yeah. Step out. Let's figure this out."

The guys at the station would give me shit about this, but traffic cops got a bad enough wrap without me giving this guy a ticket for driving while distracted. I pocketed my notebook and secured my side holster as the guy got out of his car. I went over my plan, and he rubbed his hands together, ready to get to work.

Exactly eleven hours and forty-five minutes later, I pulled out of the station, ready to head home. I knew Mom had whipped up something, and the thought of eating some more of her cooking made my stomach grumble, but there was one stop I had to make first. The lights on the vet clinic were off, but Jenna's SUV was parked in the back. She was the only one left, just like last time. And just like last time, I had to ask her for a favor.

I pulled in beside her and stared at the back door, willing my body to move. I did a breath and pit check, then looked around the empty lot for any excuse that kept me in the cruiser longer.

Why the hell was I so nervous?

Staying with her would solve all my problems. More than the looming threat of my house collapsing with me in it, I wanted to spend more time with her, and this was the way to do it. Or we'd spend one day together, realize deep down we had nothing in common but Phoebe, and part ways knowing it was nothing but a crazy mistake.

Jenna: Hey you. The back doors unlocked.
Me: You spying on me?
Jenna: Wouldn't you like to know. ;-) I'm in my office.

Talk about being called out like a kid home past curfew. I turned off my engine and headed to the back door, smoothing down my shirt and shaking out my shoulders. I got this. *Probably.*

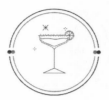

9 - JENNA

I was in the storage room, grabbing another box of medium-sized gloves when my phone beeped. One of the motion-activated cameras in the back parking lot had gone off. My office was next to storage, and I walked over and switched the security monitor back on, surprised to see Mark sitting in his cruiser. My first thought was Phoebe, but he would have texted or already been at the door if it was her.

What was going on?

Mark looked like he was deep in thought, but I was wrapping up my thrilling Friday night and ready to get home. Or maybe just glad to see him.

Me: The back doors unlocked.

His eyes darted around the empty lot, and I couldn't help but smile. Crazy or not, I liked him and was glad to see him. My palms got sweaty, and I quickly dug through my desk drawers, searching for gum while he typed out a response. I found two lone pieces and stuck them in my mouth, chewing frantically as his text came through.

Officer Handsome: You spying on me?
Me: Wouldn't you like to know. ;-) I'm in my office.

I turned off the monitor when I saw him open his cruiser door and get out. He looked like sex on a stick or sex in a uniform. His black button-up shirt hugged every muscle and hard edge, and his thighs looked like they were going to split the seam of his pants. I chewed vigorously, then spit out the gum and stood up, smoothing down my scrub top and shaking out my shoulders. I was brushing out my hair with my fingers when I heard the back door open. I kept my eyes on my dark computer monitor, pretending I was engrossed in my work.

"Hey you," Mark said, walking into my office with a smile. I stood up and moved closer, taking in his subtle scents of leather and peppermint. How had I never noticed how good he smelled? And his uniform looked better than I remembered, with his badge gleaming on his shirt, drawing my eyes to his broad chest. My comfortable office all of a sudden felt claustrophobic, with his large frame taking up all the space in front of my desk.

I wanted to lean in closer and breathe him in, but Mark stretched out his hand like he meant to shake mine. As I did the same, coming up to stand in front of him, he changed his mind and shoved his hands in his pockets, rocking back on his heels with a chuckle.

I was awkward enough without bumbling through a hello, and the silence stretched on as I desperately tried to think. Should I shake his hand, fist-bump, salute, wave, hug? A hug sounded best, but with no plan of attack, I lifted one hand in greeting and leaned forward. Instead of leaning into me, Mark took his hand out of his pocket and brought it up to shake, landing right smack-dab on my boob.

Ouch!

The sizzle of pain sent an embarrassing jolt of electricity straight to my lady bits. I sucked in a hiss, rubbing the spot as Mark shoved his hand back in his pocket like my boob was hot-lava. His eyes followed my hand as I soothed the sting, trying to cover the fact that my nipple was hard.

When he glanced back up at me, I should have looked away, but I didn't. I watched him, not hiding the mischievous glint in my eyes, wanting him to know I saw the way he tracked my movement.

"Sorry about that," he said, clearing his throat and taking a step back, only to hit the chair in front of my desk.

He put his hands on the back of the chair, squeezing the leather until it creaked underneath his strength. "Jenna, may I shake your hand?"

I paused, drawing my lip in between my teeth again. I couldn't figure out what caught me more off guard. That he asked permission to touch me, or that I found it so incredibly sexy I had to squeeze my thighs together.

"Sure," I said, leaning in with an out stretched hand. His hand engulfed mine, and when I took a step back, his hand stayed put for an extra second.

By now, I'd typically be babbling about how guys are always looking for a way to touch boobs. But that touch, that extra intimate touch, shut me the hell up and left me tongue-tied and staring into his dark eyes. You would think eyes that black would be cold and calculating, but his were like deep pools of delicious dark chocolate.

"It's good to see you, Mark. Is everything okay with Phoebe?"

"What? Oh—yes. She's fine. I hope I'm not interrupting."

"Not at all. I'm almost done for the night and have takeout waiting and an exciting evening of Netflix and Chill planned."

He let go of my hand abruptly and took a step back, rubbing the back of his neck and glancing at the open door like he was calculating how long it would take him to run to the parking lot.

What had I said? Shit. Netflix and Chill was code for bom-chicka-wah-wah.

"Oh, god, no. That's not what I meant," I said, shaking my head. "I'm literally binge-watching *Frasier* with a frozen drink and a big bowl of Pho from the Vietnamese place close to my house. Alone. I don't remember the last time I actually Netflix and Chilled with someone. So my Netflix and Chill is just that. Not that I'm standing here having a one-woman pity party. I love my life..."

Mark reached out and put his index finger on my lips, silencing my words. I could feel the color rising in my cheeks. The pad of his finger was rough, and when he pulled his hand away, I leaned closer, selfishly wishing he hadn't.

"I'm sorry, I didn't mean..." he said, his voice trailing off as he grasped the back of the chair again. I was seriously worried about the leather.

Again, his one-touch silenced my thoughts, bringing them all back to him.

His fingers.

His tattoos.

"Thank you. I ramble, remember?"

I moved back around my desk where Chick and Duck were staring at us like we were an exciting game of Ping-Pong. I leaned down and put a cat under each arm, walking over to lay them on their matching cat beds, needing the distraction to catch my breath.

"Well, as long as it's not a blow by blow of your last Netflix and Chill, I enjoy listening to you talk," Mark said, following me around behind my desk. He wrapped his knuckle on the wood, watching me settle in the office cats. His presence in my small space was powerful, and my body felt twitchy and on edge.

"Yeah?" I rubbed my hands on my pants, focusing on a poster above Mark's head so I wouldn't stare at his eyes like a creeper.

"Yeah. My brothers are always trying to get me to talk more, and it's nice you don't." He followed my eyes to the poster, and I shook my head, ignoring it to focus on him.

"Why would I try to make you talk? I mean, I assume it's part of who you are, but we've only known each other for all of five minutes, so maybe it's crazy to assume stuff. Still, you seem like the kind of person who only talks when there's something to say."

Why couldn't I stop talking? Touch me again, Mark. Shut my mind off.

He chuckled. "It's not crazy, but my question probably is."

"Well, um. Do you like Vietnamese food?"

"Hmm?" he said like I was speaking Vietnamese.

"Vietnamese food," I repeated. Whatever Mark wanted to ask or talk about would go better with food and bubble tea. "I haven't had dinner yet. Want to join me, and we can talk about this crazy question?"

"Yeah. Let me make a quick phone call first."

Mark stepped out of my office with his phone pressed to his ear, and I took his momentary distraction to check out how amazing his ass looked in his slacks. I tilted my head, staring at how the fabric was like an extension of his skin.

"Ahem." Mark cleared his throat with his eyebrows raised. Since there was no point pretending I wasn't looking, I snuck another peek, positive there was an extra pep in his step as he left.

"Sorry about that," Mark said, pocketing his phone as he walked back in a minute later. I'd barely recovered from having him in such close proximity, wishing whoever he had to call had demanded a longwinded explanation.

"My mom's been cat-sitting for Phoebe. I wanted to make sure she was good staying a while longer."

"Oh. I'm sure you need to get back. I know it's been a long day for you both."

"She was in the middle of a show on *Lifetime* and wasn't planning on leaving until it was over, anyway."

"Let me guess, either Murder Mystery or Christmas in July."

"Ha, yep. Murder Mystery all the way with her."

"My dad's the same way. We always tease him about how he should have been a detective." We stared at each other for a long moment. "So, uh, do you know where *Pho Ahn* is? Off of Rüten Boulevard?"

"Sure, but I'm not familiar with Vietnamese food." He held a small grin on his face.

"Oh, Mark. You're in for a treat. I'm going to pop your Pho Cherry."

I rubbed my hands together like an idiot, and Mark shook his head. "You're not planning on ordering me anything weird, are you?"

"That depends on what you need to talk to me about, Mark. Give me five to wrap things up here, and I'll meet you at *Pho Ahn*."

"Sounds good, Dr. Cutie. See you there soon."

Mark gave me one last look and turned on his heel, walking out the back door. I went to switch off the security monitor but paused with my finger on the button. Before he got in his car, he turned around and waved, like he knew I'd be watching. When he finally shut his cruiser door, I switched off the monitor and took a deep breath.

I peeled off my scrubs and took out the spare pair of slouchy jeans and a T-shirt I had in my office closet to change into before heading out. I was eager for Mark to see me in something different, something that hugged my curves and showed a little cleavage.

Mark was waiting for me at a two-top by the window when I walked into the hole-in-the-wall restaurant tucked in a strip mall beside a used car lot. The booths were covered in worn red leather, and the flooring was a beige tile. I'd been coming here for years, and every time I opened the door, I remembered sitting in these same booths, studying for my degree, and drinking cup after cup of sweet bubble tea.

The scenery tonight was much better. When Mark saw me coming, he stood up and looked me up and down before motioning to my chair. I sat down, and so did he, both of us waiting for the other to talk. I should pick up the menu and pretend I didn't have it memorized, but I was too busy trying to decipher Mark's face.

"What? Is there something on my face?" I smoothed down my hair and rubbed my cheeks, watching his eyes move down my body like he was noticing every curve. I could feel my cheeks flush. "You're making me blush, Mark. Is my shirt on inside out?" I glanced down at the material to check for a tag as he stared. "I've done that before, you know. One time, I went to the grocery store, and people kept looking at me funny, and when I got home, I realized my shirt was on inside out."

Mark's warm chuckle made it feel like a thousand butterflies had taken flight in my stomach. "No, I've never seen you wear jeans before."

"I also own heels and a dress."

Mark's eyes darkened, and he continued to stare until I glanced away. Luckily for me, I didn't need to stress over my inability to have a normal conversation with a hot guy because our server walked up a minute later and, I was saved from my nature channel of emotions.

"Hi, Binh," I said. His parents owned the place, and he still helped out a few days a week.

"Hey, Jenna," he said back. "Usual tonight?"

"Hmm. Maybe not." I glanced at Mark, but he looked back blankly. "Let's try something spicy. We'll start with spring rolls, then have a number seventeen, number twelve, two Saigon Red's, and a strawberry bubble tea."

"Of course," he said as I passed over our menus. Mark looked at it like it was written in Latin.

"You're not allergic to goat, ox, or squid, are you?" I said with a slight giggle, trying to keep a straight face.

"Goat? Did you say goat?"

"And squid. No allergies, right?"

His mouth opened and shut once before his eyes narrowed.

"Are you fucking with me?"

"Yep. Since me in jeans has you practically speechless."

I stared down at my outfit again as Binh dropped off the drinks. Picking up a beer, I took a long pull.

"I like you," he said, furrowing his eyebrows and picking up the beer to eye the label. He took a drink then put it down, crossing his arms to make his tattoos dance across his skin.

Now it was my turn for stunned silence. What do I say to that?

Thank you.

I like you too.

The way you wrapped your mouth around that beer bottle made me want to lick your lips like brownie batter off a spoon.

"I like your..." I whispered, watching the right side of Mark's mouth lift.

I like your mouth.

I like your lips.

He cocked his head to the side. "You like my what?"

"Hmm?" I rested one arm on the table and stared dreamily at Mark.

"You said you like my...something, and then you stopped." He chuckled, shaking his head.

"Wait—what?"

Was I saying my thoughts out loud?

"Like you. I meant I like you too, Mark." I glanced down at my hands and tapped my fingers on the table, trying to focus anywhere but on Mark's full-on smirk. "Two likes is too much, probably."

Mark laughed, and the rich baritone sound forced my eyes up to his face. He reached across the table, and his long fingers wrapped around my small hand. His palm engulfed mine in warmth, but the simple contact sent goosebumps up my arm as he stroked his thumb back and forth over mine.

"It's okay, Jenna. I said it first."

The air electrified around us, and our eyes connected. I swallowed, wishing I could convince Binh to let me use the walk-in freezer until my pulse slowed down.

"This conversation probably had a point," I said, as Mark blinked and pulled back his hand.

"Right, sorry." He ran his hand through his thick, blonde hair. "I was wondering if the offer to move in was still on the table."

"Of course it is. I meant to text you today, but the clinic was slammed."

"Are you sure?" He rubbed the back of his neck and took another sip of beer before pushing it to the middle of the table. "My hours will be crazy for the next two weeks, and Phoebe still needs extra care."

"I truly don't mind. I'm normally up by five and sleep like the dead. Phoebe can come to work with me until she makes it through her first rounds of vaccinations. It's no trouble."

"You are really pulling my ass out of the fire. You know that, right?"

"Hey, Mark. Listen," I said, reaching across the small table to take his hand again. He looked at our joined hands before bringing his gaze back to my face.

"One of my best friends is Annaleigh Mackey. Jake Rosenburg is her boss. She told me what you did for her. How you helped her with that awful guy from her office."

He blinked and shook his head, focusing on the window.

"It's my job. It's why I do this job. To help people," he said, his eyes going hard. He tightened his grip in my hand and cleared his throat, dropping his gaze to the beer like he was counting the condensation droplets running down the bottle.

"No, Mark. It's not. You could have called someone else to handle it, but you didn't. You helped your neighbor and my friend when it was out of your jurisdiction. You patrolled her neighborhood. You took the time to talk to her until she felt safe. This is the absolute least I could do for you."

Mark kept staring at our hands until I gave his a firm squeeze. Those onyx eyes met mine, and I took a breath, putting as much feeling as I could into my next words.

"Thank you, Mark."

He nodded and mumbled, "You're welcome." Before glancing back at the beer and pushing it further to me.

His lips fell into a tight frown, and he pulled his hand away, crossing them around his barrel chest. "It's good you can repay a favor then."

What? A favor? No!

I wanted him to move in before I knew about him helping Annaleigh, but sincerity might as well have been useless babble because Mark had closed himself off, glaring at the beer like it had offended him.

"Not a fan?" I said, simply to break the tense silence.

"No, it's good, but I don't drink when I'm in my squad car."

"I didn't think of that. Here, try the bubble tea." I pushed the large mason jar with tapioca pearls to him, and he looked at it, then back at me. "Just try it. I don't have cooties."

Mark leaned forward, keeping his eyes fixed on mine, and took a drink from my straw. It was by far the sexiest thing that had happened to me in a month. Maybe a year, as I watched him hollow his cheeks and his prominent Adam's apple bob as he drank.

"Delicious, thank you, but there is one issue with me moving in."

He gave me a smile that was so tight it looked forced. I clasped my hands in my lap to keep me from touching him again, but then I remembered dinner at Olivia's, and my confidence rose. I reached for the bubble tea, intentionally brushing my fingers with his as I took the glass back.

"What's that?" I said, leaning down and wrapping my lips around the straw. Mark shifted in his seat, propping one elbow on the table. Just like at the clinic, I wanted him to see me. I wanted him to notice me purposely putting my lips where his were moments before.

Binh chose that moment to drop off the steaming bowls of soup and plates of veggies, breaking whatever awkward seduction I was attempting to play.

"I can't in good conscience move in with someone who doesn't tell me upfront if I'm eating squid. So, what's really in this soup?"

Mark winked and pulled the bubble tea back, using his spoon to take out a tapioca pearl. He held the spoon out to me, and I took the offered bite.

I breathed a sigh of relief and pulled both bowls to me.

"This one is chicken," I said, pointing to the bowl on the right. "And this one is beef. Not a tentacle in sight. But how do you feel about spice?"

"I love anything hot and spicy."

"Me too."

I tore up the bean sprouts and mint leaves, adding sriracha to one bowl and hoisin sauce to the other. I mixed both and squeezed lime on top before pushing them back to the center of the table.

"Cheers," I said, lifting my beer. He clinked the tea to my glass and eyed each bowl, pulling the beef a little closer.

"Cheers," he answered back, taking another sip of tea. "Here's to the start of a beautiful friendship."

I smiled with the cheesy line, plating the spring rolls and hoping that's exactly what this was.

10 - MARK

"I can't believe the place has termite damage," Maverick said.

"I can't believe you ripped up the porch steps, and now you have a freaky floating porch," Miller added.

"I can't believe you're staying with a girrrrlllllll," Magnum drew out the syllables until Miller leaned over and punched him in the arm.

"Ouch, dick," he said, rubbing his bicep like Miller's punch was going to bruise him.

"Less talking, more cleaning," Maverick said, taking out several steaks from the fridge to move to the garage freezer.

The kitchen, living room, and downstairs office had to be emptied entirely since the damage was limited to those support beams. Most everything was already in the garage, and Mom was covering the living room furniture with plastic tarps. We were lucky we didn't have to empty the whole house.

For all the shit I talked about my brothers, the moment they heard what was going on, they all showed up to help. I was sure they felt guilty, but hell, so did I. Mom stuck her head in the kitchen right as Maverick and

I were disconnecting the oven and microwave.

"Pizza will be here in an hour. Are you packed?"

"Thanks, Mom. Yeah, my bag is in my Tahoe, and Sarge knows I won't be bringing the cruiser home until I'm back in the house."

"Once we get these appliances moved, we should be good," Maverick said, taking the large roll of plastic wrap from Mom and wiping his forehead with his sleeve. Of the four of us, Maverick was the only one who got our dad's dark, floppy hair and blue eyes. He cracked his knuckles and laid the roll down, watching Miller and Magnum make room in the garage for the appliances.

"Thanks for coming through with a recommendation," I said to Maverick, lightly punching his shoulder.

He clapped me on the back and nodded, passing me a water bottle from the counter. I wasn't much of a talker, but for every dozen words I said, Maverick said one. I looked around the living room, at all the furniture haphazardly covered, and wondered for the first time in years if something was missing.

If I needed an itch scratched, I could visit bars outside my jurisdiction. It had always been enough. Why was I questioning it now?

"...Jenna," someone said.

Yes. Exactly. Jenna.

After what? Seeing her a handful of times, I was thinking about dating? That was ironic as fuck since she made it perfectly clear she was only letting me stay to repay a favor. Maybe I was getting too old for random hook-ups.

Maybe I needed more.

"Dude? You daydreaming?" Miller said, waving his hand in front of my face.

I shook my head and sidestepped him, finishing the rest of my water. Miller picked up the bottom of his shirt and dragged it across his face before snapping his fingers to get my attention.

"Nah. Just tired."

"That's why you should sleep and let us handle this shit," Magnum said, snatching the empty water bottle from my hands and tossing it in the garbage. "Or at least if you won't, tell us more about this chick you're staying with."

I glanced at Mom, but she kept straightening the kitchen, deliberately ignoring us. I reached for another water, but Miller batted my hand away. "We're waiting."

I pretended to yawn, staring at the horseshoe hung above the sink. "Yeah, I think I'm ready for that nap now." I tried to push past him, but he shoulder-checked me.

"Nice try deflecting, dick."

"Language," Mom said in a sing-song voice while wrapping dishes in bubble wrap.

"You two hooking up?" Magnum said quietly, holding another water bottle just out of my reach.

"What? No?" I said immediately, snatching the water from him.

"Good," he said, rubbing his hands together. "Then introduce me. She's a doctor, right? Is she hot?"

I made a strangled noise in my throat as I imagined any of my brothers dating Jenna. Touching Jenna.

She. Was. Mine.

How could I possibly think that when she was only repaying a favor I did for her friend? Besides, I wasn't relationship material, and Jenna didn't seem like the type who would want a casual hookup. This was a favor, nothing more. Right? Making a move while living together had disaster written all over it.

"Oh my god, dude. You growled. You actually growled like a rabid dog when Mag even suggested meeting her. You have it bad, bro. Shit's gonna get complicated," Miller said, hefting up the microwave on the counter and walking it out to the garage.

"Maybe not," Mom chirped from the kitchen table.

She'd paused with the dishes and sat down, taking out her knitting bag to work on something pink and small with a skull on one side. Her rage-knitting was a weird-ass hobby. My eyes flicked to a pair of potholders she made that said *Don't Be A Twat-Waffle*, but it was nothing compared to her damn topiary designs. She threatened to make me a likeness of my, *ahem*, area if I kept moving them outside. "They have a whole romance genre dedicated to this kind of thing. It could be true love."

"Think of the possibilities. She might blow your mind and chain you to a radiator to be her sex slave. Hell, you have handcuffs, use them," Magnum said.

"Boys, be nice to your brother."

"Yes, ma'am," three voices chorused.

"But you should take her up on the offer if she's into handcuffs. It'd be good for you to blow off some steam, and it might lead to a relationship. I'll never meddle in your love-lives, but I hate that all of my boys are lonely."

Mom put her knitting down and crossed her arms, looking at the four of us with a sympathetic expression on her face. I don't know what threw me more. That her idea of casual sex involved handcuffs, or that she said it was a good idea for me to get laid. Magnum and Miller were leaning against the counter with their mouths wide open, and Maverick was doing his best to hide behind the pizza boxes.

"I just want my boys to be as happy as I was with your father." She shrugged and picked up her project, pulling out the needles and tying off the end.

"Mom, my brain's about to explode. Did you just tell Mark to get laid?" Magnum asked.

"Well, it releases endorphins. I mean, do you think your father and I only had sex four times?"

"Nope, three. My birth was an immaculate conception," Miller said.

"No, it most certainly was not. I remember this one time when your father was late coming home, and I surprised him with..."

"Mom!" we all said at the same time. Miller stuffed his fingers in his ears, and Magnum was shaking his hands like he was trying to dry them without a paper towel.

"The pizza guy was standing in the yard trying to figure out how to get up the non-existent steps, so I took these off his hands," Maverick said, completely ignoring the conversation.

"Nice," Miller said, grabbing the boxes and doing the same thing.

Mom smiled, then passed around paper plates, and we all dug in. The cheesy goodness made my eyes heavy, and when someone suggested I lay down again, I didn't argue. I dragged my tired ass up the stairs and eased Phoebe off my pillow, falling asleep as soon as my head hit the soft surface.

I got this. Deep breaths. It was only a month.

As my Tahoe neared Magnolia Crescent, my heart threatened to beat out of my chest. I felt like crawling up the walls or running twenty miles. Anything to keep me away from her house a little longer.

Why was I nervous?

I asked myself that question one too many times this week. Time to nut up or shut up. *Ugh.* Bad analogy. I pulled into her driveway and took a minute to look at her house. It had a one-car garage with three steps leading up to the red front door. Her small porch was covered with plants. It was a wall of green in front of her yellow house. You would think a yellow house with a red door and shutters would be an eyesore, but it worked muddled by all the green. It looked like her. My phone buzzed in my pocket, and I pulled it out, shaking my head at the message.

Jenna: Door's open.

I couldn't stop the smile from spreading across my face as my nerves settled down. I didn't know why Jenna's type of crazy was so damn cute. These random texts should be creepy, but they weren't. Even her constant babble was adorable as fuck. I wanted to be here, in her space, not because she owed me anything, but because she wanted me here.

Phoebe meowed from her carrier, so I quickly pocketed my phone, grabbed my duffle, walked up the steps, and opened the door to the foyer. There was a long table against the wall painted light blue with a huge mirror over it. A green bowl filled with sea glass sat in the middle of the table, and long, puffed cotton stems were twined together on each side. Several pictures hung beside the mirror.

One was Jenna holding her doctorate, presumably with her parents, and another of Jenna and three other girls hugging with huge smiles on their faces. There was one of Jenna when she was younger, dressed in a lab coat with a stethoscope. My eyes moved over each important moment in her life, and I smiled, enjoying every new detail I learned about her.

"Hey you," she said, walking into the foyer wearing shorts and a tank top. "Promise I wasn't being a weird stalker. I was in the kitchen when your SUV pulled up."

Her face was free of makeup, and her feet were bare. I stood there like an idiot, staring at those legs and curves. Being in such close quarters with her was going to be more complicated than I thought. I stuck one hand in my pocket and rubbed the rabbit's foot, keeping my eyes from straying down her body again.

"Hi," I said, taking a few steps further inside. Jenna came closer and opened her arms. The thought of wrapping my arms around her was something no sane man could resist, and as my hands touched her arms, she lifted her chin and smiled. I couldn't help myself. I leaned down and brushed my lips against her cheek. She sucked in a quick breath before she tightened her arms around my neck and kept them for seconds longer than a friendly hug should last.

Like last time, she fit in my arms and laid her head on my chest. She tucked her head under my neck and gave me one last squeeze before letting go and taking a step back. Her cheeks were flushed, and I could see the color creep down her neck and across her chest. I wanted to run my hands across her collarbone and down her cleavage, tracing that blush.

Fucking hell, I had to stop this.

"Did you find the house okay?" Her soft voice danced across my skin like a lover's caress, and I wanted nothing more than to grip the back of her neck and expose her throat to see how fast her pulse was racing. But I breathed in deep through my nose and pushed the feelings down, determined to get myself under control.

"Yeah, no problems. I can't tell you enough how thankful I am for this."

"I'm glad I could help. But this is weird, isn't it?"

Weird? Like she was uncomfortable? Regretting her decision?

"I mean, we hardly know each other, but I want to know you. It's a lot to take in. I want you to feel welcome, but I had about a hundred plants throughout the house, and I had to move them all to the porch. So now my living room kind of looks like nobody lives here, and it forced me to admit I have a bit of an obsession."

She blushed as she babbled, and then her mouth shut with enough force that I heard her teeth clack like she had to force herself to stop talking.

Phoebe meowed happily as Jenna picked up the carrier and walked to the living room, and I followed her like a lovesick puppy, taking in the warm colors and bright space. She had a big indigo armchair and matching couch, with a dark round coffee table set in the center. The back was all windows that had a view of the patio. Plants were stacked all over on the patio furniture. The walls were the same light color as the table in the foyer and covered with more paintings and pictures. Nothing about her house looked empty or unlived in.

"This is it," she said, sweeping her arm around the space. "Your bedroom is over here. It has its own bathroom, but the shower is on the fritz, so feel free to use mine. I'd keep your bedroom door closed for a day or two, so Phoebe can get used to the new smells before she roams the house. You're working the night shift this week, right?"

"Yeah. I work two twelve-hour shifts from three to three. Then I'm off for twenty-four hours. That's my schedule for the next two weeks, and then I'll transition back to days."

"Have you had dinner?"

"Dinner? No. I was going to pick up something on the way to the station. I'm going to put my duffle and Phoebe in my bedroom if that's okay."

"Of course, here. I'll help." She walked to the open bedroom door and sat the carrier on the bed.

The room was a decent size, with a smaller bed than I was used to, matching night tables, and a dresser with a television on top. I put the duffle bag beside the carrier and took out Phoebe's supplies. Jenna took them from me, brushing her hand on mine. I wanted more of those touches, but instead, I reached in the bag and pulled out my phone charger, slipping behind her to put it on the nightstand. When our bodies brushed, she stood up straighter, and I couldn't help leaning down to smell her hair.

The subtle scent of peaches followed her, and I wanted to carry that smell with me through my shift.

"Mark," she said, looking at me from the foot of the bed.

"Hmm," I answered, reaching out to take Phoebe out of the carrier.

I sat her on the bed, and she paced back and forth, sniffing the comforter and pillows before sitting down to bathe herself.

"Nothing. It's nothing. I'll let you get settled."

With that, she walked out of the bedroom. I could hear her feet creak across the hardwood floor as I unpacked. I hung up my uniforms and took out my small gun safe, laying it on the nightstand.

Phoebe meowed from the bed, and I sat down, kicking off my shoes and scratching behind her ears.

I had a little more than an hour before I had to leave, so I reached up and tugged my T-shirt off, folding it and laying it neatly on the dresser. I was just pulling my pants off when I heard a knock at my door.

"Ugh, shit," I mumbled. I was yanking my pants back up when the door opened.

"Oh my god. I'm so sorry, Mark."

I turned around, and Jenna stood in the doorway with her hands over her eyes, like I was naked and jerking off. I looked down, grateful my jeans had made it almost to my hips, and my briefs were still on.

"Why did you say come in?" Jenna asked, turning her back to me with a huff.

"I didn't."

"What—I thought—what did you say? Oh no—now I'm the weird creeper that just walks in on people." Jenna kept her back to me and walked out, mumbling to herself.

Fuck.

My jeans made it to my hips before I went after her. "Jenna," I called, racing through the living room and finding her talking to herself in the kitchen.

Her back was to me, but I caught the words wacko and peeping tom.

"Jenna," I repeated, coming up behind her as she stood in front of the sink, staring at a lone coffee mug. She faced me and stared at my feet before taking a breath.

"I am so sorry, Mark. I thought you said come in. I was just coming to tell you I was heating something up for you to eat," Jenna said, still staring at my stocking feet.

I traced my hand up her arm and under her chin, forcing her to look at me. She was breathing shallow with her mouth ajar, and when her pink tongue darted out to lick her lips, I had to hold back a groan.

"It's not a big deal. These things are going to happen." The uncertainty in her eyes flipped my stomach. I didn't care if she walked in on me. "We can check awkward half-naked moment off the list. I'm just sorry the sight of my chest horrifies you enough to run away," I joked. Hoping to see that smile.

The right side of her mouth turned up enough to ease my nervousness, and her eyes dropped to my chest. I moved my hand down to her arm, and she lifted one hand and traced the line of tattoos up my shoulder. Her touch was electric, and I balled my other hand into a fist beside me to keep from grabbing her and claiming those strawberry lips.

If I touched her with both hands, I wouldn't be able to stop. She followed the vines and clovers over my chest, and this time, I couldn't help the low moan that escaped my lips. My heartbeat pounded in my ears as she traced the vine down my stomach.

"Your tattoos are beautiful. Much more intricate than mine."

Her fingers danced across my abs, up to my ribs, and over the large Phoenix on my side. I flexed as she moved across my muscles, desperately wanting her to move lower. Her nails scratched lightly on my skin, making me suck in a deep breath with how good it felt. My jeans were still unbuttoned and sat low on my waist, not doing much to conceal my reaction to her touch.

Wait. Did she say…

"Your tattoos?" I tried to remember if I saw them, but all I could think about was her fingers as she moved to trace the four hawks that were tattooed on the other side of my ribs and down to my navel.

Fuck.

She was getting so close to where I needed her touch, and I swallowed hard, glancing down to her hand, and then to my cock, which was straining against my briefs.

Her big hazel eyes glanced up, and I met her gaze. "None where you can see."

Damn.

She was torturing me. We were less than six inches apart, and I continued to trace up and down her arm as she touched me. Her fingers stopped and rested against my stomach, right above where my longitude and latitude coordinates were tattooed.

"I'd really like to see those," I said before I could stop myself. I wanted so bad to drop my head and claim those lips.

I needed to kiss her, needed it more than food, needed it more than air. I leaned in closer and breathed deep, letting her peach scent envelop me. Her eyes darted between my eyes and my lips, and she took a step closer, scratching her nails across my stomach. She tilted her chin, and I lowered my head, ready to feel her, all of her.

"Mark," she drew my name out in a long breath that had my cock so hard it was painful. "This is such a bad idea. But a part of me doesn't care."

She looked down, then back at me, biting her lip and waiting. In this moment, I was ready to do anything to make her mine. But she was worth more than a casual fuck, so I forced myself to stop touching her, and I dropped my arm and took a small step back.

"This is a bad idea," I echoed, ignoring her other comment. I wasn't any good for anyone, Jenna included. She deserved someone whole.

"If you say so," she whispered, turning around so I couldn't see her face. I walked backward until I reached the living room, then turned around, wishing like hell she'd follow me.

11 - JENNA

Comfortable silence. That was our pattern. We stayed out of each other's way and made small talk when we were together. We took turns cooking, doing the dishes, and going grocery shopping. It was like we'd been living together for years. It was familiar and unnerving. Every day, I learned a little more about him, and every day, I was a little more confused.

Yesterday, I came home dog-tired to find dinner on the table and Mark outside watering my plants, like he belonged in my space. Even when he was cleaning up an ivy plant that Phoebe ate and threw up, he did it with a smile and a wink.

I was turned on and disoriented, but mostly turned on.

So turned on.

Because of the touching.

Every chance we had, we touched hands and brushed shoulders, but it was never enough. I craved more. More heat. More friction. More flesh. It felt like a relationship. It felt like more. I caught him several times covertly adjusting himself after we hugged.

At least I wasn't the only one frustrated.

He used my shower every day, and more than once, I saw him in nothing but a towel, walking back to his room. Water beaded from his blonde hair and dripped down his chest, rolling over his tattoos. His body was tanned and toned, and the dusting of blond chest hair he had was mouthwatering. Every inch of his body was a work of art, and all I wanted was to touch him, and lick him, and claim him as mine.

"Those clouds are getting dark. I'm glad I'm on days now," Mark said, interrupting my thoughts and walking up behind me in the kitchen to give my shoulder a gentle squeeze. I leaned into him, but he removed his hand just as quickly and turned around.

I watched him pad over to the fridge, taking in the gray sweatpants that sat low on his hips, black T-shirt, and bare feet. The man had honest-to-god butt dimples, and my mouth watered watching his tight butt flex perfectly as he bent down to get two beers from the bottom shelf. Mark deserved someone who fully appreciated those butt dimples for the delicious morsels they were.

And boy, did I ever appreciate them. And him. All of him.

"Yeah, a big storm's coming." I tore my eyes away from him and gestured to the small television in the corner where the local news was covering the weather. I felt my anxiety spike as I stared at the news, watching the enormous yellow and green blob move closer to Mount Pleasant.

The oven beeped, and I slid in the baked chicken parmesan before focusing on the garlic bread. Mark came up behind me and twisted the top off of one beer, handing it to me before doing the same for his. He took a sip, then rested it on the counter, taking the bread knife from my hands and pulling the loaf toward him. He passed each piece back to me to butter as he sliced, the two of us working in tandem.

"You look tense," he said, wiping his hands on a dishtowel and slinging it over his shoulder. Phoebe pranced into the kitchen, and Mark scooped her up and put her in her cat bed in the corner.

"What? No, I'm not," I said, putting the garlic bread by the oven and taking a drink of beer to cover my nerves. "I'm just trying to decide what book to read next. Definitely not tense. Nope. Loose as a goose." I shrugged and sat the beer on the counter with a clang, causing the foamy liquid to bubble up and overflow. I groaned and snatched it up, slurping the foam and ignoring Mark's obvious glare.

"Liar. Your shoulders are ramrod straight, and you're going to wear a hole in the tile with the way you're tapping your foot."

"I'm fine, really. Nighttime thunderstorms freak me out, but it's not a big deal. Do you like brussels sprouts? They don't really go with Italian, but we need something green on our plates, don't you think? I mean, I don't think the parsley counts. I can sauté them with balsamic..."

Mark stepped closer until he was right in front of me. He didn't speak, but the way he rubbed up and down my arms, fingers trailing over my bare skin, soothed my anxiety. His tongue darted out to wet his lips, and he held my gaze, silently seeing me. He was good at that.

Observing.

Listening.

Knowing.

My mind was bombarded with graphic, intense images. Images of him, of us. Of what it would be like to feel the heat of his skin pressed hard against mine.

I closed my eyes and imagined what his quiet knowing would be like in bed, what he would be like in bed. He'd be exceptional—the kind of man you didn't let leave. I imagined that intensity staring directly into my soul as he pressed me harder into the mattress. He would watch my face and know. Know the pitch of each moan and what each breath meant.

Know when to go hard, grind and adjust, and exactly how to touch my skin with his large, inked hands. He would know how hard to pinch my nipples and the exact pressure my clit needed to shatter and come around his hard, thick length.

He would know, without a word, because he could detect the change in my breath and the shift in my moans. He would know when I said his name louder it meant he needed to grab my ass and bite my neck, pushing my legs further apart to hit the spot, that spot, over and over again until an orgasm started in my toes and built up to such intensity, I would dig my nails in his back, and white spots would dance across my vision.

He would know.

Fuck me! I need a drink.

"Jenna?" he said, squeezing my shoulders. "Where'd you go?"

I tried to smile, but all I managed was a slight upturn of my lips. I was ready to snap with the slightest touch.

"I, um..." I started, desperately thinking of something to say.

I could tell him how he quieted my mind and was in my dreams.

I could ask him to kiss me.

"Did you want to watch a movie after dinner?" I said, chickening out and lifting my hands to rub my temples. Between arguing with Dr. Duvall, volunteering, and my frustration with whatever was going on with us, my head was pounding.

"A movie? Sure," he said, stepping back to pick up his beer. "I'll go pick something good. Be back in a minute to help with the brussels sprouts." He winked and walked out of the kitchen, leaving me breathless.

I sighed and picked up the beer, taking another drink. A part of me screamed to climb him like a spider monkey so we could give in to this tension. The more rational part said to take headache medicine and just be in the moment. Not knowing what to do, I opened the fridge and took out the sprouts, deciding to take my frustration out on the harmless vegetables.

After we ate dinner and loaded the dishwasher, he grabbed us another beer and sat beside me on the couch. "Alright, I've narrowed it down to two choices for you," Mark said, rubbing his hands together. "Your head still bugging you?"

"No. It's better. Tell me what you have in store for us," I said, bumping my leg against his.

"Okay. I guarantee the first choice will make you laugh." He grabbed the remote and scrolled down to a movie, looking at me and raising his eyebrows.

"Oh, *Weekend at Bernie's*. A classic."

"Yes, but if you're looking for something lighter, something quirky, something romantic perhaps, might I suggest this one." He scrolled up to another movie and paused, looking at me for a reaction. "And I am not ashamed to admit this is one of my favorites."

I grabbed the remote and clicked play, pulling a blanket from behind us to cover up my legs. Mark got up and turned off the lights, then sat back down and snatched the corner, pulling it over his legs and reaching forward for his beer. The opening credits for *When Harry Met Sally* started, and I snuggled deeper into the cushions. My eyes got heavy, and I scooted a little closer to Mark, closing my eyes for a second...

"Eek," I shrieked, jerking awake when a loud thunderclap shook the walls of the house. Mark's arms were around me, and he squeezed, but I wiggled out of his grasp and jumped up, turning on the living room lights. I jogged into the kitchen and the dining room, doing the same, then sat back on the couch and pulled the blanket back over me.

"You okay?" Mark wrapped his arm back around me and pulled me close. I let him haul me toward him until I was practically on his lap. My hands were shaking as I looked out the living room windows to see rain falling hard.

"Thunderstorms," I said to his chest, breathing in the scent of his soap. He pulled my legs on his lap and kept his hand there. His touch was soothing, calming, and I reminded myself it was just rain, just a storm.

Lightning flashed, and I braced myself for another booming clap. I tried to prepare, tried to breathe, but when it hit, I jumped and buried my face in Mark's chest, fisting his shirt. When I opened my eyes and looked at him through my lashes, he furrowed his brows and pursed his lips. I tried to move my legs, but he kept a firm hold of them.

"Tell me what's going on, Jenna."

"It's so stupid," I said with a quiet voice, focusing on the words on his T-shirt.

"No, it's not."

That was all he said. Then he waited. He didn't judge. He sat quietly and held me, rubbing his hand up my thigh.

He overwhelmed me. But in a good way, a safe way. I laid my head on his chest and wrapped one hand around his waist, taking comfort in the way my body molded to his.

"When I was five, there was a severe thunderstorm. My parents were at a neighbor's house, and I was with a babysitter. The power went out, and it really freaked her out. She left to go get them, not realizing I'd woken up. I ran from room to room, yelling, but there was only silence. It terrified me. I don't remember much after that, but my dad said they found me in a laundry basket in the garage an hour later."

"Oh, Jenna," he said, stopping his movements on my leg to give it a gentle squeeze.

I wanted to look up, wanted to see his face, but knew if I did, my resolve would crumble. I would climb the rest of the way on his lap and lick his lips like they were made of raspberry sorbet. Even though I was so frustrated, I could barely see straight. I was more worried I'd only see sympathy gazing back at me. I didn't want sympathy. I wanted fireworks.

"Nighttime thunderstorms freak-me-the-hell-out. I have to keep the lights on."

He stayed silent.

"Okay, I'm going to empty the dishwasher, then start some laundry," I said, looking around the room. I couldn't look at him. I was too afraid of what I'd see.

Mark grabbed my hand to keep me from moving and tilted my head to look at him. He ran his fingers down my face, and I closed my eyes, leaning in, but he squeezed my leg harder this time.

"Look at me, Jenna."

I did.

He shifted his hips, keeping a steady hand on my thigh, and leaned closer, brushing his lips against my forehead. His beard was scratchy, but I liked how it felt on my skin. I liked the way he could cocoon me in his warmth. Another roll of thunder rumbled outside, and Mark squeezed me harder, bringing me closer.

In the short time I'd known him, I realized something—he made me feel like a different person, not a rambling bookworm with a weird personality, but a strong, capable woman.

He brushed his lips against one cheek, then the other, tracing his hand down my jaw and neck.

"I think the movie's a lost cause."

"What movie?" I answered, pressing my hand against his stomach.

"Where do you sleep when there's a storm?"

"Normally right here, with all the lights on."

"Can we try something different?"

"Different?"

"Yeah, sleep with me."

I sat up and pushed my legs off his lap, sitting cross-legged beside him. I mean, I was up for anything that would help with my thunderstorm phobia, but I wasn't going to fuck Mark because it was raining outside.

He must have seen something in my face because he removed the arm around me and scrubbed it down his beard.

"I didn't mean sex. I meant sleep—snoring, drooling, sleep. Have you ever slept with someone else during a storm? Or hell, let's sleep on the couch. I don't know. This is seven layers of fucked up."

"What is?" I asked, silently praying any god or goddess would listen to my tightly wound heartstrings. I stretched my legs out and threw the blanket off, staring at the hardwood floor.

"This, Jenna. Us. I want you. I want you so damn bad my eyes cross, but I'm not relationship material."

Hearing him say that had me clenching my thighs together to relieve the tension.

He wanted me.

Why was I holding back? Why didn't I give in? What was so wrong with living and feeling in this moment? *With Mark.* I wanted to feel everything.

I wasn't exactly relationship material either, but that didn't stop me from wanting this, wanting us.

"Tell me a random fact," he said. "Stop me from taking what I want."

His eyes were as dark and endless as the night sky, and once again, my mind was clear. I didn't feel the need to fill the silence. The only thing I felt the need to do was climb back onto his lap and rub myself against him like a cat in heat.

I thought for a second, tapping my finger against my lips—if he wasn't going as insane with lust as me, I'd give him a random fact and take a long bath with my battery-operated boyfriend.

"Did you know your fingers have fingertips, but your toes don't have toe-tips? And you can tiptoe, but you can't tip-finger."

"Huh?" he said, cocking his head toward me and running one hand down his neatly trimmed beard.

He chuckled low in his belly and shook his head, bumping his thigh with mine. My fingertip-tiptoe fact did the trick, but if he was restraining himself because I said it was a bad idea, it was time to let him know I'd changed my mind.

"And you know, I'm not relationship material either? But I won't stop you from taking what you want." I whispered, keeping my eyes focused on the floor.

The tension in the room amped up to a thousand, and I swear I could see the ripples of lust filter through the air. Mark took a deep breath through his nose and let it out slowly.

"Everything will change," he said, resting one large hand on my thigh.

He brushed his thumb over my bottom lip, and a shudder traveled through my body. Everything would change, but that was fine. I wanted whatever this thing was with him, more than I'd ever wanted it with anyone else. I wanted to give him every part of me—even the weird, twisted, awkward parts. Steadying my nerves, I climbed on his lap and straddled him, locking my arms behind his head and tugging on the short strands of his hair.

"Good."

It was not a gentle, teasing kiss. Our lips touched, and it consumed me. With each stroke of his tongue, he stole my breath, claiming me, branding me, ruining me for anyone else. His hands wound around my neck, his fingers slipping through my hair as he held me firmly in place.

I was a willing participant, along for the ride, desperate to keep up as his tongue tangled with mine. A low growl escaped his mouth as I sucked on his lip, but I swallowed the sound, surging in to taste him, claim him, and brand him too.

This wasn't a power struggle because I wanted to give in, wanted to feel his raw power consume me, wanted him to make me burn. And burn I did. One hand traveled down my back and gripped my thigh, pulling me closer. I surged forward, brushing my core against his hard length.

Holy shit.

You know what they said about guys with big feet? Or big hands? It was all true. The equipment Mark was working with should come with a warning label for any unsuspecting veterinarians who happened to climb on for a ride.

I opened my eyes and broke our kiss to look down. Mark did the same, keeping one hand fisted in my hair. My shorts were pushed up high on my thighs, and his thick cock was pressed against my pussy with nothing but flimsy material between us. I closed my eyes and threw my head back, surging forward again to grind against him.

Mark tugged my head to the side and gave me wet, open-mouth kisses down my neck. He desperately sucked on the spot where my neck met my shoulder like he was trying to leave his brand on my skin. I let him, loudly moaning his name in encouragement. He dug his fingertips into my thigh and moved me back and forth, keeping his lips locked on my neck.

He broke away with a wet pop, gazing at me with dark, hooded eyes.

"That's it. Let me hear you. Tell me what you need."

I nodded my head, lost in the moment of his hands, his lips, his cock. Hunger, demanding and hot was pooling in my core as I grasped the front of his shirt and pulled it up, wanting to drag my fingernails across his tattoos. He let go of my hair and reached behind his head, pulling his shirt off before reaching for mine. I kept thrusting my hips as I took off my shirt, leaving me in just a thin black bra.

"Tell me," he demanded again, fisting one hand in my hair and gripping my thigh so hard my movements stilled, and my breath nearly stalled in my throat.

Mark buried his face in between my tits, pulling down the cups of my bra and licking, sucking, worshiping.

"I need your mouth here," I said, taking off my bra to bare my breasts fully to him.

His eyes were hungry, and he let go of my hair, grabbing both hips and pulling me forward to lash his tongue against one nipple, then the other. My control was slipping as I rocked my core against him, and I pushed him back against the sofa, leaning back to scratch one hand up his stomach and over his nipple. He hissed with the contact, and I did it again.

"Fucking hell, Jenna."

Then it was my turn to trail my lips over his skin, across his collarbone, down one pec, and to his other nipple, where I flicked my tongue across the smooth disk. He hissed in a breath, and I smiled into his chest, nibbling on him and loving the red, raised trail I was leaving on his skin.

He moaned and pulled my head away, bringing his lips back to mine in a soul-searing kiss. I gasped as he grabbed my hips with both hands and dragged my pussy against his cock.

"Mark, fuck. Don't stop. Please. Make me come," I moaned, lost in the moment and feeling nothing but him.

He gave me one last kiss, then broke away and pressed our foreheads together, so we could both look down. His sweatpants had ridden down on his hips, and the head of his cock was visible. A bead of pre-come was shiny on the tip, and I brought one hand down, swiping my thumb across his swollen head. I brought my thumb to my mouth and sucked, letting his salty taste burst across my tongue. Groaning with the taste of him on my lips, he grabbed my hips with renewed vigor, grinding his cock hard against me.

"Fuck yes, I'll make you come. Use my cock," Mark growled, his movements getting jerkier as he chased his pleasure. I scratched my nails up his stomach again and pinched his nipple hard. Mark threw his head back on the couch and squeezed his eyebrows together, moving me faster, harder.

I kept one hand on his nipple and put the other on his shoulder, thrusting madly against him and digging my nails into his hard flesh. A low moan started in my throat, and as his cock brushed against my clit, the moan turned into a guttural cry once, twice, three times.

"Yes, Fuck, Mark."

"More," he hissed, and something broke inside the depths of my soul like he wanted to see me unhinged and mad with lust.

I fisted his hair and pulled, so his dark, hooded eyes met mine.

"Don't you fucking stop, Mark. Grind that thick cock against me and imagine how good it will feel buried so deep inside my pussy, a piece of you will always be there. Squeeze my tits, hard. I want to watch you come. I want to watch it paint my stomach, leaving molten tracks on my skin. Don't stop, please. Pull my hair," I cried, and his eyes turned to black slits as he lost whatever shard of control he still had.

Fuck yes, he did.

Mark released one hip and grabbed the back of my neck, fisting my hair and pulling hard so my neck was exposed. He latched back onto the same tender spot he was sucking on and bit down hard enough for my toes to tingle. I cried his name, pinching his nipple and arching my back, so he had to steady me with his hand, but I didn't stop.

I kept thrusting, grinding, riding him until I felt his hand tighten impossibly harder in my hair and his whole body shuddered. I felt his cock against my stomach, then hot splashes of his come coated me as spots danced across my vision, and my orgasm destroyed my body, shattering me into a million pieces. But he was there to catch me.

Mark slowly loosened his grip and ran his hands down my back, crushing my chest to his and burying himself in my neck. We sat there in silence until our heartbeats were in sync.

I didn't want to move. I wanted to stay wrapped in his arms. He nuzzled my chest, my neck and eventually made his way up to my mouth, where he kissed me gently like he had all the time in the world to explore.

"Wow," I said, leaning down to rest my head on his shoulder.

His fingertips danced along my spine, and he sighed, sounding content. I couldn't imagine going to separate bedrooms after that, but my brain was still trying to piece together a coherent thought. We untangled our limbs and stood up, Mark tugging on my hand toward my bedroom.

"Wow is an understatement," he said, disappearing into the bathroom and returning with a wet washcloth.

He wiped down my stomach and his, then tugged down my shorts, leaving me in my soaked panties.

He traced my jaw then walked out of the bedroom. I was speechless, still recovering from my earth-shattering orgasm as I went to the bathroom, changing into an oversized T-shirt. I wanted him by my side and next to me, but it wasn't like I could march into his room and demand he snuggle. The bed creaked as I sat on the edge, wondering what would happen next.

"You didn't think you were sleeping alone, did you?" Mark said, returning with Phoebe and wearing nothing but boxer briefs. He sat her on the foot of the bed and crawled underneath the covers, opening his arms to me. I slid in next to him, resting my head on his chest, and fell asleep.

BY YOUR SIDE

12 - MARK

Things were happening down there. Not good things. Uncomfortable things. Cringe-worthy things. Tear-jerking things. I was spending more time rearranging my junk than Jenna had spent there all last night, and that was unacceptable. Especially if I wanted a repeat. And hell-to-the-yes, I wanted a repeat.

I wanted her to pick my dick out of a police lineup after he was charged with giving too many orgasms. But that wasn't going to happen unless some serious manscaping took precedent over any other plans this morning. I was three hairs away from being a full-on sasquatch, and I wouldn't expect Jenna to hang out down there if my dick looked like a Mogwai.

There was nothing better than feeling a warm, wet mouth wrapped around your cock, and I palmed myself, wondering how Jenna's mouth would feel. After last night, it was easy to imagine her standing up, then sinking to her knees, trailing her fingernails up my thighs, and swallowing me down.

And that kiss.

That fucking kiss ruined me. I was done for, content to feel her tongue tangling with mine until she ran her nails over my nipples, and I felt her hot pussy grind in my lap. Then my Universe exploded in technicolor as I grabbed her thighs, getting us both off. I'd never given my nipples a second thought, but with her on my lap, running her nails over my chest…

I stroked my cock again and reached down to palm my balls.

Shit.

First things first, I had other priorities before taking care of my hard-on. I dug through my duffle, coming up empty. Jenna said I could help myself to anything I needed, but something felt taboo about opening her bathroom cabinets. Like I was about to find out all of her secrets.

Phoebe jumped up to the side of the tub and looked at me. More like silently judging me. *Yeah. I agree, kitten.* I'd text her.

Me: Do you have a pack of disposable razors or something?
Jenna: Maybe. Check underneath my bathroom sink.
Me: Thanks. Are you sure?
Jenna: Yeah, my dildos are in another drawer.
Me: Damn, Dr. Cutie.
Jenna: Only kidding. Or am I? ;-) But seriously, help yourself if you find something that works.

I pocketed my phone and opened the bottom cabinets, searching through the mismatched bottles, and picking up a bottle of cherry-flavored lube.

Gah, it smelled like a month-old lollipop left in a hot car.

It still might be fun to play with, though. Maybe I should accidentally leave it on the bathroom counter. *Nah.* I didn't need a bottle of lube to suggest what I wanted. I'd wait until Jenna got home, meet her at the door, pull her to me, and own her body right there in the foyer. Complicated or not, feeling her last night was just an appetizer, and I was ready for the main fucking course.

Setting the lube toward the front of the cabinet, I pushed aside more random bottles until I found a tube of hair removal cream. I picked it up and pulled off random instructions stuck to the bottom.

The tube said it removed hair on and around the bikini zone. I glanced down at my dick. There was no way my junk would fit in a bikini, but the same idea worked here. Take a shower, apply, wait, remove. Dark or coarse hair might need to be left on for five extra minutes. Peeling off my briefs, I figured I'd do ten extra minutes just to be sure.

The shower did the trick, clearing my head enough to focus on my balls. Or rather, how Jenna would react to my manscaped perfection. I wiped off the mirror and dropped my towel, glancing at Phoebe, who was sitting on the toilet, staring. I shook my head and picked up the tube, squeezing some on my fingers. It felt like a mix between lotion and shaving cream. I lifted my dick with one hand and spread it over my balls with the other.

When my balls were coated in the white stuff, I set a timer on my phone and finished drying off. A minute or two in, my balls got a little warmer and tingled, but nothing was going on down there other than me looking like I had white old-man nuts. I grabbed my razor, shaved my neck, and trimmed my beard. When the timer had two minutes left, I said fuck it and jumped back in the shower.

It felt like someone had dipped my berries in hot sauce, so I grabbed the closest bottle on the nearest shelf and furiously washed off the cream, turning the water as cold as I could stomach it.

I prided myself on having a high pain tolerance. Hell, I super-glued a cut on my leg closed last year when I fell off the roof. But nothing, nothing compared to the pain that was shooting through my body. I shut off the water and grabbed a towel, walking bowlegged to the kitchen. The only thing that mattered was cooling my junk.

Thank fuck Jenna wasn't here. I opened the freezer and found a bag of frozen peas. Grabbing them and going back to my room, I sat on the edge of my bed and glanced down to see the damage. My balls were smooth as the day I was born, and I'd be impressed if they weren't an angry shade of red. I threw the frozen peas beside me and gently sat down on them, hissing out a breath as the cold gave me blessed relief.

Never again.

What the hell was I thinking, smoothing that shit all over the most sensitive part of my body? The next time I jerked off, tiny icicles and snowflakes would be the only things coming out. I'd rather pluck out my nut hair one at a time than ever do that again. I laid back on the bed, not bothering to get dressed, and closed my eyes, glad the pain was turning into nothing but a dull roar.

I woke up to the front door opening and Jenna calling my name. Phoebe was lying on my chest, and she lifted her head, annoyed with the interruption. The peas had thawed, and I tossed the bag beside me and shifted my legs. I was in that weird head-space when you're not sure if you'd been asleep for five minutes or five hours.

"Hey, Mark. I got a new plant for Phoebe that she might not barf up and thought we could go out for BBQ."

She knocked on the door, and I grabbed a pair of athletic shorts from the end of the bed and pulled them on.

"Come in," I said, rubbing a hand down my face.

"Oh, shit. What happened? You look like death warmed over."

"I made a bad decision earlier." I motioned to the peas, then laid back on the pillows, patting the space beside me and throwing an arm over my eyes.

"Oh, sorry. I didn't mean you looked bad. You could never look bad. Not with your eyes and body and elbows. You look worn out. I was kind of hoping you, um, wouldn't be. Not you know for any particular reason other than, you know, Friday. But I wouldn't assume you wanted to do that again. Unless you did, and then woo-hoo for me—and you too, because I would rock your world."

"My elbows?" I cracked open one eye.

"Yeah, they're smooth. Any man who takes the time to take care of his elbows deserves a woman who appreciates them."

She rubbed the one closest to her, then laid down beside me. I put my hand on her thigh, squeezing it so she'd take a breath and chill. I was almost ashamed to admit what happened, but she was looking forward to round-two as much as I was, and I didn't think I'd be able to get it up until my balls were back to a normal color.

"Have you ever used hair remover cream?" I faced her, propping my head on my arm.

"Yeah, I used to use it on my legs, but waxing is so much easier. Why?"

"I forgot my razor and thought using yours would be a smart idea."

"Where?" she asked, propping herself up as well to look at me. She lifted my arm and ran a hand down my chest, making my dick take notice. He wasn't in on the memo that we were out of commission for a day or two.

"Yeah, um. Not there." I gestured to my shorts, and her eyebrows shot up.

"Oh my god, you put that stuff on your dick?"

She moved her hand to my elastic waistband and tugged. I quickly put my hand on top of hers and shook my head.

"No, lower than that. And I'm good. Just need more frozen vegetables to take the edge off."

"Wait—what? Are you talking about your, your…" She gestured to my balls, then blew out a deep breath and grabbed her pussy like she was in pain. "Your testicles? Your poor balls, Mark. No wonder you look like a mac truck ran you over. Have you taken pain pills? Are you swollen? Here, let me look."

She went for my shorts again, and I batted her hand away, shaking my head.

"Not a chance. You don't want to see what's going on down there."

I cradled one hand protectively over my man-berries and tried to shove her off the bed. I wasn't rough, but there was no way she was looking at my boys in their pitiful state. When she got up close and personal with my area, it would be when I was standing tall and proud.

"Oh, shut up! I'm a doctor. Let me at least make sure you didn't burn yourself."

Burn? Holy fuck-balls!

Could I get burned from hair remover cream? I had to be at work in the morning and just wanted to spend the next twelve hours wallowing in my stupidity and sleeping. But if there was a chance I hurt myself, maybe she needed to look. That was not an area I was willing to compromise.

I patted her leg again and threw my arm up over my face. "Um. You're a vet."

She slugged me right in the pec with her elbow and sat straight up, crossing her arms and glaring at me with a look that would scare her one-day children.

"When doctors go to med school, how many life forms do they learn to treat? One, right? Guess how many vets learn? Wait. Don't even guess. Let me tell you. Just last week, last week, on top of the usual dog, cat, bird, hamster patients. I saw an armadillo, gecko, pot-bellied pig, snake, scorpion, goldfish, squirrel..."

She kept going, ticking off animal after animal, even after I grabbed her thigh. I could tell she was getting more and more worked up, and truthfully, I wasn't trying to downplay her career. There was no way in hell I could go to school for even half as long as she had. I just wasn't going to tug down my pants and have her potentially laugh at my cherry-red family jewels.

"... and a deer!"

"Baby, listen."

"Don't you *baby* me." She threw her legs off the side of the bed and was about to storm off when I grabbed her arm and tugged her down, throwing one leg over hers to pin her in place. She tried to squirm, but I kept her pinned until she was still, praying she kept her flailing arms away from my bollocks.

"The first time you see my balls is not going to be like this."

That quietened her down. She stared at me and furrowed her eyebrows, then laughed—a full belly laugh that shook her entire frame.

"So, you're saying you want me to see your balls?"

"Fuck yeah, I do, but not like this. And you know I'm not making light of your career."

I gave her a big grin and waggled my eyebrows like an idiot, earning another small chuckle.

"I know. I blame it on your toasted marshmallows. While I totally understand why you wouldn't want me all up in your business, someone should take a look if you are in this much pain. Want me to drive you to Urgent Care?"

Oh, hell no. No random dude is going to feel me up.

"No, that's okay. Fine, you can look. I'd rather you down there than an ER doctor."

"I appreciate you trusting me, Mark. I'll even kiss them to make it all better if you're a good boy and stay still."

What?

My dick twitched, desperately trying to get in the game again and play naughty nurse, but she wiggled out of my grip and stood up.

"I'm going to wash my hands. Take off your shorts, and I'll be right back."

Shit.

I pulled the elastic of my shorts and looked at my junk. I'd watched enough porn when I was younger to know my goods were above average, but I still wasn't thrilled this was the first time she was going to see them.

"Okay," she said, walking back into the bedroom with her glasses perched on her nose and a bottle of something in her hand. "Show me the jewels."

"Jesus, not pulling any punches, are you?"

"Nope, rip the band-aid off. Trust me. Here, rub this for luck." She handed me the rabbit's foot on my nightstand and patted my leg before putting a hand on her hip, waiting for me to expose myself.

I inched my shorts down and cupped my dick with one hand, getting him out of the way so she could laugh at me.

"Did you know testicles evolved to have a ton of nerves that are crazy sensitive to pain? So guys will be more likely to protect them in case of danger."

"I did a shit job of protecting them this afternoon," I said, squinting to see what she was doing.

"Nah, you have a ton of body hair. I'm sure it's not all roses and rainbows being bunched up in your briefs all day, so the lack of hair helps. I mean, after I waxed for the first time, I knew there was no going back."

Her fingertips grazed the inside of my thigh, and I sucked in a breath, waiting for her to pass judgment on my balls. She leaned down, closer, closer until she was inches away from my nads. Thank fuck I hadn't done anything strenuous since I showered.

"Okay. There aren't any burns or blisters. I have Aloe Vera mixed with CBD that will help, but it's going to be cold."

"No colder than sitting on a bag of frozen peas. And did you say CBD? You trying to get me high."

"Nope, I want you stone-cold sober and not under duress when I see you naked again. Oh, and remind me to throw those peas out, no offense to your marbles."

"None taken. So, everything looks good?"

"Yep, well above average." She leaned down and pressed a kiss to the hand holding my dick, then pointed to a bottle on the bed as I pulled my shorts up. "Take some ibuprofen and relax. You'll be fine tomorrow."

"Thanks for looking and not laughing at me."

"Um. Sure, Mark. I mean, it's kinda funny when you think about it, but you're in pain. I'm not going to be the asshole who laughs at you. Plus, I did enjoy getting a better look at your assets."

Her eyes got wide as soon as the words left her lips, and I wanted to beat my chest like a Caveman and give my dick a high-five.

"Well, your body is a fucking sight to behold. I can't wait to see every inch, including your elusive tattoos."

"Then heal up fast," she purred, leaning down to kiss my cheek. "I'll order in."

"Hey, um. Speaking of my balls…" I started, then trailed off when I realized what I'd said.

"Yes? Digging for another compliment?"

"No. I mean, yes. I mean, we haven't talked about last night."

"You're right," she said, matter-of-factly. "I liked what we did last night. I'd like to do more of it while you're here."

While you're here?

Was she not looking for anything long-term either? Not wanting to ruin the moment by letting her know this had a definite expiration date, I pulled her back on the bed, burying my face in her neck.

"That sounds like a terrific idea."

"Damn straight it does. Now chill. I'll order dinner."

I laid back down and watched her ass sway as she walked out. Phoebe hopped up from her cat bed and climbed back on the bed, settling beside me with a yawn.

"Good plan, cutie," I said, scratching her head before closing my eyes and relaxing until dinner got here.

13 - JENNA

It had been a million hours since the orgasm that shattered my life on Friday, and we hadn't slept in the same bed since. So what if it had only been a little over forty-eight hours? Not that I was counting, but I was hoping movie night wasn't a fluke. Granted Saturday, his poor man berries were the color of a ripe tomato, and he'd slept right through dinner until he left for the station Sunday.

Then he worked late, and I was asleep by the time he got home. I thought of going to sleep in his bed or locking him out of his room, so he didn't have a choice, but that would be stalker-level creepy.

Could traffic cops arrest people for stuff like that?

I was on edge and sorely disappointed I hadn't been the little spoon to his big spoon or gotten a better look at his pocket rocket. I mean, balls were balls. Some were hairy. Some were big. Some hung low. I'd never given them a second thought—but Mark's balls were impressive. Just the right size, with one hanging slightly lower than the other. It made me want to lick up the seam to the underside of his cock.

What was the matter with me? Obsessing over freaking testicles?

He said he wasn't relationship material. I wasn't either, but there was a lingering seed of doubt in the far corners of my head calling bullshit. My hours were crazy, and my brain went from spewing useless facts and babbling to sleep-deprived. I had to force myself to make time for my friends because I was so tired most days, all I wanted to do was curl up in bed with a good book. But I always made time for them, and I could see myself making time for a relationship.

Making time for Mark.

Tonight was a rare exception. My morning surgery was canceled, and my first appointment wasn't until after eleven. The day was shaping up to be a respectable seven hours. Later, we were all meeting at *B's Bar* after work. Annaleigh and Max had officially made up, and they wanted to take us out.

I added butter pecan flavored creamer to my coffee, sat at the kitchen table, and glanced at the clock. I was going to enjoy the coffee, try to entice Gretchen with breakfast, take a long, hot shower, and try not to think about the damn letter on the table.

As if it was mocking me, I saw it peeking out from under a magazine. Sighing, I pulled it forward and read it once. Then I read it again.

Wilmington.

It was an offer to be the *Executive Director* and lead vet of *All Four Paws*. I'd implement decisions without someone breathing down my neck every time I wanted to spend money. It'd be a significant pay cut, but I'd be closer to my parents and my brother.

The director and I hit it off after spending a weekend volunteering while visiting my parents in Southport, but I got a sick feeling in my stomach each time I tried to talk about it out loud. My home was here. My clinic was here. My girls were here.

Mark was here.

It was stupid thinking about him. This was temporary. Especially if I was considering accepting the position, but maybe I should invite him out tonight. He helped Annaleigh, and I was sure Max and Edward would appreciate having another guy there.

I pushed the letter back under the magazine and stood up, putting my coffee spoon in the sink and opening the fridge for vegetables for Gretchen. I was debating between cantaloupe and zucchini when the doorbell rang. Phoebe peeked around the kitchen door, and I cinched my robe and scooped her up, padding to the front door.

I opened it to an older woman standing on my porch with a casserole dish and a smile. She had chin-length blonde hair going white at the temples and kind, dark eyes. I tilted my head and furrowed my brows, putting down the one glass panel on the screen door.

"Hi, good morning. Can I help you?"

"Oh, Hi, you must be Jenna. I'm Beverly, but please call me Bev. I hope you don't mind me popping by. I was just going to leave a little something on the porch, but I saw your car and figured I'd knock. Is this a bad time?" she asked, holding the casserole with one hand so she could straighten the purse on her shoulder.

Something about her looked familiar, and I wracked my brain thinking of any clients that called me by my first name or knew where I lived. Phoebe squeaked, and I absentmindedly scratched her head, thinking as hard as I could.

"And there's my little grand kitten. I brought you something, Little Lady."

"Mrs. Hansen?" I said, reaching to unlock the screen door.

"Yes, I didn't tell you my last name, did I? No wonder you have such a strange expression on your face. I made a sweater for Phoebe and was going to drop it by, but I saw your car."

"Yes, of course," I said, a little too loud. "Please come in." I held the door open so she could walk in and locked it behind her as she marched right to the kitchen like she knew where it was.

I followed, unsure what was going on, to find her switching on the oven and opening drawers. She reminded me a little of my mom, who would always walk into a room and take charge of the kitchen.

"I didn't mean to barge in like this," she said, taking out two forks and a serving spoon. "I was heading to my other son's house to thank him for helping me in my garden and thought I would drop off a little gift."

"Can I get you a cup of coffee?"

"Yes, only cream, please, and I'll take my grand kitten if you don't mind."

"Not at all," I said, passing her over before taking down another coffee cup and adding creamer. Bev cooed at Phoebe, telling her how pretty she was and how much healthier she looked as I worked.

"Here you go." I handed her the cup and motioned to the kitchen table, where I pushed aside the letter and magazine so we could sit.

"Thank you so much, Jenna. This smells delicious."

I sat down and pulled my coffee closer, taking a sip while Bev reached down in her purse and took out a tiny pink sweater with a skull and crossbones on one side. She wiggled the sweater on Phoebe, then held her up, looking at her handy work.

"OMG, that's the cutest thing ever, Mrs. Hansen," I said, reaching for Phoebe so I could oh and ah over the design.

"Oh, Bev, please, and thank you. Mark mentioned she needed to stay warm. I should have brought this over sooner. I did it in my rage-knitting class."

"Rage-knitting?"

"Oh, yes. You'd be surprised how much better you feel after spending

144

an afternoon knitting a nice tea-towel that says *Kiss My Ass You Stupid Twat-Waffle."*

I snorted my coffee and coughed, struggling to breathe as Bev leaned over and slapped my back.

Twat-Waffle?

"It doesn't have to be so crass, you know. I knitted Miller a cap that had a hand holding up a middle finger."

"That sounds pretty amazing and relaxing, actually."

I could imagine the girls and I all sitting around, drinking, and knitting profanity onto things. Addison would live for the opportunity to shower her friends and enemies with elegantly inscribed words like *douche-canoe* and *ho-bag.*

"Oh, it is. It helped me so much after my Martin died. That and my topiary trimming and bonsai art. I had a lot of misplaced anger. You should come with me to the next class, the ladies would love you, and honestly, this is nice. I hope you don't think I'm a nosy meddler."

"What? Why would I think that? Also, you know you're going to have to elaborate on topiary trimmings now, right?"

"Oh, that. Rage knitting has taken a back seat to my topiary and bonsai designs. Here, check out this one on my porch. And all my boys have several at their houses."

I tried to remember seeing plants at Mark's house the night he brought Phoebe home, but honestly, it was all a blur. Bev pulled out her phone and flipped through her pictures until she came to the one she wanted. She turned the screen, and my eyes got wide as I stared at a giant... dick?

"Is that a—"

"Dick? Yes. My neighbor can be a real pain in the ass, if you know what I mean? So I started trimming topiary bushes. Keep scrolling."

I did and saw her patio was covered with topiaries of all shapes and sizes. There were dicks, middle fingers, vaginas, boobs, and I was pretty sure one was a giant butt.

"Wow. I'm kinda obsessed with plants myself, but nothing like this."

"You are?" she said, looking around the house.

"Yes, I'll show you."

We grabbed our coffee and walked to the patio, where Bev took in all my plants. She walked up and down, making noises of appreciation while touching the leaves and flowers.

"This is amazing, Jenna. Why are they out here?"

"Oh, Little Phoebe is a monster, and about ninety-nine percent of these are toxic to her. All my plants have been relocated while they're here. Every time I try to bring one inside, she eats it, then throws it back up."

"This is quite the collection. You should have a greenhouse, but there is one thing missing."

Bev picked up a wilted purple orchid and set it behind two prayer-plants that were thriving in the sun.

"I'm going to see if topiaries are toxic and then bring you a few. Oh! You could do bonsai plants as well. Nothing gets you over a bad day like shaping a bonsai tree to look like a labia."

I snort-laughed and stared at Bev, who had her hands on her hips like it was every day she talked about labia's and dicks.

"I'd love one, thank you."

"Of course, let's go inside. And just so you know, I honestly thought you would both be at work. Mark's almost thirty, and here I am, showing up with gifts first thing in the morning."

She shooed her hand like she was worried she'd made a bad impression.

"I had a surgery canceled this morning, so I don't have to be in until later. I'm glad to have the company. I've gotten used to having someone around."

146

Was that true?

Mark and I were almost like roommates until recently, but his presence surrounded me, and I'd gotten used to it. Smelling him in my bathroom, little signs of him all over the house, and the thoughtful gestures that made me feel treasured.

"Isn't that lucky for you," Bev said, taking a sip of her coffee. She nodded her head and closed her eyes, smelling the coffee and taking another sip. "This is amazing. What creamer do you use?"

"Oh, here," I said, standing up to take the bottle from the fridge and show her the brand. Bev reached down and took her phone from her purse, snapping a picture of the label. The delicious coffee smell in the kitchen was slowly being replaced by something that smelled even better. Something sticky-sweet and cinnamony.

"What is that smell?"

"Homemade cinnamon rolls for my oldest, Maverick. He spent all day Saturday weeding my garden, and these are his favorite."

"I guess I should feel guilty that cinnamony goodness isn't making its destination."

"Heavens, no," she said with a wave of her arm. "I can make more for him, and I wanted to thank you as well. You pulled Marcus's irons out of the fire, and I appreciate you opening your home to him."

Bev reached out and clasped her hand in mine, giving it a gentle squeeze.

"Absolutely, I enjoy his company."

"That's good to hear, Jenna. I might be overstepping here, but he always holds everyone at arm's length, occupational hazard and all that. This time will be good for him."

I wanted so badly to ask her to elaborate, to shed a little light on Mark's personality, but instead, I got up when the oven beeped and slid on

147

oven mitts, opening the door to one of the most delicious smells I'd ever encountered.

"Oh my goodness, you should bottle that smell and sell it to a candle company. You'd be a millionaire."

Bev chuckled as I plated two portions and brought them to the table. I filled our coffee cups and added a little more creamer before sitting back down.

"Thank you. Now dig in while the icing is still melty."

"You don't have to tell me twice," I said, taking a giant forkful of the sugary goodness. "I have a sweet tooth as big as this casserole."

"I'll remember that."

I brought the forkful to my mouth and moaned around the bite. Sweet, gooey cinnamon flavors burst across my taste buds, and I put my fork down and closed my eyes.

"Bev, you are my hero."

I took another bite as Bev sipped her coffee.

"Thank you. I should get going. I'm sure you have to get ready soon."

I looked at the clock on the oven and nodded, taking another bite.

"Thank you so much for stopping by. You're always welcome here."

"I'll make sure I call next time, and whatever you're doing with Marcus, keep it up," she said, standing up and lifting Phoebe from her cat bed for snuggles. "He has this crazy idea in his head he has to stay single because he's on the force, but really, he's just closing himself off from everyone who loves him." Bev reached out her hand, and I grasped it in mine. "You're good for him."

"Oh, we're not, I mean, we haven't. Not that I don't want to. Complicated," I said, stuttering through the words.

"You don't have to explain anything to me. I'll support my boys with whatever they choose. Thank you for the coffee."

"Anytime, Bev."

I followed her to the foyer, and she turned around, giving me a soft smile that made her eyes sparkle, just like Mark's.

"Bye, Jenna. I hope to see you again soon, and I'll be sure to bring you a bonsai. You have quite the green thumb."

"Thank you, Bev. Me too."

I gave her one last wave and stood on the porch with Phoebe until she backed her car out of the driveway and headed down the street. Walking back into the house, I put the rest of the cinnamon rolls in the fridge and rinsed out the coffee cups. Taking the overripe zucchini out of the fridge, I headed out to the porch to feed Gretchen breakfast before getting ready for work.

⋐⋑⋐⋑

As I pulled into the driveway, I couldn't figure out how I was home only seven hours later. Mark's truck was already here, and I unlocked the door, calling out a greeting. While I was waiting for an answer, I pulled out my phone, deciding to text the girls and see about switching things up.

Me: Anyone mind if I invite Mark tonight?
Addison: Oh, I wish you would. I'd love to meet the man that dry humped you to orgasm.
Annaleigh: Duh. Broody Max wants to thank him.
Olivia: GIF of a cat jumping up and down
Me: I need to talk about this. Are ya'll going to make it weird?
Addison: Why would we make it weird? I only want to thank his magic cock for dragging the stick out of your ass. You've been burning the candle at both ends. Something had to give, and I'm

glad it led to an orgasm.

Olivia: Damn, Addison.

Addison: What? It's true.

*Annaleigh: We won't make it weird. Mark, Max, and Edward can
talk about guy stuff at the bar for a while and let us chat.*

Me: He might not say yes. I'm so confused.

*Annaleigh: Um, yes, he will. See you soon. We'll talk about
everything.*

I put my phone back in my pocket and listened for any other sounds
in the house. It was silent. Weird, since his truck was here. I walked to my
bedroom, stripped off my clothes, started the shower, and grabbed a towel.
I was anxious to tell the girls about meeting his mom and the job offer, but
I didn't know how to start. I wasn't used to being indecisive.

I was closing the bedroom door when I heard Mark yell my name. I
grabbed my robe from the back of the bathroom door and slipped the silk
over my shoulders, cinching the waist and walking to the living room.

Mark was dressed in black athletic shorts and a gray tank top. His shirt
was sweaty and clung to his skin, but instead of wrinkling my nose and
insisting he take a shower, I wanted to lick his neck and taste him.

"Jenna," he rumbled, noticing me when he turned around.

His muscles rippled as he strode forward, fisting the knot in my robe
and pulling me flush against him. He used his other hand to grab the back
of my neck and kiss me fiercely, his tongue sweeping into my mouth as he
growled low in his throat, grinding his hips into mine obscenely. I wrapped
my arms around him and pressed my chest to his, sucking on his lower lip
and nipping lightly.

He pulled away, pressing his forehead to mine and breathing heavily.
"I missed you today."

"Woah. Going from zero to full contact, Officer Handsome."

As if to prove my point, he gave me a thrust, pressing his hard cock to my stomach, then reached behind him and tugged off his shirt, revealing miles of powerful muscles and beautiful colors. "I was the idiot that doused my nuts in murder-cream and missed two entire nights with you."

"Hmm, but I have plans."

"Maybe I have plans too," he said, smiling and pulling away to adjust himself. I shook my head and looked down, biting my lip.

"Eyes up here," he added, running a hand over his head. "Sorry if I'm a sweaty mess. I went for a run."

"Don't apologize. You smell amazing. I want to rub myself all over you like poison ivy, then lick you like a popsicle."

"Um," he chuckled, glancing down at his body.

"Oh, god, bad analogy. It's just you're so manly and strong, and when you look like that…"

His chest hair was damp and sticking to his pecs, then dipped down his abs and onto his happy trail. He didn't have a six-pack, and he didn't need one. His muscles were from hard manual work, not doing thousands of sit-ups. Every inch of him was hard and taut, except his cock. I imagined that would be like steel wrapped in velvet, and I made a strangled sound in my throat, thinking of seeing him in all his natural glory.

I trailed off, waving my hand in front of him and shaking my head, desperately trying to save myself from jumping on him like a crazed harpy. "But seriously, I was wondering if you wanted to go out with me tonight. I'm meeting my girls and their significant others at *B's Bar*."

"I'll need to shower unless you want me and my sweaty ass to go like this." He rubbed his hand down his chest and waggled his eyebrows.

"Shower first, dinner after," I said, shaking my head and pointing to the bedroom.

"You go ahead," he said, gesturing to the kitchen. "I'm going to get something to drink and feed Phoebe."

"Thanks." I nodded and turned around, digging deep for the courage to tease him a little.

I cleared my throat and untied the knot to my robe, slipping it over my shoulders and letting it pool on the ground. If he was looking, and I was most definitely not turning around to find out, he would get his first look at my tattoo and my ass. I told myself I just wanted him to see my Lotus Flower, but the thought of teasing him made me shiver, and I couldn't help but glance before I got to my bedroom door.

Mark had turned around and was staring at me with a dark, feral expression on his face. An expression that made my knees weak and my pulse race. An expression that made me crave tonight.

Crave him.

14 - MARK

Holy fuck. Talk about an open invitation I was ready to pounce on. It wasn't the beautiful colors of her Lotus Flower tattoo that started on her upper thigh and wrapped around her waist that had me following like a love-sick puppy. And it wasn't her brazen flirtation of dropping the robe and walking away with this coy little smile on her face and dare in her eyes. It was something I saw on her face when she asked me to dinner, and in the way she bit her lip when she turned those beautiful doe-eyes my way.

She was letting me into her world and inviting me into her space, something I had a feeling was rare for her. I was honored and up for the challenge. Ready to proudly have her on my arm and by my side. My hand was pushing open her bedroom door when a constricting feeling hit me square in the chest and spread throughout my body like I'd been doused in ice water.

She didn't deserve me.

Feet that were confident seconds before were now stuck like cement shoes in the hallway, and I ran my hands through my hair in indecision. Clear expectations or not about our limited time, tonight felt important, and I was thinking with my fucking dick. But what red-blooded man wouldn't?

Tonight felt like something Jenna should do with her boyfriend, and that wasn't me. No matter what the nagging voice in the back of my head said, I wasn't going to change. Turning around, I stalked to my bedroom and kicked off my shoes, closing the door and pacing in the small space. My knuckles were white from clenching them so hard, but I didn't follow her.

Not yet.

15 - JENNA

I tugged at the hem of my strappy, A-line black dress, trying to smooth it down below my knees. I was a 'jeans and tank-top girl,' but I wanted to spice things up tonight. I added a few beach waves to my normally stick-straight hair and did my eyes with a gray and smoky look. When I opened my bedroom door to see Mark waiting in black jeans and a tight black button-up shirt, I knew I'd made the right call.

His jeans hugged his muscular thighs, and I saw his substantial package that left nothing to the imagination. I couldn't tear my eyes away from it. *From him.*

He clenched his jaw as he strode forward, looking dangerous, and tracking his eyes slowly down my body. I felt exposed and vulnerable under his gaze, but more than that, I felt desired and longed to rip my dress off and press my body to his. My stomach fluttered because I didn't like the way he made me feel, as if he could burn me to ash with a single touch and crush my heart to dust.

He leaned down and nuzzled my neck, then whispered dirty things to me until I was panting. Whatever we had, whatever temporary thing this was, it was going to be something big, something scary, and something I wasn't sure I'd survive.

He pulled away and grabbed his keys, giving me a sly smile and locking the door.

"So, tell me about your friends," he said a short time later, turning down the radio and putting his hand palm up on the center console. I reached forward and entwined his fingers with mine like it was something we'd done for years.

"Hmm, let's see. Addison's in real estate. She's the one with the red hair that picked me up from your house when you first got Phoebe. Olivia owns a bakery called *Sweeter Things*. Her husband, Edward, does all the marketing for her and a little freelance. Annaleigh's uncle owns *B's*, and she recently left her job to take over for him. Max is her boyfriend and her old boss. He's in Commercial Banking at *JMS Bank*."

"Good to know. I'm glad I'm here with you tonight."

Swoon. I'm glad I'm with you every night.

He squeezed my hand and pulled into a parking spot, locking his truck and leading me to the door. This felt like a big moment, introducing him to my best friends. I wouldn't do this with someone who was a casual fling.

Would I?

"I'm glad you're here too," I said as he took my hand and gave it a gentle squeeze. He always did that. Small touches, glances, caresses. Like he was reassuring himself I was here. He was making it harder to think clearly about our so-called casual relationship.

Mark opened the door for me and put his hand on the small of my back, guiding me past the entrance. I could feel the heat of his skin through my dress, but more than that, this felt natural. *Comfortable.*

I glanced at him then looked around for the girls. I spotted Addison's fiery red hair first, piled high on her head with tendrils cascading down her face. I lifted my hand in greeting as we walked to the table.

B's Bar was a gritty dive that was big in the indie music scene and worked with up-and-coming bands and several non-profits in the area. The walls were covered with funky music memorabilia and pictures of local groups, and the bar was made of dark wood that went across one wall. The opposite side held a large stage, where several musicians were warming up. I didn't catch the band name on the chalkboard out front, but one guy looked familiar.

I hugged the girls and introduced Mark. He politely shook everyone's hand before taking a seat next to me and resting his hand possessively on my thigh. It was like he was claiming me. I loved it.

I watched him from the corner of my eye as he took in his surroundings and immersed himself in with my friends. His eyes tracked over Annaleigh, casually dressed in dark ripped jeans and a blue shirt that said *Dibs on the Bass Player,* such a contradiction from her last job as an executive assistant.

Then he moved to Olivia wearing skinny jeans and a loose purple blouse, and her husband, Edward, who had on khakis and a polo. Edward was telling the table about an upgrade he'd done to the bakery, and Mark was nodding along like he'd been a part of the whole conversation.

Addison was in her trademark power suit, green today, and Annaleigh's boyfriend, Max, was still wearing black slacks and a blue button-down shirt, cuffed at the elbows to show thick, dark tattoos snaking up one arm. He was staring at Mark with his lips pursed, giving him a crease between his eyebrows.

"Hey guys, let's get a round for the table," Max said, slapping Edward on the shoulder and tilting his head toward the bar. "I wanted to talk to you about something, Mark."

Mark removed his hand from my thigh and crossed his arms, nodding with a tight smile.

"Damn, dudes," Addison said, looking between Max and Mark. "Might as well get a tape measure out now and measure your dicks while you're at the bar so we can enjoy our evening."

Olivia snickered, and I looked between Annaleigh and Max, reaching under the table and brushing my hand up Mark's thigh. I didn't mean for it to be sexual. I only meant to reassure him I was here, but he grasped my hand like I was his lifeline and squeezed. My eyes darted back and forth, trying to figure out what was happening.

"Nothing that dramatic, I hope, Addison," Edward said, running his hand down Olivia's arm before standing up.

Max stood up, giving Annaleigh a chaste kiss on the cheek, and with one last squeeze, Mark let go of my hand and motioned to the bar, where the guys followed. We watched them leave, Mark in his tight dark jeans and shirt, Max in his suit, and Edward in his khakis, until they sat down at one of the high-top chairs and motioned to a bartender.

"The shit was that about?" Addison asked, leaning in toward the middle of the table and looking at us.

"No clue," I said, looking at Annaleigh like she would have a better explanation.

"Max has gone all growly alpha since we made up, but I know he wanted to thank Mark for his help with the Benjamin situation."

"Aww," came the collective response.

"While they're at the bar, tell us all about Mark," Olivia said, leaning in closer to the center of the table. "He's going to need a nickname too."

Everyone nodded, and I glanced one more time at the bar before meeting the eyes of my best friends.

"We decided to keep things going while he's moved in."

"Like fuck-buddies?" Addison asked, reaching out to lightly slap my arm. "Awesome. Good for you—you definitely look bang-able tonight. That dress will do all kinds of things for Mark. Oh, how about Officer Big Dick?"

"So, what happens after his house is done?" Annaleigh said, passing around margaritas a server brought over and ignoring the nickname suggestion. Annaleigh put two fingers to her lips, blowing them toward Max before focusing back on us.

"I don't know. I don't know what I want, and he's not looking for anything past casual."

"Is this you looking for an excuse not to get serious, or did he say he didn't want anything beyond a casual hook-up?"

"I mean, I've never felt like this before. I feel like we could be something real, but what if I'm the one who doesn't think we should get serious?" I took a big sip of my drink. "I was offered a job to be the Executive Director of a non-profit in Wilmington."

"What?" Olivia hissed, leaning closer. "I didn't even know you were considering moving!"

"I wasn't," I answered honestly. "But I can't keep arguing with Dr. Dumbass. The offer was well below what I'm making, but I'd be closer to home and have complete control of a state-of-the-art shelter."

"I thought *this* was your home," Addison said, staring into her drink like it was a bottomless abyss.

"Addie, I don't want her to move either, but we will always support each other," Annaleigh said, reaching out to take my hand. "And if you're considering this offer, you're right not to get serious with Mark, but to play Devil's Advocate, have you talked to Dr. Duvall?"

"Or rode that dick?" Addison added. "He shouldn't be the reason you stay, but he could be a big green check in the plus column."

Our table erupted in giggles, earning us looks from the rest of the place, mainly three burly men sitting at the bar.

"If I've learned anything about relationships," Annaleigh said, reaching out to put her hand on mine, "It's that you have to talk about stuff. Don't make the wrong decision based on a lack of communication."

"Anna's right. Agree to have fun. Agree to be more. We'll be here for whatever you decide. Just don't make a snap judgment because things are tough today, and don't leave out any of the dirty details," Olivia said, lifting her glass to clink against ours.

I noticed she hadn't touched her drink, even though I was taking the last sips of mine. I stole another glance at the guys before shrinking down low in my seat.

"I feel like a horny teenager. Like someone slipped chick Viagra or some sort of aphrodisiac in my morning coffee. And, oh my god, did I tell you his mother freaking trims bonsai plants and topiary bushes to look like dicks and butts?"

"That's a woman after my own heart and a sign if I've ever seen one. What's the chance his mother is as obsessed with plants as you are. Plus, the horny teenager thing. That's what the good D' will do to you. Make sure you take full advantage while y'all are under the same roof," Annaleigh said, giving me a wink.

"And make sure to hydrate," Olivia said.

"And stretch beforehand," Addison said, leaning her chair back as the guys stood up with another round of drinks. "Mark looks like he has some bulk." She stretched her arms wide, then wider, with a big grin on her face.

"Yeah, right…" I hissed, hunching down and leaning toward the middle of the table since the guys had just stood up. "Hey Mark, stand by with your dick out while I get a Gatorade and touch my toes. I don't think so."

"Someone say my name," Mark asked, passing another round to Olivia and me before taking a swallow of beer. I cringed, thinking he heard me, but his smile said he didn't, thank goodness.

"Thank you, we sure did," Olivia said, pulling her drink closer without another word.

I noticed Edward covertly putting Olivia's drinks in front of him and passing her a soda. She caught my eye and gave me a wink before leaning down to take a sip. Before I could give it a second thought, Mark sat down, spreading his legs wide, so one rested against mine.

"Good to know," Mark said with a smile, resting one large palm on my thigh.

"Mmm, thanks, Broody," Annaleigh said, taking a sip of her neat bourbon and leaning closer to Max.

"So, Mark," Addison started. "Tell us about you so we can give you the third degree."

"Not a problem. Addison, right? You drive the cherry red 2018 Ford Mustang GT Convertible, don't you? How many parking tickets have you gotten in the past twelve months?"

"What?" Addison sputtered, setting her drink on the table with a clatter that made the liquid slosh over the sides. "That has nothing to do with anything."

The color rose on her cheeks and down her chest, making her look like she had been out in the sun for hours and did a piss-poor job applying sunscreen. Mark squeezed my knee, and one corner of his mouth turned up a millimeter.

Oh my god, he was messing with her.

"I think it does, ma'am," Mark said, removing his hand and putting both his elbows on the table to lean closer to Addison. His lips were set in a firm line, and he cracked each knuckle, looking intimidating as hell.

I glanced at Olivia and winked at her, and she did the same to Edward, who turned to Annaleigh. It was hard to keep a straight face seeing Addie so worked up. Everyone at the table was grinning except her and Mark. He had a stone-cold poker face, and her cheeks were turning as red as her hair.

"Don't you ma'am me, Mister Man, sitting over there acting like it's not an obvious violation of police power to check my driving record? Who do you think you are?"

Mark leaned back and crossed his arms over his chest, then released one and set it back lightly on my thigh. "Just your average, humble cop that decided to turn the tables."

He glanced at me, then gave my thigh another caress, tracing his fingers back and forth, moving them higher with each pass. His touch was feather-light, and instead of being ticklish, each movement sent a jolt of need straight to my core.

"Oh my god, you're fucking with me, aren't you?" Addison said with a huff, reaching over to swat the hand that wasn't coming dangerously close to my panty line.

Mark's face broke out into a huge smile, and everyone at the table started laughing until Addison put both her hands up in surrender then lifted her glass. "Good one, dude. I'm usually not so gullible. You are welcome to hang with us anytime."

"Nice," Max said, leaning forward to give Mark a fist bump.

"Here, here," Olivia said, lifting her glass. "But seriously, we would love to know more about you, sans third degree."

"Gladly," Mark said, as his eyes cut to me.

He started talking in that deep, soothing baritone voice that sounded like melted caramel over ice cream, all while his hand moved higher and higher. I spread my legs under the table, and he took the hint, moving up until one long finger brushed my panties.

I stifled a gasp and picked up my margarita, licking the salt as he talked. He could talk about belly-button lint or the weather patterns over South Korea for all I knew. I vaguely caught the words brothers, Gamecocks, and tattoos, but nothing stuck except the heat from his fingers trailing on my thigh.

He could be on the radio or narrate audiobooks. His voice had a deep, natural timbre that rose and fell with every breath he took. I imagined us laying in bed, with my head on his chest and him reading to me. He'd be wearing these round, thick-framed reading glasses and have one hand resting on my arm. I'd turn the pages for him, and after a chapter, he'd pass the book to me, and I'd read to him.

The room had faded to nothing except his touch and the rise and fall of his voice. I couldn't hear the band warming up or the questions the girls were peppering his way. It wasn't the alcohol that was making my head swim. It was him. Mark. My so-called casual relationship.

I needed air. Or the bathroom. Or a glass of water. The bar was stifling. I had to stand up and splash cold water on my face. I wanted him so damn much I could barely stand it. More than that, this felt like it could be our weekly routine. The way he fit in and razzed on Addison, it was like he'd been doing it for years.

Pushing my chair back, I stood up and mumbled about needing to go to the bathroom. Annaleigh looked at me and raised her eyebrows, tilting her head, but I shook mine. I weaved around tables as I walked to the shadowed hallway leading to the bathrooms, with my hand pressed to my stomach. I just needed a minute to clear my head to remind myself that nothing about this was permanent. Perhaps, a minute to check and see if I had a spare pair of panties in my clutch because mine were soaked. I breathed in for five counts and out for ten, trying to steady the insane emotions that were coursing through my body.

I'd be fine in a minute.

16 - MARK

I stood up from the table, ignoring what Max was saying to follow her to the bathroom. Someone let out a low whistle, but I was too focused on watching her ass sway in that dress. Touching her all night had been pure torture. I needed more. *I needed her.* The bathrooms were past the kitchen and down a shadowed hallway, and I reached out and grabbed her arm before she could open the door. She spun around, terror flashing briefly in her eyes before she realized it was me.

"What's the matter?" she said, putting her hand on mine and looking up. Not letting go of her arm, I turned and pressed her against the wall to stroke my thumb down her cheek.

"I need something," I said, the words coming out in a low growl.

"What?" Her voice was breathy as she cupped my face, and her eyebrows were furrowed as she waited for my next words.

But there were no more words. It was just us. No one else around. I wanted to surround her, if only for a little bit. I crowded her space, driving my knee between her legs. She spread them eagerly and gave me a wicked little grin, parting her lips so I could see her tongue. I took her hand in mine and kissed each fingertip as she closed her eyes and sighed like she'd been waiting for me to do it all night.

She made me feel things I didn't want and didn't understand because I was better alone, happier.

Right?

Her kindness and vulnerability made me desperate for her. She'd willingly given me more than I could ever say, and I wanted nothing more than to throw caution to the wind and claim her as mine for all the world to see, but I couldn't. I wasn't going to do that to her, so I shut off the emotional rollercoaster that threatened to overtake my body and just lived.

I swallowed thickly and surged in, driving my tongue into her mouth. She whimpered and opened so sweetly for me, sucking on my tongue and fisting my hair. She wrapped one leg around me, and I gripped her thigh, letting my hand slide under her dress so I could hold her closer and dove in deeper.

When I pulled away, I pressed my forehead to hers. Her lips were swollen, and her lipstick was smudged.

Good.

I wanted everyone to see her, everyone to know I'd staked my claim.

"What do you need?" she asked again, leaning her head on the wood-paneled wall and glancing down the hallway to make sure we were still alone.

"I need to fuck you, Jenna. Feel your pussy come on my cock. Feel your heat wrapped around me and your heart racing." I expected her to cringe at my crude words, but she gave me that sly grin again, looking like the cat that got the cream.

"It's about fucking time," she panted, rubbing herself against my cock.

This girl.

I kissed her again, branding myself on her lips before taking a step back.

"Let's get out of here."

She nodded as I kept hold of her hand, pulling her behind me. I heard her holler goodbye to the table, but I was a man on a mission, not willing to look back until I took what I wanted. As I opened the door and felt the last of the summer heat hit my face, I heard a cat-call coming from inside. We both turn around to see Addison giving us a thumbs up.

Good enough for me. We waved in response, and then I was pulling her along again, taking long strides to my Tahoe and calculating the quickest route home. I shuffled her inside and shut the door, jogging to the driver's side and cranking the engine.

"Hurry," she said, biting her lip and stretching her hand across the console to grab mine.

I gritted my teeth and pulled onto the highway, gunning the engine. I loved that she was so assertive, telling me what she wanted. It was so fucking hot, and I was a willing participant in anything she said. I turned on a side street to miss a series of red lights when Jenna jerked her hand from mine.

"Pull over up there," she said, fanning her face and pointing to a spot just off the road.

Oh shit! Was she second-guessing this?

I pulled into an old, overgrown parking lot. Looking around, I saw nothing but my headlights piercing the darkness. I shifted into park and turned to look at Jenna, wondering what the hell was the matter. We were only about ten minutes from home.

"Jenna, what's—"

She cut my words off and scrambled across the console, lunging straight to my mouth, kissing me with a brutal ferocity of pent-up frustration. I kissed her back, grabbing a fistful of her thick chestnut hair to keep her lips locked on mine. I kissed her like she was my air, my reason for breathing. I'd been trying to be good, trying not to take advantage, but she was waving me in for a home run. If she wanted me right here, right now, I was more than willing to give her exactly that.

"Wait," I growled, tugging lightly on her bottom lip with my teeth. The seat was back as far as it would go, but there wasn't enough room. Her eyes flicked to the backseat, and she motioned with her head, letting go of me to crawl in the back. I smacked her on the ass as she went, opening the truck door, flicking the button on my jeans, and un-tucking my shirt with lightning speed.

"I should have asked you to join me in the shower," she said, slipping off her shoes.

This girl.

This girl is driving me wild and making me want things I shouldn't.

In the three seconds it took me to pull a condom from my wallet and walk around to the back passenger door, Jenna was waiting for me, naked except for a pair of sheer green panties. Her tits were perfect teardrops I knew would spill out of my hands, and her nipples were already pebbled with arousal, waiting for my touch.

My tongue.

My teeth.

God, she was beautiful, nibbling on her lower lip and spreading her legs slightly so I could see the wet spot between her thighs. I closed and locked the doors, staring at her until the dome lights dimmed.

Good.

If a stray car drove by, I didn't want anyone to see what we were about to do.

Her body glowed in the moonlight. The body I'd been fantasizing about for weeks. I was crazy for her, going straight to her lips. I braced one hand on her back and the other on her tit, kneading the smooth skin. I pulled her toward me, and she didn't miss a beat, crawling on my lap and pulling my shirt off Superman-style. Buttons went flying, but I didn't give a fuck. I just wanted her hands on me. I lifted my hips, and she raised up so I could slip my jeans to my ankles. My briefs went with them, and my cock sprang free, bobbing against my stomach. Her hand dove between us, gripping me and stroking down hard.

I grunted with the sensation, spreading my legs as far as I could with my jeans still around my ankles as she worked me up and down. There would be time for slow exploring later. Right now, I needed to be inside her more than I needed to breathe. I wrapped my arms around her, and she released my cock, bracing her hands behind my head. I thrust against her again and again, teasing against the silk fabric of her thong with what we both desperately wanted. She whimpered in my ear, and I scrambled to scoot back as far as I could to give us more leverage.

The only sound was our breathing, as our mouths found each other in the darkness. Our frantic pace grew quicker as we moved together, with only a scrap of fabric separating us. She arched her back to lean on the middle console, and I ran my hand down her body, plucking her nipples and dragging my fingertips down her stomach. I cupped her pussy, then pushed aside her panties and ran two fingers through her slit. She was soaked, and I gathered as much wetness as I could, bringing my fingers to my lips and sucking.

Jenna's gasp went straight to my cock as I sucked, letting her delicious flavor burst across my tongue. I roughly grabbed her ass and pulled her back to me, smashing our chests together to taste her lips, but she wasn't having any of that.

She bit my lip and pushed away, rearranging herself on the seat beside me on her knees so she could kiss down my chest. Her teeth found my

169

nipple, and she bit down hard enough for a hiss of pleasure to escape my lips.

"Fucking love it when you do that," I growled.

She smiled and did the same with my other nipple before kissing my abdomen. Still on her knees, she leaned forward slowly, licking her lips like my cock was dessert.

I didn't know what to expect, but it definitely wasn't her swallowing me down. Her hot, wet mouth enveloped me, and I grunted when my cock nudged the back of her throat. My hand reflexively went to her hair as she worked, bobbing up and down in the dark. I'd love to see her in the light, love to see her mouth wrapped around me, but something about the darkness and shadows was erotic, making me focus on the sensations of her mouth. I focused on how her hair felt in my hand as I guided her head up and down my cock, how her tongue felt swirling the head, and how she let one hand drift between my legs to cup my balls.

It was exquisite, unforgettable, and I was so overwhelmed I could only groan and grunt as she worked. I was giving myself to her and pleasure until I felt a familiar tingle at the base of my spine. I tightened my hand in her hair.

"I want inside you," I grunted out.

She glided her tongue up my cock, slowly letting go before sitting up and climbing onto my lap again. I cupped both her tits in my hand as she surged forward, kissing me until she was whimpering with need. I let go and tugged her panties aside, feeling her wetness one last time and plunging two fingers deep inside her eager pussy. She was so goddamned tight. I couldn't wait to feel her choking on my cock.

She grabbed the condom from my outstretched hand and tore it open, taking my cock in her hand and rolling it down my length. Aligning my cock with her entrance, our eyes met in the dark, and she lowered herself down. She moaned as she took me in.

Then there was nothing but her warm, slick heat.

"Don't hold back," she whimpered, skimming her nails up my stomach and over my nipples. "Let me feel you, Mark."

That was all the encouragement I needed. She rolled her hips as my hands fell and gripped them harshly. She rode me hard, making small cries of pleasure and taking every inch. I dug my fingers into her hip, bucking harder as she fell forward, gripping my shoulders loosely.

There was just enough room for me to lean forward and take one of her stiff nipples in my mouth. I bit and nibbled, lashing my tongue against her peak as her whimper turned into a strangled moan. I could feel the tremors in her pussy and knew she was getting close. I was right on edge, but there was no way in hell I was coming before her. I wanted to feel her spasm on my cock. I changed the angle slightly so with every thrust, my pelvic bone would grind on her clit. She wordlessly nodded her head and opened her eyes.

"Fill me, Mark. Come with me. I want to feel every inch of your thick cock as you let go."

Her pussy was tightening around me like a vise, and her hands gripped my shoulders. My balls tightened up as her first spasm hit me, choking my cock and sending me over the edge. I exploded inside of her, groaning unintelligible words and losing all rhythm. I wrapped my arms around her and buried my face in her neck, breathing in her sweet peach scent. She squeezed my shoulders and took over, slowly grinding her hips into mine as she drew out our orgasms, and we fell back down.

"Holy fuck," she said, leaning forward to put her head on my chest. The windows were fogged, and we were both sweaty and sticky, but I didn't care. I just needed her, wanted her close. No casual hook-up ever felt like this. I'd never known with anyone what I felt when I was with her, and it was all the more reason this had to end when I moved out. She had enough on her plate without the stresses that come with dating someone on the force. It would mean dating someone who works too many hours, invests their whole selves in what they do, then comes home weighed down by the burden of the things seen. I wouldn't do that to her. I couldn't do that to her. She was starting to mean too much.

My spent cock slipped out of her, and I groaned with the loss, kissing her forehead. She sat up, with her hair plastered to the side of her face and a lazy smile on her lips.

"My knees are weak."

"Mine too, baby."

I kneaded her ass and thighs as she scooted back before throwing her leg over to sit beside me, resting her head on my shoulder. I stretched my arm out and pulled her close until I could hear our heartbeats slow down and sync up.

"Sleep with me tonight—no more separate beds. I want to wake up with you in my arms," I muttered, running a hand up her thigh. As soon as the words left my mouth, I knew they were a bad idea, but I couldn't help myself. I needed her close. This was only temporary, so I was going to soak up every single second.

"Hmm." She nodded her head and blinked slowly, letting the words sink in before giving me a smile that lit up her entire face. "Yes, please. Now take me to bed."

She leaned forward and ran her fingers over my chest before grabbing her dress from the floor. Not bothering with her bra, she shimmied the dress on and crawled back upfront. When her gorgeous ass came into view, I tugged the fabric up and swatted her again, earning a delighted squeak. I stored that information away for later and tied off the condom before hiking my briefs and jeans up.

The dome lights turned on as I opened the back door, revealing Jenna's flushed cheeks and my ruined shirt. I walked back to the driver's side and got in, leaning across the console to give Jenna a tender kiss.

The truck started with a roar, and I turned on the defroster to get rid of the steam on the windows and pulled back on the main road, heading to the house. Reaching across the console, I entwined her fingers with mine, noticing how well they fit together and wondering if she'd be up for round two when we got back. She squeezed my hand and winked, making my heart feel fuller yet sadder than it had in a while.

Phoebe greeted us with an angry meow, trying to climb up my leg, and I pried her off while Jenna dropped her heels by the door and walked to the kitchen. She grabbed her food dish, and I sat Phoebe down to grab the water dish. We were in sync, and when Jenna walked to the faucet to mix a little water with the food, I couldn't help leaning down to nuzzle her neck. She pressed her back to me and sighed, reaching up with one hand to cup the back of my neck and run her fingers through my hair.

"Mmm," she hummed, giving my hair a light tug. "I could get used to this."

So could I.

"I could get used to what we did in my truck," I answered, biting down on the spot where her neck met her shoulder.

She giggled, and I kissed her shoulder, then replaced Phoebe's water before heading to my bedroom. I stripped off my ruined shirt and shucked out of my jeans, tossing them in the hamper and putting on a T-shirt and gym shorts. I was serious when I said no more separate bedrooms. My phone charger and small gun safe were lying on the nightstand with Chapstick and a cat toy. Scooping everything up, I took it to our bedroom and put it on the opposite nightstand.

Her walk-in closet door was partially open, but I wasn't going to encroach on her space that much right now. A little bell tinkled, and I turned around to see Phoebe trot in front of me with something dangling from her mouth. It was brown and spotted, and as she pawed further away, it moved.

"Phoebe," I cried, taking two steps forward to catch her.

Fucking hell, she has a toad in her mouth.

"Spit that out, crazy girl. What's the matter with you?" I wrapped my hand around the tiny toad, but Phoebe refused to let go. Instead, she hissed at me.

Me. Her Cat-Daddy!

"Gross. Let go," I said in a firmer voice, tugging lightly on the toad. The leg still in her mouth stretched and stretched, but she wasn't giving up her prize.

"Hey Mark," Jenna said, walking into the bedroom and stopping short when she saw the crazy spectacle. "Oh shit. Phoebe, drop the toad."

She ran forward and grabbed Phoebe by the scruff of her neck, lifting her up and out of my arms. Jenna gave her the smallest shake, and she opened her mouth, finally releasing the creature. I wrapped my other hand around the toad and felt a warm trickle of liquid on my hands.

Disgusting.

I side-stepped Jenna and walked out of the bedroom and across the living room to release the toad on the porch, shaking my head at how this evening turned out. I was trying to figure out how to turn the doorknob on the back door when I stopped and looked at my closed hands.

A toad. A toad crossed my path.

My superstitious mind went into overdrive, remembering the old fairy tale, *The Frog Prince.* If a toad crossed your path, it was a sign to be mindful of travelers because you'd meet your future spouse sometime soon.

So what the fuck did it mean that a black cat crossed my path with a toad in its mouth?

Nothing good.

This had to be the Universe giving me a clear, superstitious signal that I was making the right call with Jenna. She was clearly not who I was supposed to be with forever. I was meant to be alone.

"Marcus-I-don't-know-what-your-middle-name-is-Hansen, don't you dare throw that toad outside," her shrill voice cried from the bedroom before a fireball of chestnut hair with soft caramel highlights darted through the living room, waving her hands with eyes as big as saucers.

I would have noticed her hands and her eyes if it hadn't been for her tits bouncing up and down as she ran to me. It was like I was staring at the television in slow-motion *Baywatch* style. The only thing missing was *I'm Always Here,* blaring in the background and a warm summer breeze on my face.

I leapt back with a start, keeping my hands wrapped around the peeing toad and looking at her like she had three heads.

"What? What's the matter?"

She stopped short, and her eyes darted toward the toad clamped between my palms.

"Thank goodness. My heart went to my throat, thinking you'd already released the toad. Some are poisonous, and I need to examine our friend before you let him go."

Poisonous? A poisonous toad in the mouth of a black cat crossed my path? I need a beer.

She stood and held up her pointer finger, taking a few more deep breaths before putting her hand over her heart. I focused on where her hand rested. Seeing her hand on her heart made my heart ache with all the longing and loneliness I pretended I didn't understand and didn't need.

"Take the toad to the kitchen. I'll get gloves, and you," she said, pointing to the kitten that had trotted up to us like she hadn't caused this mess by picking up the damn thing. "You are a naughty little girl scaring your daddy and me like that."

She turned, carrying Phoebe, and dropped her on the living room couch before disappearing into the bedroom for gloves. The toad continued to squirm as I went to the kitchen, and I kind of wanted to squish it for all the trouble it caused.

Jenna snapped her gloves on and came up beside me. I opened my hands enough for her to peer at the toad. It was only an inch or so long with brown speckles... ugly camouflage.

"How can you tell if it's poisonous?"

"If it were, it would have nodes above the ear holes that secrete the toxin. This dude is a common toad. You can release him."

"Thank fuck. How did it get in here?"

"Probably through the garage," Jenna said, taking off the gloves and tossing them into the trash. She opened the fridge and took out two beers while I took our new friend to be released back to the wild, or at least the bushes in Jenna's backyard.

"Quick reflexes, Officer Handsome," she said, handing me a beer and clinking the bottle to mine after I came back from the porch and washed my hands.

"Right back atcha, Dr. Cutie, and my middle name is Remus, by the way."

I took a long pull of the beer and gazed at Jenna. Her eyes were sparkling bright as I stared at her, and she dragged her lower lip between her teeth.

"Come with me," she said, tugging my hand and pulling me along.

I usually liked to be the one that gave direction, but something about

Jenna made me want to follow everything she said. She led me to the bedroom, and with one swift motion, she pulled her dress off and stood there like a goddess—all curvy hips, soft skin, and dark pink nipples.

I took a moment to appreciate the view that was Jenna. Her chestnut hair sat right above her collarbone, and my eyes fell to the curve of her hips and her supple tits. Her feet were bare and small, with bright red nail polish against the cream carpet. I had a strange desire to run my hands down her thighs to her feet and rub them, running my knuckles over the arch of her foot to see how she responded. Would she moan for me real sweet or jerk her foot away with a ticklish giggle?

It felt like it had been too long since I'd touched her—since we had some sort of skin-on-skin contact, and I ached to reach out and pull her to me. I licked my lips and stared, wondering how I got so fucking lucky that a woman that beautiful was here with me. When I stared into her eyes, I saw something that made me want to share all my secrets, to have something genuinely meaningful and profound. It was like she had inserted herself into a part of my soul I'd kept hidden away.

Maybe I was a hopeless romantic under the gruffness. Maybe my future could look very different if I embraced that side. Maybe I was still high off the endorphins of being balls-deep in this beautiful girl.

I wanted to run my tongue over every inch of her body. I wanted to erase her skin of any touch but mine and brand my body to hers.

But she was better without me, my inner voice whispered like a two-timing whore. I wanted to lock that damn voice in a box and drop it to the bottom of the Mariana Trench. I was sick of this back-and-forth warring between what was right and what was easy.

"I have a strange request while I recover from that phenomenal dicking you gave me in the back of the truck," she said, glancing at the ground then back at me. She shifted from foot to foot, releasing my hand to wring hers together, all traces of her earlier confidence gone.

"Phenomenal, you say?" I rumbled, reaching behind me to pull off my T-shirt. "Dr. Cutie, I will handle any strange request you have."

Her fingers trailed up my abdomen and down my face. She was caressing me, and it felt more intimate than any touch I'd ever had. Her hands belonged on my body.

"Yes. Will you snuggle in bed with me and read me a book?"

"Read to you?"

Out of all the things she could have said, I was not expecting that, but as soon as the words left her mouth, it sounded like the second-best thing we could do tonight.

"Yeah. Will you pick out a book over there and hold me for a little while?"

She crawled on the bed and laid on her back, sighing and opening her arms. I grabbed a book from the built-in shelf beside the television and crawled in beside her, pulling her to me, so her head rested on my chest. She fit into me like she was meant to be there, and I was meant to have one arm wrapped around her to keep her safe.

I held the book with one hand and her with the other. She turned to the first page, and I started to read. Her fingers teased my chest between turning the pages, and even though I was counting the seconds until I was inside her sweet pussy again, something about this simple act felt big.

Felt like everything.

17 - JENNA

"Yes, Ms. Brown. I know it's frustrating," I said, doing my best not to roll my eyes.

She was my last appointment of the day, and I was eager to get home. I was never eager to get home, but today had sucked big, fat, hairy balls. I had *four* patients pass and was cramping like I had personally offended my uterus. Unfortunately, patients' passing was a normal, horrible part of my job, and I was no stranger to making the tough calls. I didn't know why today hit me worse than others, but I think it bummed me out because I couldn't go to my happy place.

This adorable plant nursery with funky blue shutters and an overgrown driveway was about five minutes from my house. Inside, it held a plethora of amazing and unique finds—from orchids and succulents to fruit trees and shrubbery. Going there always brightened my mood, but I couldn't because no matter where I tried to put a pet-friendly plant in the house, Phoebe would find it, eat it, then throw it back up. Hell, I wanted to try my hand at some erotic topiary trimming or bonsai expressionism, but fate had other plans.

Err, more like Phoebe had other plans.

That kitten had more personalities than a mental institution and would go from sleeping on my chest one day to drawing blood the next. I put my hand on my stomach, willing my cramps to subside until I could get painkillers.

"Don't you agree, Dr. Crews?"

Shit!

I schooled my features and focused on Ms. Brown, who was still complaining.

"If you like, we can make regular appointments for Lavender, so this doesn't happen again."

"But what about my carpets?" she cried like it was my fault her pup's anal glands were inflamed. I reached down and scratched behind Lavender's ears, and her little poodle tail thumped in time with my movements.

"Let's head upfront. I have a great enzyme carpet cleaner that will take those stains right out."

"If you say so," Ms. Brown said, gathering Lavender in her arms and petting her cute furry head.

I walked with them to the front and passed over the cleaner before heading back to my office. I popped a few pills to ease the ache in my belly and finished my case notes before shutting down my computer. All I wanted to do was go home and snuggle with Mark. He had this innate ability to quiet my mind. I didn't think he understood how he was changing me. He was making me second guess everything about myself. With him, my awkward moments, dirty talking moments, and everything in-between moments were okay.

"Dr. Crews?" Dr. Duvall nodded at me from my office door. His hair was more unruly than usual, and it set his eyes in a stern scowl that made the crease between them look as deep as the Grand Canyon. He looked like he had given up.

"Hey, Larry. I'm wrapping up for the evening. What's up?"

"I need you to cover my morning surgeries. I have an appointment I can't reschedule."

I puffed my cheeks and blew out a deep breath, pushing my glasses on my head to rub my eyes. Usually, I didn't have an issue covering, but this was the third time he'd bailed on surgeries in two weeks. My production rate was almost double his, and since we were equal partners in the clinic, I was getting irritated.

"Sure, but is everything okay? I've been covering for you a lot lately."

He walked into my office with his head down and his hands in his pockets, sitting down in the chair in front of my desk.

"I don't appreciate your attitude, Dr. Crews," he said, leaning across my desk close enough for me to see the dark purple smudges under his eyes and how his skin hung loosely over his face.

I wasn't spiteful, but if something were going on that would affect the clinic, he needed to get off his high horse and share.

"It's not an attitude, and I don't appreciate you treating me like a child instead of your partner. What's going on?" I bit back, pushing back my chair and crossing my arms.

"I'm not always going to be here, you know. I should be able to count on you to rearrange your schedule like you always do."

"Maybe I'll be the one that won't always be here." Forcing an impassive look on my face as I turned off my monitor and pushed back in my chair.

"What are you talking about?" He leaned forward on the desk. I wasn't going to get in a pissing contest with him, not again. But if Wilmington was in the cards, he needed to know.

"I'm talking about this, us—our partnership. I don't know what's going on, and you won't talk to me, Larry. I can't keep coming to work every day and arguing with you. I've been offered the opportunity to take over a rescue."

"You're going to quit because things are hard? That's not the tough as nails, bright-eyed veterinarian I brought on right out of school."

For a second, when he looked at me from across my desk, his eyes twinkled like they used to and I saw my partner, my friend, my mentor. But a second later, the twinkle disappeared like a shooting star, and the tired, worn look was back.

"No. I'm not going to bail because things are hard. But I am prepared to reevaluate my choices when every single time I walk into this office, I cringe, thinking about what petty argument we're going to have. I can't keep bickering over raises and supplies. I have the clinic's best interest at heart. As your partner and friend, it would help if you trusted me. If you can't, then we need to have a very different conversation."

Rubbing my temples as I forced a small smile, but he recoiled like I'd flicked him off. That's when I realized my smile was more like a grimace with how uncomfortable my body was right now. I walked around my desk and reached out, hoping to grasp his hand, pat his shoulder, or do something to help repair whatever was wrong with us. But he shook his head, pursing his lips, and walked out without a goodbye.

Sheesh.

I made sure Chick and Duck's food and water were filled for the night and gave them some snuggles before updating the evening vet techs and heading home. I wanted my heating pad, and *I wanted my Mark.*

18 - JENNA

Walking in the house, I heard his voice first, and Phoebe lifted her head from the pink cat bed in the living room like she was judging me for wearing a blue scrub top with purple pants. I stuck my head in the kitchen, but his voice was coming from the other direction, so I slipped off my shoes and padded down the hallway.

I was hoping he was down for some serious cuddling or copious amounts of ice cream. My body was going to be out of commission for a few days, and as much as I'd become a horn-dog these last weeks, I'd enjoyed the time I'd spent with Mark more.

"Good to hear it. Yeah, Jenna's fine."

I stopped short outside his partially opened door when I heard my name. I should have stuck my head in and waved, but I didn't. I sneaked forward like a creeper and took it as a good omen because the floor didn't squeak as I moved.

"No, man. It's casual. She knows I don't do relationships."

My heart sunk a little as I tiptoed closer, holding my breath and leaning as far as I could without peeking through the door, waiting.

But…what was I waiting for from him? What did I want?

We'd known each other a little over a month and been living together for almost three weeks. It wasn't like he'd admitted his undying love for me and told whoever he was talking to I made him believe in relationships. He commented last week something about being single because he was a cop. Unless you're a monk, I didn't see how your relationship status affected your job. But Mark had some bone-deep aversion to being in one.

Not that I was a fairy princess happily ever type, but a part of me hoped he'd want more. I guess it was because I'd finally admitted to myself I wanted more, but I wouldn't push him. Honestly, hearing him say it out loud, again, was precisely what I needed. We'd been playing house, but it hadn't been real. All too soon, he'd go back to his life, and I'd go back to mine.

It had been nice finding reasons not to work fifty hours. *Mostly him,* I scoffed at his door. He was the reason I hadn't been pulling twelve-hour days and finding ways to occupy every spare moment of my free time.

"No, man. I can't. I'm in hell here. I can't fucking wait to get back to my place. There's no connection."

What?

I backed up and walked to my bedroom, my eyes glassy with unshed tears, as I stripped out of my scrubs and threw them in the general direction of the closet. It was my damn fault for eavesdropping on his conversation.

There's no connection?

Connection wasn't about knowing how someone took their coffee, how they like their eggs, or even their favorite date night on Saturday. I balled up my fists and picked up my scrubs, throwing them in the closet before stomping to the bathroom and turning the bathwater as hot as it would go. Connection was about seeing someone's soul and bearing your own. It was about picking up on their verbal and nonverbal cues and having an innate instinct about their body, who they were, and what they needed.

My face flushed as the bathroom steamed up, and I blinked rapidly as the tears fell—stupid period. I thought back to when he first moved in. He said he wasn't relationship material, and I thought I was the one to suggest only keeping this up while we were under the same roof.

Why was I upset he was doing exactly that?

After last night, falling asleep in his arms while he read to me about a giant Kronosaurus that was alive hundreds of millions of years after it should have been extinct, my brain had done a three-sixty. Or maybe a one-eighty because I'd been second-guessing my keeping it casual suggestion since we brought it up.

With Jason, I was always on edge, always worried something terrible would happen—and forget about sex. It was a chore, another place I had to watch what I said and second guess myself, just like the rest of the relationship.

With Mark, it was different.

Of course, it was different. It wasn't a relationship.

I choked out a sob, then bit the inside of my cheek as hard as I could, willing something to give as I dumped bubble bath in the tub and watched the bubbles rise.

A sharp rap on the door dragged me out of my pity party about ten minutes later, and I glanced at the cracked door, holding my breath.

"Hey Jenna, you okay?"

I should tell him to fuck off, but some twisted part of me still wanted his arms, even if it was a fake solution. I wanted to shake him, and kiss him, and drag him into the tub with me, screaming why. My hormones and emotions were all over the place. I needed to get a grip. I lifted my hands and shook them out, stretching out my neck and breathing deep to pull myself together.

"Yeah. Come in," I said, wiping under my eyes and sinking under the suds.

"You, um, don't look okay."

Mark took a seat on the edge of the tub and leaned over, pressing his hand against my forehead. I tried to smile, but he looked at me the same way Dr. Duvall had, making me think I still had the grimace down pat.

"Ugh, I know. Tough day."

Just leave. I'll break down if you start being sweet.

"Why? What's going on, baby?"

He got on his knees and leaned down, bringing his lips to my cheek. There was genuine concern in his eyes. So much that it almost tempted me to ask him about his phone call. But then I'd have to admit I was purposely listening in, and he'd rightly get pissed, spoiling how sweetly he was acting.

"Today was pretty awful. Plus, it's, um, that time of the month." Mortification slipped through my veins.

"What can I do? Want to get out and tell me about it?" He stood up and grabbed a fluffy towel off the rack. I nodded my head and pushed down the tears that threatened to spill down my face again.

Why is he being so sweet if he hated it here? Why can't I push him away? He doesn't want me.

He held the towel open as I pulled the plug in the tub and stood, wrapping me up while I dried. My hair fell in damp tendrils around my face, and I washed the lingering mascara smudges from under my eyes. When I walked into the bedroom, Mark was sitting on the edge of the bed in his briefs. He had laid out a pair of pajamas and was holding a book. He opened his arms, and I walked into them, melting into his embrace.

"Come here, and tell me everything," he said, scooting over on the bed so I could crawl in beside him.

"Okay," I settled in beside him and laid my head on his chest. He wrapped his arms around me and put one hand on my belly like he was trying to soothe the pain. It was so intimate, so loving.

I was going to ask him why he didn't want more.

"Today started fine. But we had several routine patients get life-altering test results, and the owners put the pets to sleep. It was the right call, but four in a day was a lot to handle. Then I got into an argument with my clinic partner, Dr. Duvall. I don't understand what's going on with him. He treats me like a child, and it's so demeaning. I hoped to stop at the nursery, the one off of High Street, for a plant on the way home. I do that, you know. Whenever a patient passes, I get a plant. I know it's probably stupid because I kill plants as fast as I buy them. And with Phoebe here, I can't bring any in the house. And I am not blaming you at all, Mark, so don't even suggest that."

He gave me a squeeze and leaned down, running his nose against my hair. "I know you don't blame me. Keep going."

I nodded into his chest and took a deep breath, blowing it out to match my breaths with his.

"That's really it. But to top it off, I overheard something I shouldn't have, and it was pretty terrible. So, I'm hurt and pissed. Plus, my period, and you're being amazing and wonderful and caring and everything I could possibly want in, you know, a boyfriend..."

Mark made an audible intake of breath when I said the dreaded b-word, and I buried my face in his chest, drawing strength from the steady thump of his heart. Regardless of how he felt about labels or relationships, his pulse wasn't racing, and he wasn't trying to chew off his arm like a rabid dog, so I figured it wouldn't hurt to say a little more. Or I could be digging myself deeper. Either way, I propped my head on his chest and owned it, feeling his breath fan across my face.

"I want to ask you why you don't want to be in a relationship. But then I remember how shitty my last relationship was, and I wonder if I even want to be in one since so many things in my life might be changing. So, I'm crampy and confused, a little pissed, and tired, and so, so happy to be here with you. All the things."

I threw one leg over his, and he stroked up and down my arm, holding me so tenderly my ovaries would explode if they weren't currently trying to murder my uterus.

"Jenna…" he said, and I heard the timbre from deep in his chest.

"No, that's okay. I mean, it's not like you're my boyfriend or anything. How was your day?"

Why did I just ask him that?

All I wanted to know was why he said what he did on the phone, not how his day was. Besides, the blanket under me was feeling lumpy. Moving, I tried to adjust my body, but it didn't work. I tried to sound light and cheerful, but I was sure I failed miserably. Nonetheless, after another few seconds, Mark propped one arm behind his head and ran his other hand underneath my pajama top, resting his large palm on my stomach.

"This doesn't hurt, does it?"

"No. You feel good."

He nodded, and the thumb on my stomach caressed the skin every so softly, back and forth, as he started talking in that soothing, baritone voice of his.

"I'm sorry you had a bad day, and I'm glad I'm here with you."

Glad he was here with me? Right.

It was hard to fully focus on what Mark was saying after that line because it felt like bullcrap. Naturally, my eyes found the one spot in my bedroom that irritated me—the only spot that was still out of Phoebe's reach. The dead plant sat unloved and tucked away in the top corner of the tallest shelf on my bookcase. It gnawed at me now more than ever. It was barely more than a wilted, brown stalk and hardly recognizable as ever being green and vibrant. Kind of like how my heart was wilted by playing this less than honest verbal sparring match with Mark.

"My dad was a cop. Did I ever tell you that?"

I lifted my head from his chest and looked at him, really looked at him. Now he was being sincere, and I could feel the shift in our conversation. We were heading into deeper waters, uncharted territory.

"No, you haven't told me about your dad." I patted the center of his chest, and he caught my fingers, bringing them to his lips.

"He retired after twenty-five years, and cancer took him ten years after that. I remember it like it was yesterday, Jenna. The day I graduated from the academy and joined the force. My dad had taken me out for a beer. We were sitting at the bar, and he told me how proud he was of the man I'd become. He was the one that gave me this."

Mark paused and lifted his horseshoe pendant necklace for me to see. I held the thick chain between my fingers, feeling the cool metal on my skin as he spoke.

"He said it would always bring me good luck. I guess I got overly superstitious after he died. You probably think I'm paranoid, and maybe it's gotten a little out of hand, but it makes me feel close to him. The longitude and latitude coordinates I have tattooed on my side are where he was born and where he's buried."

He lifted one hand from my side and touched the tattoo. He had this stone-cold, robotic expression on his face like he was preparing himself for what he was about to say.

Before he could continue, I had to interrupt him. *Paranoid? I don't think so.*

"Hey, Mark."

"Hmm."

"I know you get all uncomfortable when someone tries to compliment you but listen to me. You are anything but paranoid. You are protective, kind, generous, and have one of the biggest hearts I know. If anything, I'm a better person because you're in my life, and if being superstitious makes you feel closer to your father, then I'll help you search for four-leaf clovers and make sure you never walk underneath a ladder."

He cleared his throat and looked down at me but didn't say anything. I was about to break the silence when he started talking again, quieter than before.

"I asked him if he had the choice, would he do it all over again? He looked me straight in the eyes and said no, he wouldn't. I was dumbstruck. I grew up wanting to be like him. He was my hero, my mentor, and he wouldn't choose the same path? When I asked him why he said the answer was simple. He said it was because of my mom. She worried, Jenna. Every shift, every time he left the house in that uniform, she worried. And even though he always came home, he wouldn't do that to her again. I remember growing up, how nervous she was all the time. She never said anything, but I could tell. I made a choice that night, baby. I chose to stay single. To let the job be my wife, lover, and girlfriend. I won't make someone go through what my mom did."

I leaned up the same time Mark bent down and kissed him, pouring all my frustration and sympathy into it as our lips caressed each other. One hand trailed up my arm and cupped my face, and when we broke away, he rubbed his nose to mine and sighed. His eyes held sadness like he carried the weight of the world and not just his own choices.

"If there ever was a person I'd break my rule with, it'd be you, Jenna. But I can't."

Swoon. I was melting for this man. A man that didn't want me. How could he say there was no connection, then tell me such sweet things?

190

He leaned down again and gently kissed me before picking up the book we started the previous night and opening it to the bookmark. "Want me to read a little more to you?"

"Yeah. I do. And Mark?"

"Yeah, baby?"

"I'd never ask you to break a promise you made to yourself. But times like tonight, when I'm in your arms, I wish you would."

He furrowed his brows and gave me a small smile. A smile that didn't reach his eyes as he read. A smile that held everything that wasn't meant to be.

19 - MARK

"I mean, if I have to count on both hands how long it's been since we've hung out, Bark E. Mark, it's been too long," Miller said, putting his head on my shoulder like a dork as we went over the invoice for repairs.

Stupid nickname.

I shrugged him off and crossed my arms, surveying the house. Everything was right on track to be finished late next week, sooner if the team busted their asses, and honestly, I was a little disappointed.

Fuck that. I was a lot disappointed.

I felt like I had bared my soul to Jenna last night, or at least shared with her more than I had with anyone else. She hadn't judged or asked me to change. If anything, her acceptance had me on edge more than if she'd said I was a lunatic.

What kind of chick accepted you as you were? Her.

I shook my head and moved one of my mom's ass-shaped bonsai plants back to the kitchen island from the garage. My brothers had been rewiring and upgrading the house as the construction team handled the rebuild. Apparently, they were making my place a 'smart house' by installing these

panels that looked like mini-tablets in various rooms that controlled a
bunch of shit they hadn't explained to me yet.

Miller and Magnum worked to make their business, *TriVolt Electric,*
modern and sleek to attract higher-paying clients, and Maverick did
everything behind the scenes, handling the books like a boss. The three
of them had busted their asses and made a name for themselves here in
Charleston and were expanding the business and contract with swankier
neighborhoods and businesses on Kiawah and Sullivan's Island.

Magnum was working on a panel in the kitchen as I wandered through
the open space that was once a wall separating the kitchen and dining room,
wondering how Jenna's baked Chicken Parmesan would smell as I sat at the
table before we settled in for the evening reading one of her weird-ass but
oddly entertaining marine terror books. I imagined her laying in-between
my legs in front of the re-stoned fireplace as I rubbed her back, and we
watched the flames die down to embers.

I couldn't wait to get back home so I could bring Jenna into my space.
The loft would be a gaming haven, complete with dual television screens.
There was a horrible internet connection at Jenna's house, and I had a
tough time connecting to my forums, though since I'd been with her, I
hadn't wanted to game. I wanted to spend all my extra time with her.

"When do we get to meet Jenna?" Magnum asked, drawing out
her name and clasping his hands over his heart. "You get this far-away
daydreamy expression on your face whenever you talk about her. She could
help you decorate this place with more than just mom's and dad's old
furniture. You could get art and shit."

"What I have is fine, and you're not meeting her." I gritted my teeth,
ignored him, and headed down the narrow hallway past the kitchen to
the office that was being converted into a library. My hand was on the
doorknob before Miller's voice rang through the house.

"You have issues," he called out. Retreating, I walked back to the living room like I'd been caught with my hand in a candy jar. I didn't want to think about Jenna here when I knew she couldn't stay, but I couldn't help it. She could make this house a home.

"I was just going to point out that you seem happy. You smile and shit. Maybe because you're finally getting some on the regular." Miller jack-knifed his hips, coming up behind me. I sidestepped him and darted to the living room, where Magnum was screwing the cover back on a panel.

"Hey, Maverick, is that why you're such a dick?"

"It's why I have a bigger dick than all of you pricks," Maverick answered, setting down his toolbox in the living room to grab his junk. "And it's none of your business if I'm getting any on the regular or not."

"Yeah, well. You're a freaking hermit. Living on the damn outskirts of the city and only leaving your house to go to work. You're just as bad as this guy," Miller said, jerking his thumb toward me.

I shrugged my shoulders and turned around, pretending to study one of the electrical panels as they argued. It was the same shit they'd fought about since starting the business together. Miller and Magnum were Irish Twins, born exactly ten months apart and practically inseparable. Maverick was the oldest, and I could count on one hand how many times I'd seen him smile, but they worked well together, and the business was thriving.

Maverick pushed his hair out of his eyes as he walked over and punched Miller in the shoulder. "Just because I don't get my dick wet every weekend with a different chick, then take her home to an apartment I share with my fucking brother, doesn't mean I'm a hermit. I'm a grown-up. With responsibilities."

"You're a fuddy-duddy, but I love you anyway."

"A fuddy-duddy? Really, Mag?"

"Yeah, dude. If the insult fits, now, back to what I really want to know.

Tell us, Mister Lifelong Bachelor, are you going to at least keep messing around with her once you're back here? All alone. With nothing but your black cat, topiary dicks, and X-Box to keep you company?"

I pondered Miller's question and stared at the panel. It would be easier to make a clean break, but the thought of only seeing her when Phoebe had a checkup made my chest ache. I rubbed the spot and wondered how she'd feel about keeping things casual.

It was a bad idea. The more time we spent together, the more attached we'd get. *I'd get.* It was better just to be done, no matter how much it was going to suck.

"Nah, I'll probably switch back to night shifts. No sense in keeping things going when it won't lead to anything."

"Huh," Maverick said, crossing one leg over another, then doing the same with his arms. He rubbed his hands together and hit me with a look that was so much like our dad I had to do a double-take. His forehead was creased, and there was a defined eleven between his eyebrows, but I knew whatever he was about to say was going to be important. "Seems to me you shouldn't dismiss something that makes you happy."

Shit.

He scratched his short beard and shrugged his shoulders like it was the easiest thing in the world to change something engrained so deep in my body it was a part of me. It wasn't like he was one to talk about being in a relationship. He was more FUBAR'ed than all of us combined.

"Don't you try to turn the tables and mention what happened with Autumn and me," he said, pointing his finger in my face like I'd mention something that painful. "This is you, man, and you're a fool if you're throwing away a chance at something real. Trust me. I'm heading out."

He clapped me on the back and high-tailed it out the door.

"Mom invited us to dinner tonight. Don't forget," Miller yelled as

Maverick lifted his hand in a halfhearted goodbye, leaving the three of us in stunned silence.

"He needs to get laid," Miller said, plopping down on the couch still covered with plastic wrap.

"He needs to stop living in the past," Magnum added, sitting beside him and shrugging his shoulders with a groan.

"He needs to let her go."

The two of them looked at me, and I wedged myself between them on the couch, laying my head back and closing my eyes. "Wait, mom invited us to dinner?" I snapped my eyes open and looked between them.

"Yeah, didn't you see the group text? She has some big announcement she wants to share, and I'll bet she invited your girl." Miller leaned over and punched me in the shoulder with a grin. "What do you think she wants to tell us?"

I took my phone out of my pocket and scrolled through the missed texts, scrubbing my hand over my face. "Who knows?"

My phone buzzed while I was scrolling, and when I saw Jenna's name, I smiled.

"That's the face I was talking about. I don't know what your hang-up is, but whenever you're ready to admit how you feel about this chick, we're here."

"Shut up, Miller. It's not like you're in a relationship."

"I'm not. But the difference, little brother, is when I'm ready, I'm going all in. She won't know what hit her."

I shoulder-checked him and stood up, heading to the kitchen before checking the message.

Jenna: Hey you. Your mom texted and invited me to dinner. She said she needed more estrogen.

196

Me: Ha! That sounds like something she'd say. My brothers will be there too. Want me to pick you up from the clinic?
Jenna: No. That's okay. I'll meet you at her house at six.
Me: Sounds good. See you then. Has your day been okay so far?
Jenna: Could be better.
Me: Anything I can do?
Jenna: Give me like three to five more days, then you can ravage me.
Me: Consider it done, Dr. Cutie. See you tonight.

I pocketed my phone and looked at Miller, who was still staring at me with that stupid-ass grin on his face.

"Is she coming tonight?"

"Yeah, she'll be there."

"Want to get a beer before dinner?"

I looked at my watch, then at Magnum, who was sitting on the couch.

"Yeah, let's get out of here, but I want to make one stop first."

"Whatever you say, Bark E. Mark. Magnum saddle up—it's beer o'clock."

We pulled into Mom's condo complex at six-fifteen. Miller drove. I was two beers in, and my mood was exponentially better. I clutched Jenna's present in my hand like it was made of glass as I scoured the parking lot for her car. Mav's truck was a few spaces over, and I spotted two new topiary bushes on the bottom steps leading to her door.

She lived in a three-story, three-bedroom condo complex on the far side of an expensive golf course with tons of amenities to keep her busy. Her unit had a single-car garage on the bottom and a neighbor on either side. The three of us all reached in our pockets for our keys, but Maverick threw open her front door and glared at us like we were kids out past curfew.

"You're late," he said, turning around and walking back toward the kitchen.

"And you stormed off earlier with your panties in a twist," Magnum called, pushing past us to follow him down the hallway.

Something smelled delicious on the grill, and my stomach let out a very unappealing sound. I spotted Mom in the kitchen with an apron tied around her slim waist and a smile on her face.

"Great timing, boys. Jenna brought the recipe for Mexican Street Corn, and it smells amazing."

Mom motioned to the far end of the kitchen, where Jenna was mixing something in a bowl—a similar apron around her shapely waist. She turned and waved to us, then picked up the bowl and passed it to Maverick with a spatula.

"Here you go, Maverick. Spread this on the corn and turn it after five minutes."

He nodded and took the bowl, disappearing out the sliding glass door to her large deck and patio.

"Hi, I'm Jenna," she said, reaching her hand out to Magnum. "You must be Magnum. Your mom said you were the best-looking brother."

She turned to me with a wink as Miller shoulder-checked him and crossed his arms over his chest. "I'm sure you're mistaken. I'm Miller. The handsome one. It's okay. It happens when you're faced with this much awesomeness up close and personal."

Magnum stumbled backward and looked back to where I was standing with Mom, shaking her head and watching my idiot man-child brothers jostle to introduce themselves to her first. Jenna had an unreadable expression on her face, like she was about to come back with a sarcastic comment.

Miller rubbed a hand down his green Henley and wagged his eyebrows before reaching out to shake Jenna's hand. She took it but peered around him, looking at Magnum. I stepped forward to stop him from hitting on her or making a fool of himself, but Mom put a hand on my shoulder and shook her head a fraction of an inch.

Oh. This was going to be good.

"She's good for you, Marcus," Mom whispered, leaning against the side of the door frame to watch Jenna mess with Miller.

"Mom—" I started, looking at her and rolling my eyes.

"You've been a different person this last month. Happier. More involved. Can you honestly say it's not because of her?"

Mom pushed off the door frame and took a sip of wine, stepping forward before I could respond. I pushed whatever emotion was trying to bubble up back down and placed Jenna's present on a side table as the color crept up Miller's face.

"Nice to meet you, Miller, but I'm pretty sure your mom was talking about Magnum. You know, the guy with the rugged good looks named after the infamous Tom Selleck, and—" She cupped her hand around her mouth and leaned close to Miller like she was going to whisper a secret in his ear. He leaned closer and tilted his head to one side, waiting for her to finish. "Giant condoms."

"Shit, I need a beer," he said, throwing his hands up in the air as everyone in the kitchen burst into laughter. Jenna had her hand on her knees, and Mom turned away with her head buried on my shoulder. It felt good, laughter booming around the walls of the condo.

"Alright, Bev. I got him," Jenna said, raising her wineglass from the counter and clinking it to hers. "Now, you owe me the story of how you named the boys."

"Gladly, let's take the plates to the patio and eat. Old Cam Winston is a vegan, you know. It'll piss him off even more that we're eating out there after we grill."

"Mom, is this ever going to end?" I asked, grabbing the napkins and silverware she had stacked beside the stove.

"Are you kidding, Mark? Bev told me he snuck into her garden and beheaded all of her sunflowers the other day. What kind of sick freak does that?"

"Exactly. Thank goodness I was able to make a lovely arrangement out of them, but seriously, the nerve of that man."

Mom untied her apron, grabbed the plates, and headed out to the porch. Jenna opened the fridge and passed me a beer with a smile, then patted me on the chest and picked up a tray with all the condiments and buns for the burgers.

"Wait a minute, baby," I said, setting my things down and taking the tray from her arms.

I pulled her further into the kitchen, out of the line of sight from the sliding glass door, and dragged her into my arms. She stiffened for a moment, then melted so sweetly for me. I threaded one hand through her hair and buried my face in her neck.

"I missed you," I said, spreading my legs further and pulling her closer, so our bodies were flush. She moaned and squeezed me back before letting go and tracing her hand down my beard.

"I missed you too, but we should try to keep the PDA to a minimum. I got the impression your mom was hoping we'd start officially dating, and I don't want to give her the wrong impression. Your family is freaking amazing. I'd hate to hurt them when I'm out of the picture."

She leaned up and gave me a quick peck on the lips before trying to sidestep me. I grabbed her hand and tugged her back. She stopped and smiled, putting a hand on her hip and waiting.

"Wait, a sec. I got you something."

I reached around and picked up a tiny air plant and handed it to her. "I know you said your day wasn't great, and that probably meant you lost a patient. I went to that nursery you like, and a guy there said you could keep this plant in a drawer, and it won't kill it. I've never heard of a plant with no roots, but I hope you like it."

I leaned forward and grabbed the back of her neck, pressing her forehead to mind. "Since I can't make you feel better by licking your sweet pussy tonight, the least I could do is bring you a plant you could carry around in your purse."

She took the plant and turned it around in her hands, feeling the fuzzy green leaves, then looked at me with shiny eyes and a bright smile. Her hand reached for my face, and I leaned down and kissed her, trailing both my hands up her arms. Her mouth tasted like the fruity wine she was drinking, and I swiped my tongue across her lips, longing for one more taste before we subjected her to a night with my brothers.

She caressed her tongue with mine, then pulled away and took a step back, pressing a hand to her stomach. She clutched the air plant, and I smiled, hoping it brightened her day.

"Thank you so much, Mark, truly. A plant is exactly what helps me after a hard day, but you're confusing me with these sweet gestures. Let's get through tonight, okay? Oh, and remember I'm taking Phoebe in the morning for her spay surgery."

Jenna reached out and rubbed my arms, then stood up on her tiptoes and brushed her lips to mine again. "You're a good man, Mark. This made my day. You made my day. Come on, big guy."

She picked up her wine and tray, then headed to the patio like she hadn't just told me to keep my hands to myself.

I leaned against the counter and picked up the beer, cracking it and taking a long pull. She was right, of course. Was I hoping to pull her on my lap and hand feed her dinner tonight in front of my family like a possessive Caveman? *Probably not.*

But was I perfectly ready to eat one-handed so I could keep one hand firmly clasped in hers? Where it belonged? *Fuck, yes.*

I shook my head, grabbed the stuff we needed, and made my way to the porch, opening the door with a groan.

What the fuck's the matter with me?

I'm the one with the relationship hang-up, and I'm the one that can't keep my hands to myself.

Maverick was manning the grill, and he held out one hand with a nod as I passed over the plates. Mom stood beside Maverick and headed over to the large Amish wooden picnic table my parents got on a trip to Pennsylvania years ago. My dad customized it by drilling a hole through the center and putting in a huge umbrella, so the patio was comfortable even in the summer heat.

The table sat ten, with mom at the head and dad's side empty. Miller and Jenna were on one side, and Magnum sat smugly on the other.

Fuck it.

I walked around and sat down beside her, gripping her thigh tightly before letting go and putting both hands on top of the table, like a respectable, single gentleman.

"Oh, Mav," Mom said, gesturing to a beautiful bouquet of sunflowers and daffodils tied together with twine and sitting on a table beside two oversized lounge chairs. "I thought Autumn would like those." He looked at the flowers and grunted, then focused on the grill like turning the burgers was the most essential task in the world.

"Mom, are those the sunflowers that Cam destroyed? You know, there's a fine line between a prank and harassment. I'm just a phone call away. Cam should know better than to start shit with you, especially with me being a cop."

"A traffic cop," Miller whispered with a grin. I was just about to make a comment about his dick size when a hamburger bun sailed across the table and bounced off his head. Jenna nudged me in the arm and winked. Miller picked up the bun and tore off a bite, stuffing it in his mouth with a mumbled 'thanks.'

"Well done, Jenna, and that's not necessary, Marcus. I was the one that started it, I think. I might have lobbed rotten vegetables over the fence. I don't remember," Mom said, shrugging her shoulders and passing the burgers over to Miller, who took one and put it on his half-eaten bun.

Jenna smiled and looked at Bev, rubbing her hands together in anticipation. "Okay, Bev. Unless you want me to gross everyone out with my thrilling day of surgeries and appointments, you have to share the name story. Oh," she said, raising her hand and taking another sip of wine. "And I need to know why your youngest has the only normal name. No offense, guys."

"None taken," came the response from my brothers as Mom spoke up.

"Oh, Marcus has a name just as unique as the rest. He's just the only one that's lucky enough to shorten it," Mom said, taking the first burger from Maverick and passing it down the table.

It got to Jenna, and she put lettuce, cheese, and tomato on it, then passed it to me without a second thought, all while keeping her eyes on Mom. I stared at the burger, and Jenna pushed the condiment tray toward me like it was the most natural thing in the world for her to make my burger before she made one for herself. Nothing escaped Mom, it seemed, and her lips turned up in the smallest of smiles as she started talking again.

"When I was pregnant with Maverick, something convinced me I was going to have a girl. Sorry, my favorite," she said, reaching over and patting him on the shoulder as she passed another plate to us. "Martin knew better—he always knew better. He made a bet with me. He said, if the baby was a boy, I could name him the most outlandish name I could think of, and if the baby was a girl, we could name her after Martin's mother, Rose."

Bev smiled and passed another plate. "Naturally, I took the bet because I knew the baby would be a girl and wanted to honor Martin's mother. I said we would name the baby Maverick because we were watching *Top Gun,* and there was no way I was wrong."

"She was wrong," Maverick said.

"Yep," Bev added. "When I got pregnant again, Martin made the same bet with me. This time, I knew. I just knew it was a girl and told him if it was a boy, we'd name him after his favorite beer."

Miller raised his hand and shook his head, adding ketchup and mustard to his burger.

"The third time I got pregnant, the first time we had sex after Miller was born, mind you."

"I didn't hear that," Maverick said, taking the last corn on the cob off the grill and putting the large plate in the center of the table.

"Well, I said if it was a boy, we were going to name him after my favorite television show."

Magnum raised his hand.

"And the last time I got pregnant with my youngest and favorite son. I knew he needed a powerful name. A bold name."

"Oh god, Mom. Please, no," I said, hanging my head as Jenna looked between us like we were an exciting tennis match.

"I told Martin if this last baby was a boy, I'd name him after a Roman Emperor and Philosopher. So we gave him a hyphenated first name, Marcus-Aurelius, and threw in a Roman middle name for good measure.

"Four boys and four utterly unique names. Here, here," Jenna said, raising her glass.

We all did the same, clinking them together before digging into burgers, corn on the cob, and fruit Mom and Jenna prepared.

We were quiet for a time, with nothing but the sounds of twilight and our silverware clinking on the plates to fill the space.

"Tell me a random fact," I said, not looking up from my plate as I took another bite of the street corn.

Damn, that was good.

"Hmm. Did you know that your middle name is also my favorite Harry Potter character?"

Magnum snorted with laughter and put his fork down, covering his mouth to keep from spitting out the last bite of burger he took. "Your favorite character's the werewolf? For shame. Couldn't even pick a pureblood."

"Ouch," Jenna answered. "I guess that means your favorite happens to be a certain white-haired, wealthy family with an affinity to peacocks?"

"Damn right."

"I suppose that's better than ginger blood-traitors."

Jenna winked, and Magnum picked up his beer and tried to take a drink, but he kept laughing until Maverick reached over and slapped him hard on the back. He was shaking his head like he was put out that his brother would dare laugh, but I swear I heard him mutter filthy *mudbloods* under his breath, whatever that meant.

"Mom, tell us this big news," Miller said, spearing another burger without a bun. We all looked at her, and she finished her wine, then steepled her fingers on the table.

"I've made a decision that you boys are probably not going to be happy about."

My heart started racing as Mom looked at us. Was she moving? Was she sick? A million worst-case scenarios ran through my brain, but Jenna let her hand drop to her lap, then drift to my leg, entwining her fingers with mine and scooting closer, so our shoulders were touching. I gripped her fingers and moved my other hand to rest on her thigh, but it still wasn't enough. I was tempted to pull her onto my lap and wrap my arms around her waist. The more of me that touched her, the better I felt.

"I'm not saying this is going to happen today, or tomorrow, or even next month, but I'd like you all to start warming to the idea of me dating again."

"Dating?"

"You?"

"Are you serious?"

My brothers peppered her with questions, and I relaxed my hands on Jenna. Mom wanted to date? She deserved happiness. She didn't deserve to be alone for the rest of her days, and I'd support her. After I thoroughly vetted the guy with my nine-millimeter.

"I'm happy for you, Mom. You deserve to share the rest of your life with someone," I said, drawing everyone's eyes to me.

"So do you, Marcus."

Touché. I walked right into that one.

I cleared my throat and stood up, stacking some empty plates and mumbling about doing the dishes. As I opened the sliding glass door to head back to the kitchen, I heard Jenna ask about the proper way to trim a bonsai plant. By the time I turned around to close the door, Miller was joking with her about trimming her own dick topiary, and Maverick had retreated to the far corner of the patio with another beer.

She looked like she belonged with my family—like she fit it. As I turned on the water and started the dishes, I felt like an outsider.

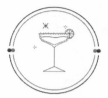

20 - JENNA

"Okay, Kim. You're doing great. Check the pulse oximeter and make sure Melissa has the area thoroughly cleaned with chlorhexidine scrub."

I pushed down my nervousness at having a veterinary student handle Phoebe. I felt crazy overprotective of the little pipsqueak and her growly owner but kept my hands by my side instead of snatching the instruments out of Kim's hands and doing everything myself like a lunatic.

Kim was competent, with steady hands and a whip-smart memory. She was going to be an asset to whatever practice snatched her up. Hell, she correctly diagnosed malignant hyperthermia in a beagle last week, and that case stumped Dr. Duvall and me.

She picked up the scalpel and made a perfect incision below the umbilical scar, all while talking through each step, exactly how I preferred she handle every surgical procedure. I nodded, barely having to adjust her movements as she worked. As she finished the last intradermal suture, I blew out the breath I swear I'd been holding for the last half hour and checked Phoebe's vitals for the hundredth time.

Both patient and student did terrifically, and I followed Melissa as she carried Phoebe to her holding area and placed her on one of Mark's shirts, taking a moment to send Mark a selfie of a thumbs up with her in the background, sound asleep. Mark called, but I didn't have time to answer, only grabbing a donut hole and a drink of coffee before moving on to the next patient.

It was already lunchtime when I finally had time to call him back, but he was on shift and didn't answer. Probably for the best. I slumped down at my desk and slipped off my shoes, untying my scrub cap and leaning back. Dinner last night with his mom and brothers was amazing, but I was getting too close, getting attached.

Something changed since the night at the restaurant, since the night in his truck, and it wasn't just fucking in his truck. Well, it wasn't only fucking in his truck. I could see myself with him, but I couldn't let myself fall for someone that wasn't available. My phone buzzed, and I dug it out of my pants pocket, smiling at Addison's message.

Addison: Taco Tuesday and Margaritas?
Me: Normally hell to the yes, but I'm beat.
Olivia: You mean you're too tired from beating off Officer Big-Dick?
Addison: All aboard the train to pound town. Choo-Choo!
Me: I wish. My period is ruining my life for at least another day or two.
Annaleigh: All the more reason to get toasted, but how are things with Mark?
Me: Confusing.
Olivia: ???
Addison: GIF of head exploding
Me: He made it clear he doesn't want a relationship, even though he

calls me baby and reads me books. I think I'm catching feelings.

Olivia: Oh fuck.

Addison: Fucking feelings or feelings feelings?

Me: Both?

Annaleigh: You need to pull back. Give yourself space.

Me: I know.

Olivia: Are you okay? What about Wilmington?

Me: I don't know, and I'm still talking to the director.

Addison: Well, keep us in the loop. Hey, want me to send you a silicone mold kit so you can make a replica of his dick? That way, you can always have a reminder of him. I found one with purple sparkles the other day. Oh, we can call him Sparkle-Dick!

Annaleigh: When the hell do you have time to google shit like glitter silicone dildo molds?

Addison: I might have gotten some good dick the other week that made me wish I had a replica.

Oliva: Omg, It's times like this, I'm glad I get the same dick every night.

Annaleigh: Me too.

Addison: Y'all are missing out. This guy had a curve that hit me in exactly the right spot. I mean, my toes were throwing up gang signs.

Me: I was so desperate for Mark after B's I asked him to pull over and jumped him in his Tahoe. We did it in the back, and I'm sure he had to deep clean the seats afterward.

Olivia: GIF of breakdancing

Addison: GIF of girl fanning herself

Me: GIF of a sly smile

Annaleigh: He seems so good for you. I hate this.

Me: Me too. Drama sucks. Lunch soon?

Olivia: Definitely.
Addison: Talk later. Love to all.

"Hey lady, brought you some Tuesday motivation," Melissa said, walking into my office with the coffeepot and a bagel. I smiled and lifted my mug as she refilled it for me.

"Thank you. How's everyone recovering?"

"Oh, are you interested in the other patients, or just the little blue-eyed beauty back there?"

"Why do you have to call me out like that, Melissa? How is she?" I said around a mouthful of bagel.

"Fully awake with good movement. She hasn't eaten or gone to the bathroom, but she's been drinking water and has already removed her cone once."

"Ugh, thank you."

"Anytime."

Melissa gave my coffee cup one last top off, then headed out, letting me focus on my computer. Nothing stood out except a client bringing in her pair of sugar gliders named Ginger and Juniper for nail trims.

Ugh, this client.

Some patients stood out because you looked forward to seeing them. Others stood out because they were 'trouble' with a capital T.

I mentally prepared myself for the craziness that followed in the wake of this client and stood up, slipping on my shoes and running my fingers through my hair. I peeked in on Phoebe, and she hissed as soon as she saw me. I took a picture anyway and sent it to Mark before picking up the folder outside the first exam room and opening the door, preparing myself for the onslaught of appointments for the rest of the afternoon.

"Everything looks good, Molly," I said, looking over Ginny's chart with a smile. "She's—" I stopped what I was saying and listened.

It sounded like there was a commotion in the lobby. That was bound to happen with all manner of animals that came into the office, but this was louder than usual.

"Sorry," I said, shaking my head. "Ginny's healthy, and her teeth look fantastic. Keep using the dental treats and brushing them regularly."

I stopped again and looked at the exam room door that connected to the lobby. Something was definitely going on out there. It sounded like the receptionist was squealing, or someone was squealing, and there were footsteps. Loud footsteps. Like people were scrambling back and forth.

Molly noticed as well, and she stepped closer to Ginny, comforting the bulldog who started whining, then pressing her ear to the door. I shrugged my shoulders and did the same, coming up beside her and pressing my ear to the door. As soon as I did, a loud thump whacked against the door, and Molly and I both jumped back.

"What the..." I said, leaning forward again. "Do me a favor and put Ginny on a leash, Molly, and stay here, please."

"Sure. Sure, Dr. Crews," she said, clipping on Ginny's leash and wrapping it around her wrist.

I nodded and cracked open the door, peeking out into the lobby.

"Jesus Fuck," I hissed, looking out onto what I could only describe as complete fucking chaos.

I had enough sense to turn and mouth sorry to Molly, who shrugged before I headed into the lobby to contain the nightmare that had unfolded while I was checking a Bulldog's teeth. I shut the door behind me as my eyes darted to every corner of the front of our office. Supplies were scattered on the floor, and animals were barking and hissing. Owners were yelling as Melissa and Danielle were trying unsuccessfully to calm everyone down.

Our receptionist, Dana, was standing up behind the counter and dancing from foot to foot with her brown hair billowing around her head and her hands flapping around her ears like she was on fire while shrieking, "There's a rodent on my head. There's a freaking rodent on my head. Get it off. Get it off!"

A Goldendoodle had gotten off its leash and was weaving in and out of Dana's legs, barking at the rodents and trying to jump on her chest. The owner was going between trying to grab the dog and trying to catch whatever was in Dana's hair.

A cockatoo was flying by the grooming supplies, and a cat was trying to climb a shelf to get to the bird. Melissa and Danielle were trying to wrangle the cat and bird, and the owners and Dr. Duvall were staring at the craziness with vacant expressions on their faces.

Honestly. Had I walked into the freaking Twilight Zone?

Nope.

Because smack dab in the middle of the chaos, wearing a pink housecoat with a leopard fur coat buttoned over it, was Ms. Freaking Lovejoy with her hands on her hips, wagging her finger at Dana like she was in the wrong.

"They are not rodents, you nitwit. My babies are members of the marsupial family, like kangaroos. They are adorable and have pouches to raise their young. Ginger even has two vaginas, and Juniper has a forked dick. Now calm yourself, girl, so I can help."

I took a deep breath and strode into the middle of the lobby, holding both my hands out like a badass crossing guard. "Everyone stop."

Aside from the noise of the animals, all the people stopped and looked at me. I took a deep, cleansing breath and met their eyes.

"Dr. Duvall, please take Ms. Lovejoy to exam room three. Dana, please calm down, and Melissa will help remove Ginger and Juniper from your hair. Danielle, please help with the Goldendoodle. Then come over here and help me with the cat and bird. Everyone else, please take a seat, and we'll work to get back on schedule shortly."

"Dr. Crews," Dana started, blowing her teased bangs out of her face.

I held up my hand and shook my head. "Let's get the office back in order and our patients handled, then we'll chat. Are you okay?"

She gave me a sheepish nod, and I nodded back, turning to the shelves where the cat was unsuccessfully trying to catch the bird. I stretched up to get the cat down, turning around to find her owner waiting with an open carrier. I smiled and put the cat back in.

"I'm sorry, Dr. Crews. The bird wasn't in a cage, and the receptionist gave me a treat. I shouldn't have opened the carrier."

"Don't sweat it. It was like the perfect storm of animal opposites." I patted his shoulder as he zipped up the carrier and took a seat, staring at the cockatoo perched on the television in the corner.

The bird's owner let out a shrill whistle, and she flew down and perched back on her shoulder. I nodded again and looked at Melissa, who had one sugar glider in her scrub-top pocket and the other in her hand. Aside from some sore feelings and extra cleaning and straightening up to finish, everything looked okay.

"Okay. Now, are you sure you're alright?" I asked Dana, taking the sugar gliders from Melissa and rubbing her arm. "Did these little guys scratch you at all?"

"No, Dr. Crews. I'm so sorry. They came out of nowhere, flew at me, landed in my hair, and got tangled. Then that crazy lady started yelling, and the dog started barking…"

I squeezed her shoulder and gave her a sympathetic smile so she'd stop talking. "It's fine. I get it. Let's talk about requiring all small animals to be in carriers at the next employee meeting or something. Why don't you take the rest of the afternoon off?"

"Oh no, this was all my fault. I need to help clean."

I put my hands up and shook my head. "Dana. It's four-thirty. There are three appointments left, and they are all here. It's fine. Head home."

"Thank you, Dr. Crews. If you're sure."

I nodded and headed to the back, passing Dr. Duvall in the hallway.

"Great job handling that mess, Jenna."

Stopping short, I turned and looked at him, tilting my head and furrowing my eyebrows. Not only had he called me by my first name, but he complimented me. I smiled, waiting for the other shoe to drop, but it didn't. Larry nodded, awkwardly patted my shoulder, and continued down the hallway.

"Well, this day is just full of surprises," I said to the sugar gliders in my lab coat pocket. They just stared at me with their unblinking, enormous eyes as I headed to the exam room.

"It's about time, Dr. Crews. I hope that lady didn't traumatize my babies," Ms. Lovejoy said, reaching her hands out for Ginger and Juniper.

"It's good to see you too, Ms. Lovejoy. How's Pepper doing?"

"Oh, Pepper is fine. She'll need her hooves trimmed soon, but my little gliders need their nails trimmed today, and you need to talk with your receptionist. She offered a cat treats when there was a bird unrestrained in the lobby! And her hairstyle. This isn't the set of an eighties hair band video, you know."

"An eighties hair band video, really? I'm pretty sure I've asked you multiple times to bring Ginger and Juniper in a cage and not your pocket. What if they escaped? A fur coat is not proper transportation, you know. Plus, there are a ton of trees outside. What if they decided to pull a *Braveheart* and jump to freedom in the parking lot?

"Oh, the coat is fine, Dr. Crews," she said, shooing her arm at me like I wasn't making sense. This lady was going to drive me to open up those mini bottles I kept in my bottom drawer for emergencies.

"Hmm," I said, taking back Ginger and giving her a once over before trimming her nails. We switched, and I did the same with Juniper, making notes on the computer and checking that they didn't need vaccinations or bloodwork. I checked to make sure Dana left, and the lobby was empty before walking Ms. Lovejoy to the front and waving her off.

Dr. Duvall was finishing the last appointments, so I headed back to my office and sat down, slipping off my shoes and laying my head on my desk.

I needed to check on Phoebe, and I wanted to text Mark, but I remembered my text chat earlier with the girls—I had to pull back.

A mental image of me dragging a kicking and screaming Mark toward a giant blinking sign that said 'Relationships This Way' flashed across my mind, and I snorted, pushing the image aside and shaking my head.

My emails were probably getting away from me, so I sat up and turned on my computer, determined to make some progress. There was the usual junk, bills, and coupons, but one stuck one.

It was an email from Kelli, the nonprofit director of *All Four Paws*. She wanted me to come up this weekend to tour the facilities and take a deep dive into the financials. My finger hovered over the reply button. I didn't want to leave, but I owed it to myself to see if I had what it took to take this next step in my career. Heading up a nonprofit was always my big picture plan, and this could be my chance.

Before I could let myself overthink and second guess, I clicked reply and told her I'd drive up first thing Saturday and spend the day with her. I'd text my mom in the morning and tell her I'd spend the night. It would be good to see her and my dad and get out of my head for a few days. Hopefully, if I took a break from pretending to play house with Mark, I'd get my head on straight.

I opened my bottom drawer and stared at the mini bottles. I wanted to get out of the office, but I wasn't ready to go home. Blowing out a deep breath, I stood up and slipped off my white lab coat, then pulled my phone out of my pocket and texted the girls again.

Me: I changed my mind. I don't want to go home yet. Who's up for tacos?
Addison: ME! PS I totally ordered that purple sparkle dick kit. I ordered one for all of y'all, each in a different color.
Olivia: No, you didn't.
Annaleigh: Are you serious?
Addison: With express shipping.
Olivia: I can be at El Guapo's at seven.
Me: I'll have chips and salsa waiting.
Annaleigh: With cheese dip?
Me: Duh.
Addison: See you then!

How hilarious would it be if I asked Mark to make a purple sparkle mold of his dick before he walked out of my life? The thought of using a big purple Mark-shaped cock with that thick vein on the underside that felt so good on my tongue instead of that grossly inadequate buzzing thing in my nightstand sounded incredibly appealing.

Thinking about Mark had me thinking about Phoebe, and I stood up and headed to the kennels, grabbing my stethoscope and bending down to open her cage to take a peek. Her incision looked pink and healthy, and her intestine function sounded perfect. Aside from her looking pissed that she had to wear the dreaded cone of shame, she was healing perfectly. I sent Mark another selfie, one of just Phoebe, then sent him another message letting him know I was going out with the girls for dinner and not to wait up.

He responded with okay, and I stared at my phone, hoping three little dots would appear and he'd text more. Just because I was pulling back didn't mean I wanted to go back to a comfortable silence. I cradled Phoebe in my arms and carried her to my desk, setting her on my lap and thinking. Chick jumped up and sniffed the newbie, and I petted them both, trying to think of a fun fact or something to say. I'd even take a heaping dose of my weird awkwardness at this point.

Me: Phoebe wants to tell you a fun fact about the wheel.
Mark: Tell me, baby girl.
Me: Cat Daddy — Did you know paleolithic art dating back thirty thousand years showed people using dildos to pleasure themselves and others? That means people invented sex toys before they invented the wheel.
Mark: Phoebe, what are you and Dr. Cutie doing?
Me: She's making me wear this stupid thing on my head, and my tummy hurts. I need a nap, daddy. The mean doctor is laughing manically and drinking something that smells funny. Phoebe, for shame. Bedtime,
Young Lady.
Mark: Lol. Have a better day?
Me: I did. How's yours going?
Mark: Wrapping things up soon. See you later on.
Me: Sounds good, Handsome. Be back after dinner.
Mark: Later, Cutie.

I put my phone down and picked up Phoebe, tucking her into her kennel with fresh food and water. Chick and Duck followed behind me, and I refilled their food as well before giving the place a once over and checking in with the evening vet tech. I felt a little better heading to the restaurant, but it still felt like this was the beginning of the end—the end of us, and there was nothing I could do to stop it.

21 - MARK

Something was the matter with Jenna. Since coming back from Mom's house two nights ago, we'd been off. Not even bringing home three bonsai trees and two giant topiary plants brought a smile to her face. It was more than her period and more than a bad day at work. Something was pushing us further apart with each second that went by. Sure, we still joked, and kissed, and found every excuse to touch, but our dynamic had changed.

The day of Phoebe's surgery, she went out with her friends, and even though she crawled into bed later that night and wrapped herself around me like a spider monkey, it wasn't the same, and I was struggling. The next day she was gone before I woke up, and when she came home, she had Phoebe with her, and we were both distracted for the night, trying to keep the damn cone on her tiny head. We hardcore snuggled again that night like we were trying to repair whatever had broken.

Today was a double shift that, thankfully, was almost over. Mom was over for her second day in a row, and not even her selfies of Phoebe crawling in a giant boob bonsai could get me out of my funk. I usually loved patrolling. Driving was calming and cathartic, for the most part, but today, everyone on the road pissed me off. I finally parked in the shade underneath an overpass to do paperwork and get my head on straight.

My duffle bag was halfway packed on my bed. The last freaking thing I wanted to do was leave, and I felt like a failure for thinking about moving out early, but it was what I'd do when the house was ready. I knew I could make a few rooms livable if worst came to worst.

You could always man-up, tell her how you feel, and get your head out of your ass; a voice whispered that sounded suspiciously like my dad, but that was stupid. I was doing this because of him, and I'd never heard his voice calling me out before.

And I couldn't do that, Dad, because I didn't know how the fuck I felt.

Yes, you do, the traitorous voice mockingly said back. *You're just too chicken-shit to admit it.*

Even if I was prepared to face the fact that maybe, just maybe, this whole single decision was a mistake because most cops were married and happy. The cold, harsh reality was this job *took* lives, and I refused to do that to someone.

But was that refusal worth your chance at happiness? The voice tried one last time, echoing deep inside my head, but I was done listening.

I scrubbed my hand over my face and scratched my beard, picking up my phone and staring at our last message thread. There wasn't anything new, so I threw it in the cup holder, flicking on the radar and staring out my front windshield.

There went a car three over the speed limit, then one going two, then four. I usually looked the other way unless they were at least going over five, but I kind of felt like being an asshole and pulling over the white minivan driving by doing four over. Still, it was probably a mom on her way to soccer practice, and I wasn't that much of a douche, even if it would make me feel better taking my frustration out on someone.

I could always ride down to Battery Park or around Boone Hall Plantation. Cruising past the giant oak trees, marshes, and southern palm trees with my windows down might help. It was impossible to stay in a bad mood with the sun shining, the September weather a balmy eighty-one degrees, and big, white, fluffy clouds in the sky. I smacked my head against the back headrest and closed out of the program on the laptop installed in my Interceptor. My mind was swirling with more thoughts and colors than one of those giant rainbow suckers at the checkout counters at grocery stores.

Puzzled at the bizarre thought, I barely noticed the black car zipping by me in the far left lane, registering twelve over the limit until my radar buzzed, snapping me out of my funk. I flipped on my flashers and clipped on my seatbelt, ensuring the coast was clear and pulling onto the highway. I felt bad for feeling giddy about pulling over this person who thought they thought they were above the damn rules.

The rules were there for a reason.

They kept people safe. They protected people. They keep jack-asses in black sedans from causing five-car pile-ups on the freeway and untold amounts of personal heartache and damages. I gritted my teeth as I darted between cars to get closer to the vehicle. He tapped on his brake lights and moved to the center lane as soon as he saw me.

Good.

At least I wouldn't be making a call about an idiot that wasn't going to stop for blue lights. As I got closer, I radioed in the plate number and found out it should be a guy in his mid-fifties with no outstanding warrants and a resident of South Carolina with no points on his license. He moved to the right lane, and I followed, getting right on his bumper as he pulled off the road and turned off his car.

I let him sweat it for a minute while I got my attitude under control and reached over for my campaign cover, making sure the strap was correctly adjusted across the back of my head.

Unless his attitude called for it, there was no reason for me to take out my piss-poor mood on this guy. Most people respected the badge and the blue, but you always have to be on the watch for those who didn't. You had to treat each person and each incident with attention to detail, compassion, and above all else, integrity.

After radioing my position, I opened my door and switched on my body cam, walking slowly to the sedan with my clipboard in hand. My boots crunched on the asphalt, and I unclipped my taser, calming my breaths like I always did before a stop. I touched the back bumper above the taillight and kept my hands by my side as I approached the driver's side door, taking in every detail.

The backseat and passenger seat were spotless, giving no indication he was driving under the influence, and the driver matched the description dispatch gave me. His hands were resting loosely on the steering wheel, and his posture was straight and confidant. I leaned forward and nodded my head in greeting, noticing the smell of the car's interior and the dilation of his pupils.

"Good afternoon, Sir. My name is Officer Hansen with the North Charleston Police Force. May I see your license, registration, and proof of insurance, please?"

"Yes, Sir, Officer Hansen," he said, meeting my eyes with a nod and reaching into his back pocket.

I followed his movements, my hand automatically moving to my gun and resting lightly on top of the holster. No matter the situation or how polite someone was, things could turn sour in the blink of an eye, and you always had to be prepared. Always had to be aware. He passed over the cards without issue, and I took them, clipping them onto my board and quickly scanning over the expiration and issue dates.

"I take it you know why I pulled you over."

"Yeah," he said, shaking his head and gripping the steering wheel. I could tell he was pissed, but I couldn't discern if it was because he was caught or because it was an honest mistake. "I have a date with my wife tonight and was stuck at work. I'm already on thin ice for my hours lately, and I was speeding to get home. You were right to pull me over."

He said the last part, gritting his teeth, then looked at me with a sheepish smile.

I grinned and nodded. "I understand, and I'll be right back, Mr. Parkinson."

By the time I was back in my cruiser, I'd decided to reduce the ticket to only five over the limit. The guy admitted he was speeding, and even if he was lying, he owned up to it. Muscle memory took over as I followed procedure and completed my requirements.

It felt good.

Well, not writing this guy a ticket when he was only trying to get back to his wife, but rules, policies, procedures, plans. They steadied me, grounded me. This last month with Jenna, and really since I got Phoebe, my life had been one massive disruption. I needed to find my bearing, give my life a hard reset, get back to what I knew.

Jenna was what I knew, wasn't she? Was I ready to lose her?

I shook my head and finished writing up everything, then got back out, still keeping my guard up. I touched a different spot higher on the back bumper, greeting Mr. Parkinson again and handing him his information.

Hell, I should try for a bit of humor. This was probably my last stop of the day, so I might as well try to snap myself out of this funk. I mean, what's the worst that could happen?

223

"Alright, sir. Thanks for cooperating with me this afternoon, and I apologize for holding you up even later for date night. I guess the only other thing I need is your pilot's license for flying that fast. Then you can be on your way."

I said it with a smile and leaned in closer, not expecting the color to drain from Mr. Parkinson's face.

"Seriously? Does my license say my occupation? How did you know my last flight was delayed? Or was that just a seriously lucky guess?"

He reached over to where he'd laid his wallet on top of his center console and opened it up, passing over his pilot's license with a smile. I reached out and took it, barking out a laugh and shaking my head.

This guy was legitimately a commercial pilot.

"Seriously lucky guess, and it's your lucky day. I'm tearing up this ticket. Get out of here and get home to your wife. Just slow down. If I pull you over again, I will not go easy on you."

"Rest assured, Officer Hansen, I will drive two under the limit all the way home."

"Good to hear. Have a nice evening."

"You do the same."

I tipped my campaign cover and walked back to my cruiser, feeling like I was doing some weird walk of shame. I slammed the door and tore up the ticket, stuffing the scraps in the cupholder.

Good thing I hadn't inputted it into the laptop.

Mr. Commercial Pilot Parkinson pulled back onto the highway, and I took off my hat, checking the time and typing a warning into the laptop instead before radioing that I was heading back to drop off my cruiser and pick up my Tahoe.

Mom: Are you almost home? Phoebe seems off, and Jenna's not

answering her phone.
Me: I have to drop off the Ford. What's going on?
Mom: Her stomach is really red, and she hasn't touched her food.
Me: I'll be home in twenty. I'll try Jenna.
Mom: Thanks, Marcus.

I snapped my phone on the mount and dialed Jenna, pulling onto the highway and heading to the station. She didn't answer, so I hung up and tried again. This time she did, and I could hear the stress in her voice, hating that I interrupted whatever she was doing.

"Hey, what's up. Your mom called too, but we're having a little crisis here."

"Sorry to bug you, but Mom thinks something's off with Phoebe. Says she's not eating, and her stomach is red."

I made a left-hand turn, checking the time and calculating how many miles there were between the station and me.

"Okay. I haven't had a chance to look at my messages. Did she say anything else?"

An image of Jenna pushing her glasses on her head and rubbing the bridge of her nose flashed in front of my eyes as I drove, probably pacing in whatever room in the clinic she was in.

"No, but she sounded concerned, and if she already called you, it has me worried."

"Right, I understand. I'll grab some supplies and head home as soon as things are handled here. If you beat me there, take a picture of her incision and thank Bev for the plants and kitten-sitting."

"Will do. See you soon."

"Okay, bye."

She hung up without another word, and I felt like an ass for not asking what was going on that had her ignoring our calls, but Mom texted again asking if I was close, and I pushed my speed higher, making it to the station in eight minutes flat.

"Holy shit, Mom. Her incision," I said, picking up Phoebe and bringing her to the kitchen table where the light was better. She felt hot and gave out a meek little squeak in my arms as I pushed aside a pile of mail and laid her down. "When did this start?"

"It was like night and day, Marcus. I kept that stupid cone off her when I'd been here, and I guess she's been licking the incision. At lunch, I noticed she didn't follow me in the kitchen, demanding part of my BLT, and she didn't want to play and fussed when I picked her up. I started looking up her symptoms on the internet, and I think this is my fault. I should never have taken her cone off."

I looked closer at her stomach, and sure enough, the incision was puffy and red.

Shit.

"Mom—"

"I'm so sorry. I'll stay, everything should be fine. I think all she needs is a drug called, hang on, I looked it up."

Mom was getting worked up and frazzled, and I hated it for her. I'd been just as slack with that damn cone as she had. Phoebe had a neck the size of a damn thimble, and no matter how many times I put the cone on, she wiggled free. Jenna could fix this. Fix Phoebe.

"Mom. She'll be fine. Jenna's on the way back with supplies. You head on home. I didn't use that stupid cone either. She probably spent all night licking her incision. This is no one's fault."

"But—"

Mom put her head in her hands, and I leaned forward and put one arm around her, pressing my lips to the top of her head. "This wasn't your fault, and it's been a long day. Here, I'll walk you out."

She nodded her head and gathered her things, following me down into the foyer. Phoebe stayed cradled in one hand, and I hated how warm she felt, but I tried to stay calm, not wanting to worry Mom any more than she already was.

"I'll text you later with an update, don't worry, and Jenna says thank you for the plants and for watching her."

"She's so good for you, Marcus."

Yeah, Mom. I agree.

"Hmm," I responded, not wanting to give her ammunition either way.

She waved as she pulled away, and I watched her drive down the road. Then, I hightailed it back to the kitchen, opening the freezer for a bag of frozen vegetables. I went to the bathroom and got a thick towel, putting the vegetables between the folded layers, and laying Phoebe on top. Her blue eyes were at least alert, so I grabbed a spoon and an opened jar of baby food from the pantry, offering her a little.

Babying her was doing the trick, and she slowly was licking up the baby food, already looking perkier. My eyes strayed to open mail I had carelessly pushed aside, and something caught my eye. Feeding Phoebe another bite, I leaned forward and moved it closer as a roaring noise that sounded like a freight train was barreling through the kitchen overtook all other sounds in the house. Words tried to pierce through the noise, but the first thing that made it through my thick skull was sheer panic.

Jenna was offered a job in Wilmington. She could be leaving.

She couldn't leave.

Not when I…

I couldn't grasp at the words my brain was trying to form, not when my temper was rising like the steam from the barreling train, but I took a deep breath and pushed it down. I'd never felt more conflicted as I did at this moment, reading over the words.

I shoved the letter away, disgusted and hurt. All this anguish. All this temptation. All this second-guessing *everything* was for nothing because she was leaving. I ran my hand through my hair and yanked on the short strands, focusing my attention back on Phoebe, but my subconscious was screaming.

I was right.

I was right for holding back.

I took a deep breath because there was something else bubbling to the surface. Something more than the anger and the frustration now that the steam from the train was dissipating. Some big, important, heart-swelling emotion that felt like—

"Hey, Mark," came Jenna's tired voice from the foyer.

She looked exhausted and beautiful. My stupid subconscious had miraculously produced a bouquet of roses and a bottle of wine, holding it out like a peace offering to ease the exhausted look on her face.

I'm a fucking lunatic.

I finished the spoonful of food I was feeding Phoebe and stood up, bending down to kiss her. No matter my anger, or disappointment, or whatever twisted emotion I had going on, I was happy she was home. I crushed her to my chest, breathing her in like it would fix whatever was wrong with me, wrong with us.

"Let's take a look at your girl," she said, putting both hands on my chest and giving me a tired smile.

She still had a stethoscope around her neck, and she put an old-school black doctor's bag on the table before bending down to listen to Phoebe's heart. Then she cooed softly and picked her up, checking her over and paying particular attention to her stitches and incision.

"Okay, Cat-Daddy. She has a minor infection, fever, and is dehydrated. Luckily, I have everything we need here. Kim handled her surgery like the pro she is, so I'm—"

"Wait," I interrupted, coming up to stand right beside Jenna. "You're not the one that did her operation?" My anger roared back tenfold, and my eyes flashed red as I stared at her.

"No, one of our students performed the surgery. I was there the entire time, of course."

"You let a student operate on my cat? Look at her. Obviously, she screwed up because you couldn't be bothered to do it yourself. Were you too busy considering your move to Wilmington?" I gestured to the letter on the far end of the table.

She gently put Phoebe down on the towel and stood up. Her cheeks were scarlet, and her chest was flushed, but her eyes were no longer soft and hazel. She stood up to her full five-foot-five frame and squared her stance, crossing her arms over her chest and making her tits press against her scrub top.

"Get the fuck out of my kitchen."

"But, Phoebe," I said, pointing to the kitten like Jenna didn't know she was laying there on the fluffy bath towel.

Jenna didn't raise her voice, and she didn't move an inch. She only stared at me, unblinking, not moving a muscle.

"I said, get the fuck out of my kitchen."

I clenched my fists and cracked my neck, staring at her, expecting her to crumble under my gaze. If anything, her eyes got more brutal, and I gave in, like the asshole I was, and walked out, pulling the sliding door closed behind me.

As soon as it was closed, I turned around and slumped against it.
What a dick move.

I was pissed, worried, confused as fuck, and a little turned on seeing her aggressively take charge like that. I knew she'd take care of Phoebe and give her the treatment she needed to feel better.

The real question was, after she fixed Phoebe, what the fuck was she going to do with me?

22 - JENNA

As soon as my kitchen door closed, I took a deep breath and counted to ten, shaking out my shoulders and bouncing on the balls of my feet.

How dare he think I would ever not have Phoebe's best interest at heart?

I spread my legs and stared at the floor, stretching out my neck for five counts, then tilting it to the right, left, and ceiling, repeating the process until my heart rate was under control. We were at a breaking point, a crossroads, a boiling teapot on the stove someone forgot about, and it just bubbled over, but I had to hold it together until Phoebe was better.

Emotional detachment.

It was one of the first phrases taught at med school, and I had to dig deep right now because I was too emotionally attached to Phoebe and Mark, and I was especially emotionally attached to Duck, Chick's best friend. This evening, we operated on him because we found a small mass in his stomach—I was emotionally attached.

And I fucking hated every second.

Drawing one more shaky breath, I sat down at the kitchen table and pulled Phoebe closer. She needed a shot of antibiotics and intravenous fluids. The fluids I could give easily through the loose skin on the back of her neck, and I took the liquid from my bag and put on sterile gloves before prepping the needle. She squirmed and squealed when the needle pierced her skin, and that was good. You wanted a kitten that reacted to pain, not one that was out of it.

About ten minutes later, she already looked fifty times better, so I took out the IV and gave her antibiotics. Also, I made sure Mark had the prescription needed for the additional antibiotics, gave her an extra shot for pain and inflammation, and slathered ointment on her incision before sending a selfie to Bev, knowing she was probably worried sick.

The last item Phoebe needed was a cone that worked. Luckily, Melissa had already figured that part out, and it was brilliant. Her solution was to reinforce another cone of shame, so there wasn't any way Phoebe could take it off. Phoebe struggled with the cone while I cleaned up. Finally, she quit fighting it, turned in a circle, and laid down on the towel. Her glare was not happy.

"You're welcome," I mumbled, capping the needles and putting them in a separate sterile bag to take to the office and dispose of later. Then I snapped off my gloves and threw them in the trash.

Now there was nothing left to do but face Mark.

My body vibrated with the intensity of the emotions I was feeling. Anger, pain, and desire rolled off me in waves as I slid open the kitchen door. He was waiting for me on the other side. His body snapped taut with tension. He'd removed his vest and equipment, standing before me in nothing but a tight white T-shirt, slacks, and those black boots polished to a high shine.

"How is she?" he said, biting off the words and reaching for the bundle.

I'd removed the frozen vegetables Mark stuck on the bottom to bring down her temperature, but passed her over, curled up on top of the fluffy towel. He lifted her to eye level, and she raised her head, trying to head-butt him but only bumping him with the cone.

His little girl was going to be just fine.

"She's already on the mend. That cone's been Phoebe-Proofed, so she shouldn't be able to take it off, and there are two scripts for you on the kitchen table."

"I'm going to put her in the bedroom."

"Yeah, I'm going to change. Then we need to talk."

"Yes, we do," he said, turning and walking to his room. Not mine.

What did I expect?

I peeled my shirt off as soon as I got to my bedroom, shutting the door before undressing the rest of the way and grabbing a comfy shirt from my pajama drawer and leggings. When I walked back out to the living room, he stood by the couch with his legs spread and arms crossed. His muscles rippled, and his tattoos seemed to dance across his skin.

He was stupidly good-looking, and it pissed me off even more that I was thinking about his freaking muscles when he dared to question my competence. Giving up trying to remain level-headed, I settled for passive-aggressive and sat down on the couch, crossing my legs and looking in the other direction.

I glanced at him from the corner of my eye and watched him grind his jaw back and forth like he was waiting for me to talk first, so he could unleash whatever shit he wanted to get off his chest.

"This isn't working anymore," he said, staring at the wall like he was trying to bore a hole through it. "And you don't have a right to kick me out when you're treating Phoebe because you don't like what I have to say. You wouldn't have done that to any other client."

"You never had the right to question my competence and suggest I would do anything to compromise Phoebe or any of my patients."

"Yeah, I get it. That was uncalled for, and I apologize, but why the hell didn't you tell me about Wilmington?" he said, throwing his hands in the air and pacing back and forth in front of me. "That seems like a pretty big decision, don't you think?"

Wilmington?

I lowered my head and ran my fingers through my hair, taking a deep breath to calm the roaring thoughts pulsing around my brain.

"A big decision? A big decision? That's an understatement. It's a huge decision, but it's also my mine, Mark, because you are nothing more than the King of Mixed Signals. You call me sweet nicknames, but you've been clear you're not relationship material from the start. Don't catch feelings, Jenna. What makes you think you deserve to be a part of any decision I make, hmm?" My voice was getting louder, but as I got worked up, he continued to pace, keeping his emotions guarded.

I watched his body language. His shoulders were tight and bunched, and he kept running his hands through his hair. His mouth was set in a flat line, and his lips were so thin they were barely visible. He wasn't spewing hateful words my way, but his silence was deafening.

Good.

If he was angry, maybe this wouldn't hurt as bad. I wouldn't feel the persistent ache in my chest whenever I thought about our expiration date. I could push aside every instinct that cried out to hold him tight and never let him go.

"I overheard you the other night on the phone," I said, lowering my voice but still holding onto my courage. He stopped pacing and looked at me like he was trying to remember. I leaned forward and met his eyes, reaching my hand out and looping my finger in his belt loop. I wanted him to look at me as I told him. I wanted him to see my pain.

"I believe your words were: I'm in hell here. I can't wait to fucking

234

get back home. There's no connection." I paused for a second to let the words sink in, my eyes never leaving his. His eyes narrowed, and he sucked in a breath, shaking his head a fraction of an inch like he couldn't believe I overheard his careless words. He put his hand over mine and stepped closer, and cradling my head in his hands.

"We were just each other's itch to scratch, right, Mark? Nothing more than fuck-buddies. That's all this was," I said, spitting venom in his direction as I remembered how casually he tossed his words around about us like garbage.

"You have no idea what the hell you're talking about, Jenna," he hissed through tight-pressed lips, running his thumbs over my cheeks. His actions were contradicting his voice and muddling my exhausted brain. "But moving without telling me? Without evening mentioning it? That's all I need to know about how you feel. Do you think I'm a fucking joke?"

I crossed my arms and stared up at this mountain of a man, pushing his hands off me and scooting back on the couch. "You have no idea how I feel. I don't even know. I'm a fucking joke, Mark. I'm the joke because I thought I could do casual with you. I thought I was strong enough to keep this up. But I'm not. I'm plain, awkward, boring Jenna who can't do casual because I've fallen for you, Mark. And you? You can. And I get that, I do, but I'm done pretending."

I stared at this man who's made me feel more in the last month than I had in my entire life. This man—who was still glaring at me with a mix of anger and lust swirling across his handsome features.

His hands were fisted by his side, but his bottom lip was dented and swollen with the way he'd been worrying it between his teeth. The moment I focused on his lips, the electricity in the room fizzled and crackled, charging our emotions to ten thousand degrees.

"I'm done pretending," I whispered to nothing at all, keeping my eyes anywhere but on him. I guess I needed the assurance that this last month meant something, if only for myself. I looked at Mark through my lashes, seeing the beginnings of something else shining through his eyes.

He wanted me.

No matter the outcome, the chemistry we had was undeniable, but I wouldn't give him the satisfaction of knowing how much I wanted him.

How much I needed him.

But the truth was written on my face, and the truth was in my words. As soon as they crossed my lips, he knew. He knew I'd fallen when I said I was done pretending.

Now that the words were out there, some sick, twisted part of me wanted to make him hurt like I was hurting. Make him ache like it would help the hollow, desperate feeling that had overtaken my chest. I wasn't going to make him change for me. If he didn't want a relationship, I would make sure I burned our bridge so severely he wouldn't have regrets. I'd be the bad guy. I'd be strong enough to end this.

"Did you fuck me because I was convenient?" I uncrossed my legs and planted them firmly on either side of him. His hands went to my hips, almost dimpling the skin as I narrowed my eyes and set my lips in a firm line. Unyielding.

He would not break me.

"No, baby. I fucked you because I couldn't, not fuck you. Because I couldn't let one more second pass without feeling your tight pussy surround me. Because there has been no one, and I mean no one, that I've ever wanted more."

He pulled me closer, spreading my legs further and wedging himself between them. I could see his eyes looking fierce, but somewhere in the unyielding darkness, I saw a spark—the smallest sliver of light.

Below the rugged plains of his face, I saw the clench of his jaw and a tick near his left eye. He looked pissed that I called him out about his stupid conversation on the phone, but more than that, he was turned on.

And fuck, so was I.

I wasn't sure if he heard my admission through the haze of lust I saw in the depth of his eyes, and I was a glutton for punishment because my body ached to feel him one more time.

I wanted to push him over the edge, to see him lose control. To have him take all the lust and frustration out on my body. I wanted him to snap like a rubber band. If we were going to end, I wanted to go down in flames.

I wanted to burn.

"You're a coward," I snarled, leaning forward and rolling my hips against him. "That's what you won't admit."

"You're insufferable," he growled, burying his face in my neck and dragging his cock against my center. "And you'd rather talk at me than have a real fucking conversation."

"At least I'm willing to talk." I gripped his hair and dragged his head back. He was still close enough for me to count each eyelash framing those dark as sin eyes.

"Yeah, right, and when things get hard, you think moving away is the answer."

"Then you know what to do, right?" I popped up, making him jerk backward with the sudden movement. "Do what you do best. Fucking leave, Mark."

His hand shot out. He grabbed my arm, yanking me toward him, so I was flush against his body. He leaned down to rub his nose against my neck, and goosebumps appeared on my arms. I tilted my neck to give him better access to my skin and could feel his restraint snapping. My stupid body was betraying my mind.

"What are you going to do?" I whimpered, daring him to take his frustration out on my aching body. "Spank me?"

"Is that what you want?"

Was it?

Thinking of his hands on me, fulfilling something I'd never spoken out loud but always wondered about, was too tempting to ignore, especially when this felt like the end.

"Yes. Make me feel everything, Mark."

"Then fuck yes, I am," he said, turning me around roughly to face the back of the couch.

He kicked my feet apart and manhandled my body, so my knees were resting on the couch cushion. He yanked down my leggings and grabbed a handful of my flimsy blue boy shorts, tearing the material from my body.

"Are you sure you want me to?" he hissed between his teeth, running one hand up my thigh.

"I dare you," I replied, trying to turn my head around to face him, but he grabbed a fistful of my hair to hold me steady and cracked his palm across my ass.

My back arched, and I hissed out a breath. The sting of his palm was exactly what I needed as I listened to his ragged breath as he guided his fingertips over my swollen flesh. He tugged my hair harder, turning my neck, so my cheek pressed against the back of the couch. Draping his entire body over mine, he let go and licked a line up the side of my neck, then bit down, grinding his hips to my ass.

"That's a dare I'd take every time, baby."

"Ahhh," I moaned, lifting my head enough to shake the hair from my face. "Is that all you've got, Mark? Let me fucking feel you."

He hissed in an audible breath, and then I heard the telltale sound of his belt buckle and zipper as he worked his pants down. My pulse was racing, and my heartbeat was roaring in my ears, but I wiggled my hips enough to let him know I wanted more.

He stood up and popped me again. Once. Twice. Three times. Never in the same spot. He kneaded my stinging ass and leaned over me again, breathing in my ear.

"What do you want, Jenna?"

"Again. Make it count," I said, panting and egging him on. I needed him raw and uninhibited. I needed him more than oxygen. I needed everything he was willing to give.

Crack!

My breath hissed out between my teeth, but he didn't let up, smacking me two more times in the same spot. I could feel the heat pouring off my skin as he let go of my hair and sunk to his knees, spreading my ass cheeks apart to expose everything to him. Tracing his tongue through my wetness, he growled low in his throat.

"Fuck, you're soaked for me. This pussy is everything, baby. This is what you really want, isn't it?"

I nodded desperately, turning my head to see him and not confident I could form a coherent sentence. Not when his tongue, his cock, and his overwhelming essence were so close. He stood back up, shoving his pants and briefs the rest of the way down to his ankles. His cock looked painful, the head dark and swollen as he gripped the base and gave himself a harsh stroke.

"You want me?"

There was no point denying it. He was everything I wanted. I didn't want to leave Charleston. I wanted this, him—*every day.*

"Yes."

"You want this?" He grabbed my hair and angled my head so I could see him drag his cock through my pussy. I whimpered with the sensation, nodding and pushing my hips back.

"No, baby. You want this? Beg for it."

I could see the last shred of restraint disappearing from his gaze, but he was going to make me work for it. He was going to make me beg.

"Fuck me, Mark. Please. Please," I whimpered as he let go of my hair and ran his hand down my back, then leaned forward and kissed the places his hands smacked. He licked and soothed the tender skin, running his hands over my ass, over my back, and through my hair.

There was nothing I could do but whimper. It felt too good. He felt too good, and this was the end. I could feel it as much as I could feel the wetness from my pussy sticking to my thighs. Everything had come full circle.

And I ached.

I ached for his touch. I ached for his cock. I ached for not being enough for him.

"Please, Mark," I said in a choked whisper. If I spoke any louder, he'd hear my voice cracking with the realization this was it. And I wasn't ready to give him up.

I'd never be ready.

"Tell me you want my cock bare, Jenna," he growled, continuing his slow torture up and down my slit. The anger in his voice was gone, replaced with cracked, consuming lust that matched mine.

"I'm safe, and I'm on the—"

"That's not what I fucking asked. Tell me you want me like this, no barriers, nothing between us. Just you and me. Like it should be."

Yes. I wanted to feel him, all of him—nothing but his thick shaft filling me, owning me.

"Yes. Please. Fuck me bare. Let me show you how sweetly I can grip your thick cock."

He gripped himself again and ran his length through my folds, getting himself nice and wet and prolonging the pleasure and torturing me at the same time.

"I know you will, baby—my Jenna. I'll give you what we need. You know I will."

I felt the head of his cock at my entrance as his fingers danced over my hips. Then he gripped them and thrust in with one hard stroke.

Bliss.

There was nothing, nothing, like feeling him in me bare, nothing but his slick, velvet cock plunging in and out. I gripped onto the back of the couch like it was my lifeline and let the sensations wash over me, throwing my head back and moaning.

He set a punishing pace, grunting with every thrust and giving me everything I needed. His cock stretched me open, bordering between pleasure and pain, but he kept thrusting, grinding, slamming into me over and over. I closed my eyes, determined to hold back the tears threatening to cascade down my face. Because he felt too good, he felt too real.

It was better than I could have imagined, better than anything I'd felt before—he relentlessly pounded into me without a hint of slowing down. I knew his fingers were leaving bruising marks on my hips, but I was glad. I wanted his mark, wanted the reminder of how he felt. The slap of his balls on my pussy…the friction was almost too much. I could feel myself racing toward orgasm.

It was too soon.

I didn't want this to end.

This was too good.

He was too good. I leaned my head back and took a deep breath as he slammed into me again.

"Give it to me, Jenna. Don't hold back. Give me what I need."

"Don't stop," I panted. Each word was punctured with a breath and a thrust, and I knew as my body tightened around him, the spiraling orgasm I was heading toward was rapidly approaching the point of no return. I hoped he could feel me because I wanted to jump over this cliff together. I wanted to freefall into oblivion with him.

With Mark.

"I feel you, baby," he growled. "I'm there too." He released one hip and snaked a hand between my legs to rub my clit.

I threw my head back and exploded into nothing. Spots danced in my vision, and I screamed his name, feeling his cock swell impressively inside me before he painted my inner walls with his release. There was no finesse, no gentle movements. Only violent, shaky, breathless grunts and thrusts as a riptide of waves rolled across our bodies. Tears streamed down my face, and my knees were trembling, but I kept coming. Like my body knew this was it and was determined to wring every single drop of pleasure from me.

He slowed his movements, and I lowered my head to rest my cheek on the back of the couch. The silence was deafening. There was nothing but our shaky breaths and rapid heartbeats. Mark took a step back, and his cock slid out of me, coating the inside of my thighs with his come. With that one step, I felt walls erecting between us, and I wanted to turn around and pull him to me, begging him to stay, but I wouldn't.

My hair was plastered to the side of my face as I rose up and furiously wiped my eyes before I turned around, falling back on the couch with my leggings still around my ankles. I kicked them off and pulled my knees to my chest, looking up to see Mark towering over me and breathing hard.

His eyes were glassy, and a sheen of sweat covered his forehead and matted his blonde hair to his chest.

"Do you feel better?" he asked as his eyes roamed over my body.

No. Because I'm going to lose you, and it's going to break me.

"Yes."

"Good."

He leaned down and pulled his pants up, not bothering with the button, then turned on his heel and walked toward his room. I pressed my hands to my cheeks, feeling how flushed they were, then stood up with shaky legs, pulling up my leggings and padding to my bedroom before shutting the door.

I felt like I was closing the door on him, on us.

Maybe it was for the best, but I knew down deep in my soul that was bullshit.

BY YOUR SIDE

23 - MARK

*H*oly shit.

I shut the door, dragging my spent body to the bed and sitting on the edge, resting my elbows on my knees. My body was vibrating with the intensity of the evening, and I threaded my hands behind my head, digging my fingertips into my neck to relieve the tension brewing through my body. I was wound as tight as a pocket-watch ready to spring.

My palm was red and tingling from where I'd spanked her, and damn if that wasn't the hottest sex of my entire fucking life. I'd never felt anything as good as her bare pussy gripping me. I'd never been with someone like that before, and the thought of having anything between us after that was a moot point. Not after what we'd been through.

But what had we been through?

That was the million-dollar question. I looked over to my pillow where Phoebe was laying, already looking healthier and pissed as fuck to be back in the cone of shame.

I rubbed my face, jerking my hand away when I realized I smelled Jenna on my fingers. It was like she was seared into my skin, a piece of me.

I couldn't stay here.

After our fight and what we shared? I shook my head and stood up. I was lost.

My brain felt five times too big, like it was about to leak out of my ears. She was sexy wrapped in a big awkward rainbow with purple glasses and so damn sweet I'd probably have ten cavities the next time I went to the dentist. But it was all worthless because of my words to her the other night.

If there ever was a person I'd break my rule with, it'd be you, Jenna, but I can't.

I was grasping at straws. It was better to have her think I said those horrible words about her and not my stupid fucking video game set-up than to admit otherwise. Though some dark part of me wanted to march into her bedroom and pink the rest of her ass for even thinking I'd say those awful things.

How could she think there was no connection?

What reason did you give her to think otherwise? That damn voice from earlier whispered.

My duffle bag was half open on the floor, and I picked it up, carelessly stuffing my clothes and toiletries in with reckless abandon. Jenna's door was closed when I opened mine, and I partially zipped the duffle, cramming it with Phoebe's toys as I walked through the house. I grabbed my keys from a bowl on the table in the front hall, tossing the duffle in the Tahoe along with two cat beds and her food. My second trip was for the rest of Phoebe's supplies, along with her medicine and instructions.

When I walked back in, the house looked empty and cold without the scattering of cat toys, so I took a few minutes and brought Jenna's plants in from the back porch. The bonsai boobs went on the coffee table, and smaller topiaries went in the kitchen. I left some of the larger plants on the porch, but her place looked more like her when I was done.

Phoebe was my last trip. I grabbed my wallet and put her in her pink cat bed, making sure Jenna's door was locked behind me. I contemplated leaving the key under the mat but felt safer taking it and dropping it in the mail or at *AMC* when Phoebe needed a follow-up. I stared at her door, willing her to open it, praying I'd see a light switch on, a blind flicker, anything.

Who knew how long I was in her driveway, but when Phoebe meowed, I leaned over and made sure she was secure, then cranked the engine and backed out.

Do what you do best. Fucking leave, Mark.

Something about Jenna's cold, harsh words stuck with me as I pulled out of her neighborhood and onto the highway. My heart and my head were at odds with each other. My heart was screaming for me to go back, grab her and kiss her and tell her I wanted nothing more than her to be by my side, but my head was rational, not my heart.

There was a reason the right choice wasn't easy. If it were easy, no one would ever feel pain, and everything would always be sunshine and fucking butterflies.

Phoebe slept while I was lost in the white lines on the highway, and before I knew it, I was turning into my driveway and marveling at the finished wrap-around porch, lit up with motion-activated lights as I parked in front of the garage.

Several rocking chairs were moving slowly in the late summer breeze, and Mom had been by because there were topiary plants on either side of the bottom steps and baskets with leafy vines hanging from the porch ceiling. I shut off the Tahoe and took in the completed look, my face blanching at the realization that the house looked livable from the outside.

"Come on, Baby Girl. Let's go in," I said, opening the door and walking around to collect Phoebe on her cat bed.

I walked up the porch steps and couldn't help but do a lap around the house, letting out a low whistle. Even in the moonlight, I could see the porch was freshly stained, and several fans with those large low-hanging blades shaped like palm ferns were on each side, giving the place a classic southern vibe. The house had a fresh coat of paint, sticking with the green we had growing up, but deeper and matching the darker stain of the porch.

I looked out to the backyard and saw the large oak trees, sadly smiling with the realization I was home. My key slid smoothly in the lock, and I walked into the kitchen, tossing them on the island and taking in the smells of wood and paint. There was still one light switch in each room, something I insisted on, and tonight I was glad for it because I was too damn tired to text my brothers and have them walk me through the smart panels.

The kitchen flared to life with clean lines and warm colors, and I sat Phoebe on the floor in her bed while I walked back to the Tahoe for the rest of our things. Once I got everything for her situated, I opened the fridge to grab a beer.

Wait. The fridge? The appliances?

Everything was not only back in its place, but my fridge was stocked. Not with anything extremely perishable, but I had beer, bread, cheese, jelly, and other essentials. If I weren't feeling so shitty, I'd be excited I could hold off on shopping. Grabbing a beer, I took a long pull and scooped up Phoebe as I walked into the living room. Aside from a plastic tarp by the front door with some tools laying on it, everything looked finished.

I did a three-sixty, walking down the hall, through the dining room, past the half bath. "This is the kind of place a family deserves to live in," I said to Phoebe, stopping in my tracks when I got to the far back room my dad had kept as an office.

I always thought this room would look great with built-in bookshelves and floor-to-ceiling windows, and fuck if the construction crew didn't deliver.

"She would love this room, Phoebe. I could see her sitting on the bench underneath that big window reading. Couldn't you?"

My shoulders fell as I backed out of the room and turned off the light, shutting the door with a click and walking back down the hall. I put Phoebe in her cat bed on the kitchen floor and pulled out a barstool on the far side of the island, looking around the space. Jenna should be here, laughing at me as I pulled her through the house, pointing out all the things I changed and all the things that stayed the same. She should be here, drinking with me, smiling with me, just with me.

If there ever was a person I'd break my rule with, it'd be you, Jenna, but I can't.

Alone in my space, the words felt like an excuse, a copout, a reason to hide behind my fears.

I pulled my beer closer and finished it in one swallow, remembering a night not long after I joined the force when we took a buddy out to celebrate his return to duty. He was shot during a routine traffic stop, and that night he got trashed and confessed he walked in on his wife cheating on him the week prior. It turned out, the shooting fucked her up pretty badly, and her way of dealing with it was to stop caring about him. When he confronted her, she told him point-blank, you couldn't get hurt if you stopped loving someone.

I'd forgotten about that. He was shot less than a month after I joined.

How did Jenna deal with death and sickness every day? She didn't choose to stop practicing when her first patient died. She loved her job and wouldn't stop on days she came home in tears. Was I making the easy choice all this time because I was scared of giving my heart to someone? Was I that emotionally stupid it took losing Jenna to make me see everything clearly?

There was nothing good about what was happening. My choice for staying single was imploding around me because I was finally fucking realizing I wanted to share this big, empty house with someone.

I wanted to share my big empty life with someone.

With Jenna.

The emptiness was spreading through my body like I submerged it in ice-cold water, but for once, in my solitary existence, I let everything hit me head-on instead of exploding in anger or pushing things below the surface.

I let the harshness of Jenna's words tonight flow through me, absorbing how I'd hurt and used her. How I'd treated her, asked so much of her, and given nothing in return.

I hung my head and closed my eyes as another wave crashed into my body like a Tsunami. It was what was threatening to crack my chest in two. What this was, what this had always been, was deeper than trust, deeper than desire.

Connection.

The basic recognition of finding someone in the billions of people on this planet that truly made you a better person. The person you were willing to change for—the person who was worth it.

Do what you do best. Fucking leave, Mark.

And I did.

24 - JENNA

"It's easy to see why this shelter has the highest adoption rate in all of North Carolina," I said, taking in the five-thousand-foot facility Kelli Jacoby, the owner, and Executive Director, was showing me.

The last time I was here, I didn't get the entire tour, and it was even more impressive than I remembered. She beamed at the praise and tossed her honey-colored hair over her shoulder, motioning me to follow her into the back offices.

Kelli and her husband, Ralph, had been philanthropists their entire life, having a particular passion for helping animals. She was in her late forties and dressed impeccably in a pair of white designer pants and a green button-down blouse. Casual sneakers completed the look, and I couldn't help but notice both the knees of her pants were dirty, suggesting she didn't have a problem jumping in to help when needed.

They spent a fortune renovating an old warehouse and turning it into an animal shelter and a state-of-the-art surgery facility. They focused on rehabilitating animals and finding the best adoption matches. Volunteers and employees darted around the bright, open area. They walked dogs, cleaned spaces, and showed families different animals.

I stopped and watched a young kid sitting in the corner of a large kennel. He was probably in college, and he had a textbook open on his lap. In the opposite corner was a skinny black dog, hunched over with his tail between his legs. The food and water dish were beside the dog, but he wouldn't move. Every time the boy turned a page in the book, the dog jerked and moved closer to the corner. The boy noticed and stopped, putting both hands on his lap. The dog stared and inched closer to the food with the boy, completely ignoring him.

"That's our goal," Kelli said, crossing her arms.

As much as I was taking in every detail of the day-to-day operations, she was watching me just as closely. "You can't put a dog like that in a tiny cage and then wonder why no one wants it. It took Tom a week before Oliver would let him in the kennel. Now, look at them. Oliver is going to be someone's best friend one day."

Kelli patted my arm and motioned me to follow her. We walked down a hallway past a room designed for reptiles and birds and to her office. She had a large cherrywood desk with two computer monitors but motioned me to a small round table with two comfy chairs. I took one, and she took the other, giving me a kind smile that made her blue eyes sparkle.

"So, what do you think? We have a shortlist of candidates to take over, but you're at the top. You're young, dedicated, and talented. It's time for Ralph and me to retire, and your reputation precedes you, Dr. Crews. This facility is a well-oiled machine, but it's a full-time job, seven days a week. Between fundraisers, board meetings, volunteers, hell, just the schedule is enough to turn your hair gray." She shook her hair and smiled, crossing her arms over her chest.

I grasped the folder I'd been carrying with me through the tour—my ideas for upping the ante, if you will, to bring more money in and not only help more animals but more people. I'd been brewing this idea in the back of my head since Annaleigh quit her job and took over her uncle's bar, *B's*. The business plan was solid, and the income it would generate would provide the shelter with so much.

"This opportunity is amazing and everything I could ask for." I paused for a second and moved to open the folder when Kelli put her hand over mine.

"I sense there's a but coming," she said, scooting her chair closer and pushing the folder to the far side of the table.

"What, no," I said, with a little more vigor than necessary. "This place is like a dream come true, and everything I've dreamed of doing."

"I think the word you are looking for is badass," she said with a wink.

"Yes, you're badass. This place, what you have accomplished. Hashtag goals, lady." I shook my head, and Kelli got up, walking behind her desk and opening a mini-fridge. She took out two water bottles and brought them back, passing me one and opening the other.

"Thank you." I cracked the seal and took a sip, gathering my thoughts and pulling the folder closer again.

"If this is your dream, then what's stopping you from accepting on the spot and taking a seat behind that desk?"

I thought for a minute.

What was stopping me?

I loved my job at the clinic. Even if things were shit right now with Dr. Duvall, could I see myself giving it up? And my friends? My lifelines? My ride-or-dies that would help me bury a body now and ask questions later?

"Talk to me. I have an intuition about this stuff. We hit it off the last time you were here, remember? We went to *Eastern Prime* and talked about upgrading all the lights to day-bulbs."

"Oh my goodness, how did I forget about that? And your husband picked us up in a limo."

We both laughed, remembering Ralph sticking his head out of the sunroof as the poor driver tried to maneuver his way into the parking lot of the bar.

"Your husband is all kinds of extra," I said, taking another sip of water.

"He sure is. Now tell me what the real issue is." I glanced at the floor, then the ceiling, trying to gather my thoughts. "Honestly, Kelli, it's not one thing or another. I love *AMC*, but my partner and I have been on the outs, and it's made coming to work almost unbearable. I guess I'm having guy trouble, but it can't be guy trouble when the guy doesn't want a relationship. I hate the thought of leaving my best friends and a town I love, but coming up here, I'd be closer to my parents."

"Hmm," Kelli mused, running a hand through her hair. "I was going to invite you out tonight, but if I did, I'd spend the entire time convincing you to move, and that's a shit thing to do. You don't go and upend your life because you're going through a rough patch. You need to think about what you want. Tell me this, if you had unlimited funds, what would you do?"

"Turn the clinic into a no-kill sanctuary, or at least add one on to the practice. I'd gut the building and expand, putting in windows and large kennels with lots of natural light. I'd make a place for exotic pets and work to bring on round-the-clock volunteers. Pretty much what you have here, but on a smaller scale in Charleston."

"Hmm," she said again. "Seems like you have some thinking to do, and I hope you seriously consider moving here. This place could use you."

"I will," I said, standing up and reaching out my hand. Kelli grasped it in hers, then pulled me in for a hug. I reached for the folder, but she grabbed it before I could.

"I'm sure this is filled with brilliant ideas, and I'd like to review them if you don't mind."

"Um," I said, clutching the folder to my chest, suddenly unsure about handing over something I poured so much time and energy into over the years.

"Hey, don't feel obligated at all. I'd never tell anyone or do anything without talking to you first," she said, putting her hand on my arm with a kind smile.

I nodded and opened the folder, taking out a high-level overview of my ideas and passing it over.

"Thank you."

I followed Kelli out of her office and through the building. We lingered for a minute at Oliver's cage and saw he was sleeping in the corner, his food gone, with the college kid back to reading his textbook. He waved his hand in greeting before focusing back, and I smiled, knowing all the good Kelli and her shelter were doing. She walked me to my car, and I promised to call her within the week with my decision.

I pulled out of *All Four Paws* and made it exactly two point three miles before I pulled into a little hippy organic grocery store parking lot. My brain was about to explode. I was sure smoke was ready to pour out my ears and fog up the entire damn car.

What the hell was I thinking? Verbally spewing my life's problems to a millionaire, then just expecting her to turn over the reins to a nonprofit to me with nothing but a copy of my business plan in her perfectly manicured hands?

I needed to find a bar. I scanned the parking lot, but unless I wanted an organic shot of wheatgrass and pressed alfalfa sprouts, I was going to have to settle for drinking at my parents' kitchen table. At least my mom always kept good vodka on hand for such an occasion. I was going to put a dent in her supply tonight. A cop car drove by, and I was tempted to give it the finger, but of course, I didn't.

I wasn't that petty. Actually, I was that petty, but the last thing I needed was to get arrested and have to call my dad for bail money on a Saturday night that should be spent doing a perfectly respectable thing, like drinking.

I laid my head down on the steering wheel. I needed one of those meditation apps on my phone or something, so I could relax enough to make it to my parents' house. My phone startled me out of my pity party, and I looked down to see Dr. Duvall requesting a FaceTime call.

What the hell?

I picked up the phone and stared at his picture, wondering if I should answer it. Worrying over one of the animals at the clinic for the weekend, I swiped to answer and secured my phone on the dash mount. Larry's face filled the screen, and he looked happy. He had a huge grin spread across his face and what looked like tear tracks running down his cheeks. There were people behind him and beside him, and I leaned forward, focusing on his eyes. They were different. They were full of life, of vigor, of happiness. It was like I was staring at a different person.

"Jenna, Jenna, oh, Jenna, I have the most spectacular news," he cried, walking away from the commotion behind him to a quieter room. He plopped down in a chair and held the phone up high. It looked like he was in a waiting room, but it was hard to tell. His hand was shaking.

"Larry? Are you okay?"

That seemed like a pretty stupid question to ask with the way he was acting, but it wasn't like I could reach through the phone and shake him.

"I am better than okay. I am fantastic. I am better than I've been in a year, and before I tell you anything else—I owe you the biggest apology I could give. There is nothing I could do to make it up to you, but I'm hoping once I shed some light on things, you'll find it in your heart to forgive me."

"Okayyyy," I said, drawing out the last syllable as Larry ran one hand through his white hair.

"About a year ago, Lily was diagnosed with stage three breast cancer."

"Oh my god, Larry."

"We took her to MUSC, and she started on very aggressive treatment, Jenna, and had two surgeries, then more treatment. I was miserable. I'd given up."

He paused for a second and looked at the ceiling, his eyes glassy. He wiped them with the back of his hand, then his face broke out into a gigantic smile again, and he tugged on the collar of his button-down shirt.

"Today, Lily got her test results back. She is one hundred and ten percent cured. There is no cancer anywhere in her body. She rang the bell today."

My eyes got a little misty, and I covered my mouth with my hand and smiled, feeling Larry's happiness pulse through me. Everything that had happened this last year made sense. Even though he deserved to be junk-punched for not sharing his pain and letting me help, I understood. I couldn't imagine how hard this had been.

"She rang that bell, she beat cancer, and I'm spending the rest of my time with her. I'm retiring."

What?

"I want you to buy me out, Jenna. Take over the *AMC*. Make it your own. I'll stay on long enough for you to bring on someone else or downsize it to something you can manage, whatever you need. But I'm not going to spend another moment without Lily."

"Larry, I don't know what to say."

"Well, I know what to say. I'm so sorry, so very sorry. And my wife is cancer-free, and I'm retiring. We'll hammer out the details next week. I'll be here, really here for you for as long as you need to transition, then I'm taking Lily, and we're going to Europe."

"That's absolutely incredible."

"It is, it really is. Talk soon, Jenna."

Larry's smiling face winked off my screen, and I put my head back down on my steering wheel. Raising it a moment later, I looked out my windows, hoping a bar magically appeared in the minutes since I'd hung up. The messed up part about all this was that my first thought after talking to Kelli and hanging up with Larry was calling Mark.

I should want to call the girls, my parents, or even my younger brother, but I didn't. I wanted to call Mark. To ask for his advice, share the good news, and have him tell me he was proud of me or happy things were falling into place. Hell, I'd take him yelling at me not to move because he didn't trust anyone else taking care of Phoebe. Even though the dipshit still blamed me for her incision infection. I started my car and pulled back on the road, dialing Mom to let her know I'd be there for dinner after all.

"Hi, honey," she answered. I could hear the television on in the background and figured she had already retreated to the kitchen to drown out the sounds of Dad's football game from the *Den for Men* as he and my brother had affectionately renamed the front room.

"Hey Mom, are the guys already watching the game?"

"Oh, yeah. The boys just started pre-gaming in the Den for Men. You heading out with the couple who runs the shelter?"

"No, I'm on the way home."

"Did everything go okay?"

I nodded like she could see me and made a right-hand turn onto the interstate. "Yeah, I didn't go over my business plan, but she offered me the position and reminded me I shouldn't accept something just to run away from my problems at home."

"Smart lady."

"No joke, Mom. Then Dr. Duvall called and dropped a bombshell. He's been insufferable because Lily had cancer. Had, as in doesn't, anymore. He wants me to buy him out. He's retiring."

"Holy shit, Jenna."

"Understatement of the year, Mom."

"What are you going to do?"

"In the ten minutes since I've found out? I'm going to hope you have the good vodka in the freezer."

"Two bottles. And copious amounts of ice cream and Oreos, but even the good vodka isn't going to help the decisions you're going to have to make."

"I know, but it will make me feel better. I don't think I have the funds to buy him out, and I don't even know if I want to do that. It's not like I'm rolling in the collateral to put down to own the practice."

"Well, don't worry about all that tonight. You just focus on getting home, and we'll drink on it."

"You're a wonderful mom. You know that, right?"

"Yep."

"Good, I'll see you soon. Love you."

"Love you too, Jenna."

⁂

"Okay, Jenna-Bean, time to rise and shine. I'm making French toast," Dad said, sounding way too chipper for whatever ungodly hour it was on Sunday morning. I groaned and turned the other way, wishing my twin bed with the frilly pink comforter was my queen-sized mattress in my own house with memory foam.

"Come on," he said, pulling the pillow out from under me in that same chipper voice. "I don't have all day. For posterity, I recorded you and mom singing *I Get By With A Little Help From My Friends* last night while Annaleigh, Addison, and Olivia were backup dancers over Skype. I have no problem calling your brother over to help me hook it up to the big screen."

"Oh my god, I thought that was a dream," I said, sitting up and putting one hand on my head.

"Nope, not a dream. Not with the amount of vodka the two of you put away. There's ibuprofen with coconut water by your bed. Take that, then a shower and head down."

I nodded and slumped back down on the bed, groaning as the night started to come back. After Mom and I finished the first drink and I gave her the whole story about Kelli's offer and Dr. Duvall, we called the girls, and my dad and brother joined in on the fun.

At one time, I think I remembered Max and Edward on Skype arguing about who would win an arm-wrestling match, but by that time, my head was swimming. I know I poured my heart out about Mark, and my dad and Caleb covertly left, then appeared back when Addison propped her phone on something and started singing. Pretty soon, Mom and I were arm in arm, dancing and singing off-key at the top of our lungs.

The shower helped a little, and by the time I made it downstairs, my head at least felt like it was only one size too big. Dad pushed a plate piled high with French toast and bacon toward me with orange juice and coffee, and Mom was sitting across from me with her head on the kitchen table.

"Where's Caleb?" I asked, taking a bite of bacon and pulling the coffee and creamer closer.

"He headed home about a half-hour ago," Mom said, raising her head and giving me a tired smile. "I guess your dad and brother were more innocent bystanders last night."

"Yep," Dad said, leaning down and placing a kiss on Mom's head, then turning around to refill her coffee.

"I'm probably going to get on the road after breakfast. Thanks again for talking through everything with me last night, even if it got a little crazy."

I speared a piece of French toast with my fork and bit into it, savoring the syrupy goodness as it melted in my mouth. I felt a little better, a little clearer-headed, and leaning a little more toward a decision with every bite I took.

"Jenna-Bean, Mom and I were talking this morning. We will, of course, support you with whatever you decide, but if you want to stay in Charleston and need a little help, we'll be glad to step in. You're young, and we don't want you going broke doing this."

I was speechless. I looked between them with my mouth hanging open and a piece of bacon hanging limply in my hand. If I stayed in Charleston, the amount of money, time, and work it would take to convert *AMC* would be insane. I still wasn't sure I was in the right mindset to take on a project like that. I didn't know anything about interior design.

"Close your mouth and eat your bacon. Why wouldn't we help you? Caleb lived here through law school and after failing the bar exam the first time. Who do you think paid for him to retake it? You're our children, and we're here to help. You are both hardworking, and you don't take advantage. We'd kick your asses if you did."

"Wow, Mom. If things were different, you and Mark's mom would either be best friends or mortal enemies," I said, stabbing another piece of French toast and putting it on my plate.

"Oh, pish. I'm friends with everyone. Though I would have words with her after some of the things you said last night." Mom crossed her arms and peered over her green framed glasses, looking so intimidating I felt like a five-year-old reprimanded for talking back.

BY YOUR SIDE

"Oh god. What did I tell you?" I said, praying I didn't go into detail about our spanky-angry sexy time.

"Nothing terrible," Mom answered, glancing at Dad, then back at me. "But I'm going to make you squirm and not tell you right now. You need to focus on what direction your life is going to go. Take the drive home and do some deep reflection."

"That's the plan, and you're evil," I said, snagging one last piece of bacon, then pushing my plate away. She gave me a wink and took another drink of coffee before cinching her robe and taking my plate. My dad stood up and stopped her, taking the plate from her hand and kissing her cheek.

"Go lay down on the couch, babe. I'll do the dishes."

"I'll help, Dad," I said, standing up and reaching for the bacon plate.

"That's fine, Jenna-Bean. I've got this. Go pack." He gave me a side hug and a wink, taking the plate from my hand and walking to the sink, humming to himself. It sounded suspiciously like Joe Cocker. I shook my head and walked upstairs, glad to have such amazing parents but already dreading the enormous amount of brainpower it was going to take to decide about what I wanted to do.

262

25 - JENNA

I forced out a harsh laugh and tried to hide the guilty expression on my face as we finished our pitcher of sangria on Annaleigh and Max's rooftop terrace. I never told Olivia and Addison details of the angry, aggressive, spanky, amazing sex that was apparently my kink now. I could have if our epic ending hadn't been so final and epically terrible. It was enough that I'd completely given my heart away to someone who wasn't at all available. I didn't need to relive the night again.

Annaleigh was the only one who knew I'd made a decision about the clinic. Olivia and Addison had left me alone so far, though I knew it was killing them to do it. I still wasn't sure why I was afraid. It was like saying my decision aloud meant it truly was an end to that part of me. So I laughed as if all was right in the world as Addison followed me down the spiral staircase, asking if we'd made our silicone dick replicas yet. I still wanted to ask her where she ordered those things from because I know it couldn't have been a prominent place.

"Hmm, never got around to asking Mark before he left," I said, leaning down to let Baxter sniff my hand as we walked down one more flight and then through her kitchen.

"Oh, I'm sorry, babe," Addison said, turning around to rub my arm. "I didn't mean to bring him up."

"It's fine," I said, shooing her hand away. "I mean, not really, but it would have been a nice parting gift. Still, I don't want to be with someone who doesn't want to be with me. At least this whole ordeal got me over stupid-ass Jason and made me realize he was the problem."

"Damn right," Annaleigh said.

"What about you, Liv? I gave you the green dick kit, right? Can we nickname Edward *the Hulk*? Oh! What about the *Jolly Green Giant?*"

"Oh my god, I am not having this conversation," Olivia said, opening the front door with a flourish of her wrist and a wave. "Bye, y'all."

"But she didn't say no," Addison said in a sing-song voice, waving two fingers and following Olivia out the door, turning around to waggle her eyebrows. "Get you some Hulk dick!" she called after Olivia, who turned around and flicked her off. "Oh yeah. She's getting Edward and his sparkling green replica. Bye, ladies."

"Bye," we called back.

I followed Annaleigh back inside and started to the kitchen to help with the dishes, but she motioned to the living room and sat on the couch. I did the same, pulling my legs underneath me and turning to look at her with a question on my face. She held out a plate of cookies, but I shook my head. Since coming home from Wilmington, I'd been living off of nothing but carbs, and my body desperately craved water and things not made with processed sugar.

"Why didn't you tell them you'd made a decision?" she asked, kicking off her sandals and crossing one foot over the other.

"I couldn't without a plan."

"Like they would care."

"Yeah, probably not, but I'd feel better."

"I know you would," Annaleigh said, looking past me as her eyes lit up. "Which is why we want to help you."

Max strolled around the corner wearing a navy-blue suit and a matching vest. His crisp white shirt peeked out from underneath, and his sleeves rolled up to the elbows. His dark hair was perfectly coiffed to one side, and he pushed his round tortoise-shell glasses up as he bent down to run his fingers down Annaleigh's face and kiss her cheek. She leaned into his touch and sighed. It was hard not to swoon at how sweet they were together.

I was fully prepared to admit I was much more a man-in-uniform type, but something about seeing a good-looking guy in a put-together three-piece suit was a sight to behold. Especially with the sleeves rolled up to the elbows. That simple gesture of exposing something as sinfully delicious as the forearm was enough to make my mouth water. Forearms to me were like ankles to eighteenth-century gentleman.

"Hey, Blue. You ready for me?" he asked, using Annaleigh's nickname and taking a seat beside her and spreading his legs wide, so she melted into his side.

He laid a manilla envelope on the coffee table that I didn't realize he was carrying because I focused on one thick tattoo that snaked up his arm. I wasn't staring in a creepy way, but seeing that lone tattoo had me remembering the colors and swirls and miles of ink that seemed to cover almost every available inch of Mark's skin, and that made me miss him, something I'd been trying not to do.

"Yeah, Broody," she said, using his nickname as well and picking up the folder and looking at me. "So Jenna, I told Max your decision and, well, I'll let him tell you. I'm too excited." She uncrossed her foot and started tapping it on the carpet, practically bouncing up and down.

I understood how she felt, remembering her idea to have the local bands that play at her bar partner with drug rehab clinics, teaching the patients music. If she could take her best friend's overdose and turn it into something positive, why couldn't I take the same concept and apply it to an animal shelter?

Max chuckled and shook his head, taking off his glasses to clean them on a handkerchief. "Anna gave me a high-level overview of your business plan and decision about deciding to stay here in Charleston. I have to say, not only am I extremely impressed with the depth of the plan, I'm happy you're staying. I'll always remember how you helped with Baxter."

"Thank you, Max," I said, side-eyeing Baxter, who was lying on his dog bed in the corner staring at me like I had a vaccine in my pocket.

"I've never shared much about my parents, but they're assholes. Rich assholes."

I nodded, remembering when we had a *Southern Charms* intervention for Annaleigh and learned about the depth of Max's rightful hate.

"The point is, Jenna," Annaleigh said, interrupting Max, squeezing his knee in a sweet gesture. "The fact that your business plan revolves around partnering your shelter with drug rehabilitation clinics is brilliant, and we want to donate. I mean, training rescues to be therapy dogs? Jenna, it's genius, and it aligns with my big picture for *B's*. Oh, I'm sorry Broody. I stole your thunder."

"You could never," Max said, picking up the manilla envelope and passing it over. I opened it, and my mind short-circuited looking at the enclosed papers. There was no way Max had access to that many zeros.

"Max—" I started, but he cut me off before I could offer a word of protest. I couldn't let him do this. Even if he and Anna were married, this was absurd. I had to raise funds the right way.

"The money is not for you, Jenna," Max said, leaning forward to rest his elbows on his knees.

"Max, be tactful, you ass," Annaleigh said, slugging him in the side. "Jenna, listen. Look, it's all broken down here. Max is working with your brother's law firm, setting up a trust. The first check is made to *AMC* to help with the buyout, downsize the practice, and reassign the staff. Those kinds of things. This isn't a favor. We believe in you and want this money to help you fulfill your dreams."

"Anna. There's a part in here about partnering with you," I said, scanning over the pages.

"Yes," she said, nodding and shoving her thumbnail into her mouth. "I was going to leave that up to you. I'd love to work with you once you're up and running and I'm fully immersed in *B's*. We could bring fosters into drug treatment centers as well as musicians. Think of what we could do together, Jenna. Think of all the people and animals we could bring together and heal."

"I'd love to. I can't believe this is happening. I can't...." My voice suddenly got tight with the enormity of the situation. I looked at the light blue carpet and blinked, taking off my glasses and laying them on the table. Max stood up, giving us space, and I watched Baxter's feet trot out behind him. Anna scooted closer on the couch and put her arm around me, pulling me close.

"Let it out. You've been brave too long, babe," Anna said, and it was her sweet words that started my tears. I cried for falling for a stupid man who wasn't available and for never being able to say goodbye. I cried because everything professionally I'd wanted was happening, and it almost seemed too good to be true, and I cried because sometimes it just made you fucking feel better, snot-bubbles and all.

"Thank you," I mumbled, my voice sounding steadier as the sobs slowed down several minutes later.

"Duh, you dragged my drunk ass out of the tub when Max and I broke up. Have you talked to Mark at all?"

"Not a peep and Phoebe has a vaccine appointment Wednesday." I sniffed and grabbed my glasses, wiping my face before putting them back on. I clutched the manilla folder to my chest like it was a lifeline, nervous at the thought of seeing Mark.

"What are you going to do?"

"Honestly, he'll probably ask to see Dr. Duvall or send his mom. I can't think about that anymore. There's too much to do." I thumped the folder and stood up, pulling my best friend in for a tight hug.

"Just so you know, this was all Max's idea."

I squeezed her harder and closed my eyes, wondering how the hell I got so lucky.

"Let me ask you one thing before you leave," she said as we moved to her foyer. "If he was waiting for you in your driveway when you got home with some grand gesture, what would you do?"

"Grand gesture?"

"Yeah. You know, letting you lay on the door while he freezes his ass off in the water, standing with a boombox over his head professing his undying love to you, grand gesture. What would you do?"

What would I do?

I thought back to all I'd learned in the short time I'd known Mark. Sure, there was fear of relationships, but it was based on some pretty heavy stuff he needed to work through.

"I'd let him inside and hear what he had to say," I said, nodding to myself as much as I was to Annaleigh.

For as angry and as hurt as Mark made me, the prickly idiot had my heart, and I wasn't going to give up on what we could have if he would admit what he wanted. After all, wasn't I a better person with him by my side?

ↄ·ↄ·ↄ

"So good news and bad news," Melissa said, catching me as I walked out of one of our exam rooms. "The good news is there are three tall, tan, and gorgeous men waiting for you in the next room. The bad news is, Mark's not with them."

Three guys?

"He's not?" I said, not bothering to hide the disappointment in my voice. I kind of figured Mark wasn't just going to stroll up into *AMC* like all was right in the Universe, but a girl could dream. "Thank you," I added, swinging by my office to chug the rest of my sugar-free energy drink.

Dr. Duvall and I worked well past closing this week, coming up with a game plan to transition some patients to other clinics since we were downsizing, and agreeing on a fair buyout. He was also willing to see patients part-time while I oversaw renovations. Not that I knew anything about turning a doctor's office into an animal shelter, but I could learn anything, and I already had a kick-ass name picked out.

"Jenna," three baritone voices said as I opened our largest exam room that suddenly looked about as big as a broom closet with the amount of testosterone and muscles it currently held.

Maverick, Miller, and Magnum surrounded Phoebe, sitting in the middle of the exam table looking like a healthy, petite princess. They were all wearing stonewashed jeans that looked painted onto their thick thighs, black work boots, and matching hunter green polos with the company lightning bolt logo in the corner.

"Hey, you three. I figured Bev would bring her by today. How'd I get so lucky?"

I shook Maverick's hand and clapped the Irish Twins on the shoulder before picking up Phoebe and giving her a once over. I couldn't help holding her close and cooing to her a little, not even taking offense when she hissed.

"So you going to tell us about Wilmington?" Miller asked, suddenly turning around and focusing on a poster describing how to tell if your cat is overweight.

"Not pulling any punches, are you?" I asked, holding Phoebe by the scruff of her neck and flipping her over to check her incision. "You going to at least look at me or keep pretending to read that poster?"

"Damn, Doctor," Magnum said, raising his hand for a high-five. After slapping his palm, I handed Phoebe over to Miller, who cradled her like a baby before facing the three-amigos like it was our very own Mexican stand-off.

"Listen, guys. I'm not moving to Wilmington. Actually, I'm going to buy Dr. Duvall out of the clinic, downsize, and turn it into a shelter. I want to gut the whole thing and put in huge windows and daylighting. I don't know a thing about commercial interior design, of course," I said with a shake of my head.

Maverick tilted his head and looked at Magnum, then nodded toward me, like they were having a silent conversation.

"So yeah. I, um, didn't grab her vaccinations. I'll be back in a jiff."

"You're not going to ask about him?" Maverick said, crossing his arms over a chest just as broad as Mark's.

"I was respecting his space, guys. He could be here," I said quietly, looking at the floor, then up, and up some more until I met the eyes of Mark's brothers.

"He's working nights again, Jenna, and he's not doing great," Maverick said, taking a step forward as Magnum and Miller flanked behind him.

"I understand, and it's not all butterflies and unicorns in my personal life right now. I can't even sleep in my own damn bed, so my back feels like I'm an eighty-five-year-old arthritic woman, but I'm also not the one with the relationship-cop-dad-thing," I said, waving my hand in front of me like they would understand and drop this conversation.

"What cop-dad-thing-relationship," Magnum said, mimicking the gesture.

"Nope," I said, shaking my head and waving my hands in front of my face. "Not my circus, not my monkeys."

"Guys, go flirt with the receptionist," Maverick said.

"Oh, eighties hairspray chick? On it," Miller answered, passing Phoebe over to Maverick and walking out the door with Magnum in tow.

Maverick stared at me, tall and intimidating with dark hair, miles of rigid muscles, and sad eyes. He cradled the kitten as if his head was also full of a thousand reasons he was steering clear of relationships.

"Tell me what's going on, Jenna. Please," Maverick said.

I looked into his sad eyes. Eyes that held pain I never wanted to see echoed in the depths of Mark's beautiful, soulful, black orbs.

"It's not my place to share something he hasn't told you."

"Maybe. Maybe not. But I know about love, and I know about loss. And if Mark is throwing away a chance at something real, I need to know why. He deserves happiness, and so do you."

I could see this was a losing battle, and Maverick made sense...sort of.

"Mark chose to stay single when he joined the force because of a conversation he had with your dad. Your dad said if he had to do it all over again, he wouldn't be a cop because of the stress it put on Bev. Mark decided to end things. Wait, that's not right. It was his decision never to start anything, but somewhere that got muddled."

"Oh shit," Mav said, passing me Phoebe so he could run his hand through his hair in such a Mark-like gesture I couldn't help but smile.

271

"Mark's got it all wrong. I have to go. Tell Tweedle-Dee and Tweedle-Dumb to meet me back at the office."

"Wait a second!" I said, grabbing Maverick's arm as he put one hand on the doorknob. "It's not your responsibility to fix this. Hell, we never even said goodbye."

I let go of his arm and looked at the floor, taking a step back into the small space. Maverick didn't answer, striding out of the exam room and leaving me with a bewildered expression on my face. Magnum and Miller turned from talking to Dana to see him go, not bothering with a wave or goodbye. I motioned them back to the exam room, and they shared a knowing look before following me in and closing the door.

"What was that about?" Magnum asked, reaching for Phoebe, who gave a little squeak before climbing up his shirt and attempting to bury herself in Magnum's neck. He nuzzled her close, looking back at me for an answer.

"I meddled."

"Nah, he's meddling," Miller said, punching me lightly in the shoulder. "Someone needed to help Mark figure his shit out. So you're going to take over and remodel this place? That's badass, Doc."

"Thanks, Miller. I'm feeling overwhelmed. It's all so real now, you know?"

"I, um, can help you with that," Magnum said, the timbre of his voice lowering like he wasn't his confidant, usual self.

"Hmm?"

Magnum passed the kitten to Miller and rubbed the back of his neck, looking at the floor, then at me. "Listen, I've wanted to expand our business for a while. Take on more customers, do more than electrical work. Commercial interior design is a huge untapped market, and I'd love to help you. We could work something out. Pay for the materials at cost and maybe do some advertising?"

"Dude," Miller said, clapping Magnum hard on the back. "This is amazing. You'd fucking rock the shit out of designing. Why didn't you say something?"

"I've been working with Mav, but you know…" Magnum shook his head and took a step back, the color rising in his cheeks before he looked at Miller. "I wasn't sure how you'd react."

"How I'd react?" Miller said, slapping Magnum on the back again before pulling him in for a guy-hug. "I can't believe you held out on me."

"Thanks," Magnum said, as a big smile spread across his handsome face, and he reached over to scratch Phoebe under her chin.

Holy Amazeballs.

"I'd love to work with all of you. This place needs an electrical overhaul as well," I said, taking a step back to fan my face. I couldn't believe this was happening. I put one hand on my chest, hoping to keep my heart from beating straight out of my ribcage.

"Oh, shit. Mav took the truck, didn't he?" Miller said, pulling me back from a panic attack or a happiness attack.

"Why don't y'all take my truck and come back with a couple of pizzas or something tonight, and we'll go over ideas for the place."

"Good idea," Magnum said. "Thank you."

"Sure, let me get her vaccines and my keys," I said, making a beeline for the door.

I needed a minute to compose myself or stick my head in a freezer to cool down. As soon as I left the room and was safely in the hall, I sagged against the door, dropping my head to my chest and breathing deeply.

Why was I freaking out?

The pieces of my life were falling into place, but I didn't feel complete. I shook out my shoulder and bounced on the balls of my feet.

It didn't matter how I felt.

I had to kick ass and take names. People were counting on me. Animals depended on me. I wasn't going to wait around for someone that didn't want me.

It was time to make my own happiness.

It was time for me to live for *me*.

26 - MARK
- One Week Later -

"**O**h my god. What the fuck," I screamed, jumping off my couch as *Ride of the Valkyries* played as loud as movie theater speakers through every smart panel in my house. I ran to the panel in the kitchen, pressing every button on the screen until the noise stopped, then turned around and sagged against the wall, wiping my arm across my forehead.

I looked down at my watch. It was only eleven in the morning. I'd barely been asleep for an hour after coming off of a fourteen-hour shift. Just as the adrenaline wore off from that stupid song, it started again, louder than before, and this time accompanied by a loud banging at the front door.

It was the fucking doorbell.

My brothers made my damn doorbell *Ride of the Valkyries*. I was going to torture them. *Slowly.*

Tomorrow.

I groaned as I pushed myself off the wall, making my way to the door, not giving a fuck that I was only in briefs. Whoever they were could deal with it for waking me up at this ungodly hour. Digging my knuckle into my eye, I was about to yank the door open just as a screeching voice pierced my skull, sounding like a mix between one of those whistling firecrackers and an angry seagull.

"Marcus-Aurelius Remus Hansen. I am sick of you sulking in this dark house like a freaking teenager who had his favorite toy taken away. Open this damn door, or I will kick it down."

Good freaking god.

I was too damn tired to deal with this today. I laid my head against the front door, hoping she'd take the hint and leave. Believe me, I was beating myself up enough without bringing my mother into the mix to tell me what an asshole I was.

I already knew.

I stepped away from the door as quietly as I could and sank back down on the couch, keeping my feet on the ground but laying sideways and scratching my beard. It had gotten out of control, the blonde scruff growing every which way, but I couldn't care less. Working nights, Chief went easy on us with the way we looked, and he let it slide that I looked like a filthy motorcycle gang member.

My mother had thankfully given up, and my eyes were getting heavy when a shattering crash sounded on my front porch. I jerked up with a start, wiping drool from my mouth and running to the door, throwing it open, thinking Mom had hurt herself or someone was vandalizing my property. I was not expecting to see her on my sidewalk with her arms crossed and a down-right pissed expression on her face standing beside a shattered topiary pot.

"What the hell happened? Are you okay?" I hollered, stepping on the porch in my bare feet and briefs. Shards of broken orange pottery littered the sidewalk, along with a shit ton of soil. Mom kicked aside a huge piece and marched up the steps, pushing past me and inside.

"Did you just break one of my plants?" I asked, shielding my eyes from the sun like some sickened vampire before following her inside and closing the door.

"No," she said, throwing open the curtains in the living room and walking to the kitchen to do the same. I closed them behind her, picking Phoebe up from her corner of the couch and laying her in her cat bed before following Mom into the kitchen. "I just broke one of the plants I brought over to your house. I would have broken the other one if you hadn't opened the damn door, Marcus."

"My shift ended at nine-thirty, Mom. I'm dead on my feet," I said, picking up a discarded T-shirt and gym shorts from the floor and pulling them on with a yawn. "I don't feel like cleaning up broken pottery right now."

"I truly couldn't give two shits at this point. Your brothers and I have sat back and watched you cocoon yourself in this house and throw yourself into your work, and it has to stop. Enough is enough."

Don't be an asshole to your mom. Don't be an asshole to your mom.

I closed my eyes and repeated the mantra two more times, breathing through my nose with my eyes closed until I felt my anger subside.

"You better stop whatever shit you're saying in your head right now, Marcus. Open your eyes and talk to me. Your brothers are your family, and you shut them out." She leaned forward and grasped my hands, pulling me down to her level and patting my cheek. "You and I need to talk, okay?"

My shoulders slumped in defeat, and I nodded my head. If it would get me to sleep faster, I'd throw some sappy feeling her way. It was a copout, but I wasn't going to rip the band-aid off my freshly scabbed wound. Yesterday was the first time I'd slept for more than a few hours, and I didn't want to do anything to jinx it.

"Come on," she said, motioning to the back porch. I followed her, grabbing two beers from the fridge, then opening the sliding glass door and lowering myself to one of the oversized Adirondack chairs with a groan.

I cracked one and passed it to her. She took a long swallow, grimaced at the taste, then sat it on the small table between us. "You look like shit, by the way. And what the hell are you building back here? You're ruining the landscaping in the backyard."

"Nothing. Just a bunch of crap I have to throw away. It's always so good to see you, Mom."

"Don't be a smartass. Now, did I ever tell you what happened on your father's first day on the job?"

"I don't think so," I said, cracking my beer and leaning back, crossing one ankle over the other and looking at a lone squirrel in our large oak tree. I closed my eyes, and my head sunk to my chest, hoping I could catch a few winks as she talked.

Nope.

She leaned across the table and slapped my chest, making me jerk forward with a start.

"Jesus, Mom. I'm awake."

"Sit up and drink your beer, or I will give you a titty-twister that will bring you to your knees."

I cringed, and my arms immediately covered my chest before I sat up, swinging my legs to one side. I took a swallow, doing my best not to glare at her, mostly for threatening to pinch my damn nipples.

"That's better. Anyway, it was right after we bought this house, and I was pregnant with Maverick. Your dad wasn't gone five minutes before he got his first call. It was freaking Loony, Marcus. Back then, even when she was married to Neville, God rest his soul—she always got these insane ideas in her head. She wanted to raise goats, fucking goats. Somehow, one of those square-eyed little weird-o's got on her roof."

She paused and shook her head before taking another drink of her beer and leaning back in the chair. She kicked off her white tennis shoes and looked over the backyard like she was looking thirty-five years into the past.

I could imagine Dad in his old Dodge Diplomat squad car, pulling up to Loony's house with his partner, probably rolling his eyes wondering how the hell this was his first-ever call on duty.

"Your dad got a ladder from her shed and climbed on the roof trying the get the damn goat. He managed to get the stupid thing off, passing it to James, his partner, but he fell coming down the ladder."

I threw my leg over the chair so I was facing her and finished my beer, putting the empty bottle on the table, but she still had that far-away expression on her face.

How had I never heard this story before? He fell off Loony's roof?

"It was so stupid, Marcus," she said, wiping underneath her eyes. "He fell off the ladder, broke his leg in two places, and accidentally discharged his gun."

"What?" was all I croaked out as I watched Mom relive the accident.

"He was on desk duty for I don't remember how long, and there was an incident report for the gun firing, even though the bullet only hit a damn tree."

Mom stood up and paced the length of the freshly stained deck, picking up her beer and finishing the bottle. My mind was muddled from hearing her story, and something was pushing through the exhaustion.

Her calm demeanor was gone, replaced with a woman unsure and anxious. No wonder she hated every moment of Dad being a cop.

"Marcus, listen to me. I've kicked your asses when you've it needed and made my opinion known, but I've always respected your decisions, even when I disagreed. That said, you need to understand something."

She walked up to me with glassy eyes and clasped my hands in hers, looking up with a silent promise that her next words were not meant to hurt. They were meant to heal.

"Your father had been on active duty for five-fucking-minutes, and he fell off a ladder, broke his leg in two places, and accidentally discharged his weapon. I was pregnant and scared. I worried every day after that. I worried something ridiculous and stupid would happen. My mind came up with all these whack-a-doddle scenarios. I guess I didn't hide it as well as I thought I did."

She shrugged and let go of my hands, walking back to the sliding glass door. She opened it to pick Phoebe up, taking her back to the Adirondack chair and sitting down.

My choice to stay single was based on a stupid-ass accident Dad had five minutes into his first shift?

Holy. Fucking. Shit.

"Mom—" I started, rubbing my palms into my eyes until brightly colored spots danced in my vision. I spread my legs wide and put my head between my legs, threading my hands behind my neck and waiting for my vision to clear.

"No. Listen. I didn't come here to change your mind about being with Jenna, and I have no clue if what you have is even something you want to pursue. Hell, maybe you ran away screaming because she's into some weird kink that freaks you out. I don't know."

"Mom," I hissed, sitting up and digging my palms in harder, so the spots turned into zig-zagging lines. I couldn't think about what-ifs and maybes. I'd go crazier than I already was.

We were over.

Finished.

Done.

"I'm serious. You cannot base your chance at love, at happiness, at maybe a family, and a future with someone on my anxiety born from an accident thirty-five years ago. You just can't."

I blinked rapidly, focusing on a tree in the backyard until the spots disappeared and the leaves faded into view. The midmorning light shone through the trees, throwing the yard into hazy greens and reflecting off of the unfinished project I'd started last week on a whim. I stared at the large panels of glass propped against the porch, watching a lone drop of dew sliding down to the grass.

Mom had laid back on the chair with Phoebe on her lap, staring out into the backyard, letting me process whatever the fuck my brain was trying to sort out.

"How did you find out?" I said, finally stringing together a coherent sentence.

"Maverick stopped by last week and told me. The boys took Phoebe to her appointment because my book club ran long. He wanted to come out here himself and talk some sense into you, but this felt like something I needed to do."

She paused for a minute and looked at me, but my mind was still reeling.

How was this not a hilarious story heard around the office? Or something shared when he died?

"She's not moving to Wilmington. You know that, right?"

"What? No? Yes? What?" I said, tearing my eyes away from the glass panels and metal skeleton to look at Mom.

"She's staying here. You should drive over and see what she's doing. It's pretty amazing."

"That's not a good idea, Mom."

"If you say so. Seriously, what are you building back here?" she asked, flawlessly changing the subject back so quickly it took me a second to recover from the whiplash.

"Oh, you know, nothing," I deflected again, rubbing the back of my neck.

"Seriously, what it is?" She pushed, looking again then back to me, determined to make me say it out loud.

"It's a greenhouse," I said, standing up and reaching for Phoebe. Mom passed her over without so much as a smile, brushing nonexistent dirt from her pants and slipping her shoes back on her feet.

"Are you taking up gardening, Marcus?"

"You know I'm not," I answered, rubbing Phoebe's back before opening the sliding glass door and walking back inside. Mom followed, throwing the beer bottles away before heading straight through the living room and to the front door.

"Yeah, I know you're not, Marcus, and it seems to me you wouldn't be building a greenhouse for your backyard if you truly believed in your heart that things were over. I'll bring another pot by to replace the one I broke tomorrow," she said, reaching out to scratch Phoebe behind the ears, then pat my cheek.

"Thanks, I'll clean up the mess later."

"Okay, I love you very much, Marcus. Dinner this weekend. No excuses."

"Love you too, Mom," I said, shutting the door and collapsing back on the couch with a sigh. Phoebe kneaded my chest, but even her little needle claws digging into my flesh couldn't stop the gears from beginning to turn in my fuzzy brain, burning through the exhaustion like a wildfire.

All the weariness and anger that had seeped through my muscles were gone, replaced with something else. It was time to push aside my fears, admit I made the wrong damn choice, and embrace the fact my heart might get stomped to smithereens.

Actions spoke louder than words. If there was any chance of earning Jenna's heart, it wasn't by sending her a text or showing up at the clinic with flowers. She deserved something big. I rubbed my chest and glanced past the kitchen and to the backyard, where a half put-together greenhouse laid pitifully in the grass.

Determination? Hopefulness?

Sheer insanity?

Whatever it was that had taken root in my chest, sleep wasn't happening, not when there was work to do to bring Jenna back where she belonged—by my side.

BY YOUR SIDE

27 - JENNA

That stupid, stupid doggie doorbell was barking. I looked at my watch and groaned, pushing out from behind my desk and standing up. My back gave an uncomfortable twinge, and I leaned over and twisted from side to side to relieve the tension.

Had I forgotten to lock the door?

I stood up, smoothing down my shirt and looking at my mismatched ensemble. My old shirt was covered with paint splotches, and my jeans were faded and ripped. But my appearance was the last thing I cared about until the renovations were done.

On top of seeing patients until we successfully transitioned, my workload had tripled when you added in the million-and-one-things that went along with starting a shelter. I still wasn't sleeping for shit, so I was at the clinic at all hours. I should be giddy with joy, but my mind kept taking me back to the empty void in my life where he used to be. I didn't know if it was the persistent ache in my back or because after trimming a bonsai tree for an hour last night, I'd realized I had made Phoebe's cute little face, but something else was off.

I stepped over a large sign with our new name, *Feathers and Fur*, and trailed my fingers over the lettering as I walked down the hall past boxes of lightbulbs, fixtures, and paint cans. When I looked up, my heart stalled because Mark was standing right in the doorway with his hands shoved in his pockets.

I stopped and stared, not believing my eyes.

He isn't supposed to be here.

I blinked and shook my head, putting one hand on my chest and the other on the wall. It felt over-dramatic, but it was like the aching emptiness I'd felt since he'd been gone somehow recognized its chance at becoming whole.

"The door was open," he started, walking the rest of the way in and locking the door behind him.

He had on dark jeans and a green Henley, pushed past his elbows. His hair was a mess, like he hadn't stopped running his hands through it, and his beard was trimmed close to his face, showing off his sharp, chiseled jaw. I gave myself three seconds to breathe him in before looking away. I wasn't going to let myself hope. I wasn't going to let myself feel anything. For all I knew, he was finally returning my damn key.

"What are you doing here?" I said with a voice that didn't sound like my own. It was even, empty, emotionless. I focused on his shoes because if my eyes stayed on his for more than one millisecond, I'd force myself to see the pain I was feeling mirrored back tenfold.

"You were right," he said, clenching his hands at his side. "I was scared shitless, so I left. Because if I didn't, I'd have to admit to myself that choosing to stay single was fucking wrong."

He ran his hand through his blonde hair and took a step forward as I took one back.

He wasn't supposed to be here, looking every bit as miserable as me, like these last few weeks hadn't gutted him.

"Mark—"

He stepped forward again, and I lost my train of thought, watching his muscles flex beneath his clothes and his jaw move back and forth.

I sucked in a breath listening to his words, not realizing he had moved closer. I longed to close the distance and wrap my legs around his waist, thrusting my tongue in his mouth to forget about our fight, but we'd always had crazy naked chemistry.

That wasn't going to fix this cluster-fuck. Talking would if it was fixable. And I wanted it to be fixable so damn bad. I wanted the hurt to go away. I wanted him to claim the part of my heart that belonged to him and make me whole.

I let myself take one step closer, one step toward him, and the tension ricocheted through the roof as I met his eyes.

"Don't you think I don't question myself, my quirks, my personality, wishing I could be different some days?" His voice echoed through my body. "Everyone does. It's what makes us human. It's also admitting we have faults and admitting we need help. It's admitting that some people are better together than apart and not walking away."

I took a deep breath and shook my hands out. My body felt like it was asleep. That awful pins-and-needles feeling had crept up my arms and legs, making my whole body shiver.

"Why are you here, Mark?" It was a stupid question to ask, but I had to say something to keep my brain from spitting out random useless facts.

I took one more step forward, but he put both hands up, shaking his head. I was close enough to see his Adam's apple bob as he swallowed, thinking of his next words. He was nothing if not meticulous. When he spoke, it wasn't to fill the silence or hear his own voice. It was because he had something to say. And the emotions I saw flickering across his face said he had a big something to say.

"I remember you said I calmed your mind. Well, you calm my soul. I never thought I needed anything, but I need you. You give me peace, and you give me love. You give me happiness when I didn't know I was missing it, and the stupidest thing I've ever done is walk out your door."

He looked down and dug a palm in his eye, and my feet moved before I knew what I was doing, reaching out to grab his hand. He drew in a deep breath and closed his eyes, blowing it out so hard I heard it in the empty building.

"Jenna, I'm sorry I didn't tell you I'd fallen for you too, and I'm sorry I didn't fucking ask you if you wanted to be mine. I love you."

The tingling feeling had moved up my arms and to my face, where my eyes were getting glassy. All the useless facts that filled my head minutes ago were gone, just like the empty ache I'd carried with me these last weeks. It was replaced with something new, bright, and beautiful. It was replaced with hope.

His other hand swept up and gently brushed my hair behind my ear. "You get me, Mark, and the thought of you walking away and giving up because of a choice you made when you joined the force almost broke me, but I didn't want to let go."

That's why I was here, in front of him, grasping his hand like it was my lifeline.

I didn't want to give up on someone who was a part of me, someone I'd given a part of myself to—I didn't want to walk away from this man.

Mark closed the distance between us, so our bodies were nestled together, and my heart got caught in my throat as his hand skimmed down my cheek and tilted my head up, his hand falling to my jaw, holding me firmly in place as his mouth moved closer to mine, like he was asking for permission.

I licked my lips and tilted one side of my mouth up, removing my hand from his to put it in his back pocket.

"Jenna, baby. I choose you. It's always been you. I was just too stupid to realize it."

"I chose you a long time ago, Officer Handsome," I said, bringing our joined hands to my lips and kissing his palm. "And I love you too."

One corner of his full pillow lips ticked up, even though his eyes had purple smudges underneath. He licked his lips and took another deep breath before meeting my gaze and nodding his head. "I don't want to hurt you ever again. I want to wake up next to you and fall asleep with you in my arms. I'm a greedy bastard, baby. I want both, you and my job. I want it all."

His mouth relentlessly crashed into mine, sucking all the breath from my lungs and the oxygen from the room.

Claiming me.

Branding me.

Marking me as his.

One hand fell from my face, and I felt his long, calloused fingers run through my hair, tilting my head exactly where he needed it. He groaned into my mouth as my tongue danced with his, demanding more with another swipe of my tongue over his lips.

"I need you." He broke the kiss to lick down my neck and pull my T-shirt to the side to suck on the tendon where my neck met my shoulder.

"I need you more." I yanked his hair so I could claim his lips all over again, but he pulled away and muttered something unintelligible before striding to the door to make sure the lock was secure. I could only describe the look in his eyes when he turned back around as raw animalistic lust. He stepped forward, confident and steady, picking me up and throwing me over his shoulder as if I weighed next to nothing.

I was panting, staring upside down at the delicious globes of his ass in those jeans as he walked to my office, setting me down and pulling off my shirt in one smooth motion.

"Jeans," he growled, taking a step back to watch as I kicked off my sneakers and peeled off my jeans and panties, leaving me in nothing but a front zip sports bra. He crowded my space, stepping closer until my back hit the hardwood of my desk. Lifting me up, he sat me down and reached between us to unzip my bra, sucking in a breath as my breasts spilled out of the thin material.

He grabbed my desk chair and sat in front of me, spreading my legs wide like I was his next meal. Using both hands, he parted my pussy and, not breaking eye contact until he was millimeters away from my sensitive nub, he buried his head between my legs, his tongue dancing across my clit.

"Oh, fuck yes," I cried, throwing my head back as my senses were flooded with him. His tongue, his breath, his hands. One hand stayed on my pussy, keeping it spread open so he could continue his assault on my clit, while the other traveled up my stomach to my nipples, where he pinched and kneaded until I was whimpering and thrusting against his face.

I was gripping the desk so hard my knuckles were turning white, but I removed one hand to grab Mark's hair, needing to feel as much of him as I could. No more denying ourselves, no more staying away. Just this connection that felt so right, so deserved, like where we were both meant to be.

The only thing that mattered was his hot tongue on my clit, tracing maddening patterns, bringing me closer to orgasm, and his fingers pinching and tugging my nipples in time with his tongue. His beard was rough on my inner thigh, and I relished the burn, feeling like he was branding himself on my skin.

"Please, right there, Mark," I panted, nodding my head and gripping his hair like it was my only connection to this plane. I could feel my orgasm building at the base of my spine, contracting my muscles, diverting every sensation, every feeling, to one particular spot where Mark was focusing all his attention.

Lick after lick, he took my body higher until I removed my other hand from the edge of the desk and braced both on his head, knowing I needed to feel every part of him so I could stay grounded. As if he knew what was coming, he took his hand away from my nipples and pushed my thighs as far apart as they would go before looking up at me and smiling with glistening lips, lidded eyes, and messy hair.

"Let go, baby."

And with those words, he dove back in, wrapping his lips around my clit and sucking for all he was worth. I threw my head back and screamed, free-falling over the edge to oblivion, coming harder than I ever had before, and holding onto the only person who could take me there and bring me back, the only person I wanted with me when I fell.

Mark.

BY YOUR SIDE

28 - MARK

Ididn't come to the clinic to lick Jenna's pussy on her desk until she filled my mouth with the sweetest juice I'd ever tasted, but fuck, if that wasn't the best way this evening could have turned out. I pushed back from the chair, keeping a firm grip on her thighs with a dazed expression on her face as she opened her eyes and came back down. There was nothing sexier than how she looked right now, naked and spent, with red splotches on her cheeks and a far-off look in her eyes.

Fuck and the way she tasted. I could spend a lifetime between her legs, exploring her sweet flavor. Her eyes looked as dazed as mine felt, with this lazy little grin pulling up the corners of her mouth. Running my hands up both of her thighs, I stood up, adjusting my cock in my jeans and stepping in between her legs to run my nose up her neck before claiming her lips. She needed to taste herself on my lips and see how much I got off licking her sweet pussy. I wanted her to know how fucking crazy I went whenever she was around.

"I love these lips, this pussy, these curves," I whispered, skating my hands over every available inch of exposed skin I could feel. "You ready to get out of here?"

"You might have to carry me," she answered, grasping my shirt and pulling me close so she could lay her head on my chest. "I think you just scrambled my brain and turned my legs to jelly."

I chuckled and ran my fingers through her hair, holding her to me because the thought of being without her again was more than I could bear. "I would carry you anywhere, Dr. Cutie. Come home with me."

I meant it as a question, but it came out like a demand. Either way, she nodded, lifting her head from my chest and wrapping her legs around my waist to drag her naked core against my cock. I sucked in a breath with the friction, my cock painfully hard in my jeans.

"You sure I can't take care of that first?" she said, releasing her legs but reaching a hand between us to squeeze my cock.

"Fuck yes, you can, but not here. I want you in my house. In my bed."

"Hmm, then hand me my panties, and let's get the hell out of here."

I stepped back and helped her off the desk, scrambling to grab her clothes as she pulled them on and turned off her computer. We rushed out of the office, hand in hand to my Tahoe, not caring about leaving her car exactly where it was.

Good.

The thought of not touching her for even fifteen minutes as we drove to my house was unacceptable. She sat as close as she could on the drive home, hand squeezed in mine, glancing over every few seconds to smile or bite her plump bottom lip.

When we pulled into the neighborhood, she leaned forward, looking out the window to see my finished place.

"Oh, Mark. The house. It's finished, and it looks—"

"Empty," I interrupted, pulling into the driveway and turning off the engine before hightailing it to Jenna's door and opening it for her.

I leaned forward and ran my fingers across her jaw before cupping her cheek and lightly kissing her lips.

"It's been empty without you." I pressed my forehead to hers, never being more certain of my words. "I want, no, I need you here with me. Will you move in, turn my house into ours, fill it with plants, and let me read to you every night?"

"Are you sure that's what you want? I'd never ask you to change a part of yourself for me."

Uncertainty peeked through her eyes, and she cast them down. My heart ached for what I put her through, and I tipped her chin so she would know how serious I was.

"I've never been more certain of anything, baby. I'm going to stay on the force, and I want you here every day, so I can support you as you follow your dreams with the shelter."

"You don't think we're moving too fast?"

I chuckled deep in my belly and moved my hands to her hips, pulling her to me so her ass was barely on the seat. Her legs wrapped around my waist, and one side of her cherry lips tilted up in a sexy little grin.

"We've never done anything slow, and that's okay. The only thing that matters is what we want."

"Then take me inside, Mark, because I want you and everything you just said."

I stepped back and pulled her out of the truck, shutting the door and leading her up the walkway and porch. The front door was locked, and instead of pulling her inside, I led her around to the back of the house.

"I want to show you something before we go inside."

We walked to the back porch, where the moonlight shone through the trees and reflected off the greenhouse. She tilted her head to the side, looking at it, and I watched her face, registering the moment she understood what I'd done.

"Mark, is that a greenhouse? You built that? Here?"

"Yeah. I meant it when I said I want you to fill our house with plants. We know for sure the greenhouse will be safe from Phoebe and safe from rogue squirrels."

She let go of my hands to walk down the steps, running her fingers along the glass panels.

"This is big."

"That's because what we have is big," I said, standing behind her and wrapping my arms around her waist. She leaned into me, and I brushed her hair to the side, bending down to kiss her shoulder.

"Mark...I... Thank you." She stuttered through the words, and I held her tighter, not needing to hear anything else. The time for words was over.

"Come inside."

Nodding her head, my hand trembled as I unlocked the back door, but the moment we got inside the house, the reality of having her in my space, in my life, and getting her in my bed, came crashing down. I grabbed her around the waist and lifted her in one swift motion. She let out a squeak of delight and wrapped her legs around my waist as I headed up the stairs and down the hall to the bedroom, our bedroom, kicking the door closed behind me.

I set her down on the bed, pulling off my shirt and kicking off my shoes. She did the same, both of us getting naked in record time. Sitting on the edge of the bed, I took her in, all smooth skin and soft curves as she straddled my lap, leaning directly over my raging hard-on and slowly dragging her hips back and forth. My hands went to her ass to guide her, and a low moan escaped my lips, feeling her slick heat glide up and down my cock.

Her hand reached down between us, and she found my length, gripping me to the point of pain and stroking down firmly. I hissed out a breath as she leaned forward to place a kiss on my chest and flick her tongue over one nipple, then the other, scraping her teeth against my sensitive flesh until I was bucking into her hand.

I leaned back, propping one hand on the bed and using the other to knead her full breast, pinching the nipple until it was stiff, tight, and begging for my tongue. Her hand continued to pump my cock, slick with her wetness even as she slipped off my lap, pressing kisses to my chest, my abs until I felt her breath hovering over my cock and looked down to see her licking her lips.

Holding me by the base, she rose on her knees as I spread my legs wide and reached out to grasp a handful of her hair. She positioned her mouth over my straining cock and sucked in the tip, hard enough for my hips to thrust off the bed and my hand to fist harder in her hair. I was lost in the feeling of her warm mouth sucking me, her soft fingers wrapped around the base, and her heavy tits brushing against my legs as she worked me in and out of her wet mouth.

"Fuck," I groaned as she swirled her tongue around the head, lapping, sucking, and making me dizzy with need.

Everything turned me on. Every sound, every sensation, bringing me closer and closer to the point of no return. The point of coming down her hot throat and missing the feeling of her pussy gripping my cock. This was not how I was going to come. I wanted inside her.

I needed inside her.

I pulled her hair and forced her to look up at me, and she did, grinning with hooded eyes.

"I want your pussy," I said. "I need to come in it, claim it. To feel you grip me so I can make up for all the time I wasn't there."

Her eyes widened, but she didn't have time to respond because I stood up and grabbed her, tossing her on the bed and loving the sight of her tits bouncing. She giggled and scooted back on the pillows, spreading her legs and beckoning me closer with a crook of her finger. I gripped my cock and gave it a few languid strokes before kneeling on the mattress and staring at her glistening pussy, counting the seconds until I was balls deep inside.

Her hands smoothed over her tits and trailed down her stomach, but I crawled between her legs and batted her hand away, leaning down to lick her belly button.

"Tell me you want this. Tell me you're ready for me, baby."

"I'm so ready, Mark," she said, wrapping her legs around mine to pull me down closer. "Please. Show me what I've missed."

I didn't need to hear anything else. I leaned closer and notched myself at her entrance, already feeling her heat waiting to suck me in. Her heels dug into my ass as I slowly inched my way in. When the head was in, she sighed. When I was halfway in, she closed her eyes, and when I was all the way in, she smiled.

"So fucking good, Mark," she moaned, opening her eyes and pulling me down for a kiss. After tasting her lips, I broke away from her mouth to bend my head lower, taking one nipple in my mouth and sucking until it came to a point. I nibbled on it, licking and sucking while she moaned underneath me, urging me on, living in the moment of complete pleasure. After a few seconds, she threaded her fingers through my hair and brought her lips to mine, kissing me unlike she had ever kissed me before.

It was full of love, passion, and want, but on a deeper level than anything we'd experienced. After knowing my deepest insecurities, she not only accepted me exactly like I was, she showed me she wanted me for the man I am.

It was in the way her arms wrapped around my neck and the way her hand weaved into my hair. The way her legs were around mine, urging me forward, holding me close. And I knew what I felt—I never wanted to be apart from her again.

So I rocked into her, showing her exactly that.

I kept my mouth on hers, licking her lips, sucking her tongue, owning her lips, and fucking kissing her for all I was worth. My hips fell into a slow, lazy pattern, feeling every sensation as her pussy gripped my cock. It was then I realized we weren't fucking. There was no urgency, no rush for us to finish or chase our orgasms. Instead, we were making love, connecting on a deeper level, feeling more with each other. And I fucking loved it. We were letting ourselves feel more than just fucking. We were becoming one, searing our souls together.

"I love your mouth," I said, breaking away from her lips to pepper kisses along her jaw and neck.

"I love yours more," she answered, tilting her head to give me better access to her glistening skin. She gave my hair a sharp yank, drawing my lips back to hers and thrusting her tongue in my mouth. I lifted one of her hands above her head, pinning it in place, and reached between us to squeeze her breast. She exhaled my name and propped her legs on the mattress, giving me a deeper angle.

"Fuck, Mark. Just like that."

I squeezed harder, moving my hand to pinch her nipple and threading my fingers into the hand pinned above her head.

"Yes, baby. Tell me what you need. What you want."

"You, Mark. I need you," she whispered, squeezing her thighs against me as I palmed her tit harder.

"Make me come on your cock, Mark. I've missed this, you. Please show me, let me feel you. All of you."

She moved her hips, and I let go of her breast, grabbing her other hand and pinning both above her head. My hips took over like they had a mind of their own as her panting grew shorter and her moans got louder. Her fingers dug into mine, and I leaned down, biting her neck, sucking her tits, licking along the length of her collarbone.

She opened her mouth, but nothing came out, and I pushed harder, deeper inside of her.

"Fuck, again. More, Mark."

I wanted to slow down, make it last, prolong our pleasure, but my hips had a mind of their own. They followed the signals of the writhing, sexy woman pinned beneath me. I moved my lips back to her tits and, with one last hard thrust, I sucked her nipple into my mouth. Her back arched off the bed, and I felt her pussy contract around my cock. I let go and threw my head back as I bit my lip so hard I tasted blood.

Fuck, she's tight.

My hips pounded at an ungodly pace, thrust after thrust, plunging into her.

"Yes. Yes, Mark. Fuck, Mark, I'm coming," she yelled as her pussy squeezed my cock so hard my vision turned black, and I saw nothing but spots. All I felt was her. Her tight pussy made my balls pulse with white-hot pleasure, and my cock erupted as I came violently inside her.

I held her close, pressing my chest to her, drawing out our orgasms and every drop of pleasure until there was nothing left but quivering muscles, shaking breaths, and my cock, completely satisfied inside of her.

"Holy fuck," I muttered, letting go of her hands and wrapping my arms around her before collapsing. I immediately sat up and tried to prop up my arms, so I didn't squish her, but she pulled me back down, pressing my weight on top of her.

Her hands slowly traced up and down my back, nails lightly scratching my skin as she let out breathy little moans. I buried my face in her neck, breathing her in and pressing small kisses to her scorching skin.

"That... hell, Mark. That was everything," she said, wrapping her arms tightly around me.

"You're everything."

I pushed myself off her and leaned down for a kiss before rolling to the side. My spent cock slipped out, and I ached at the loss, but she leaned forward and pressed a soft kiss to my lips. Her kiss made me feel like I could finally breathe for the first time since I left her. Like she was breathing life back into me.

I stood up and made my way to the bathroom, switching on the light and running a washcloth under the faucet. I glanced at my reflection. I saw dark circles under my eyes, but I also saw red scratches on my biceps and a grin that wouldn't disappear.

It was her.

It had always been her.

I walked back from the bathroom, holding the warm washcloth for Jenna and taking my time cleaning her before tossing the washcloth back toward the bathroom.

"I'm going to need to take you again real soon. But lay with me for a little while, first. I want to hear all about the clinic and tell you about a room in the house you're going to love."

"I'd like that," she answered, turning around to wrap her arms around my neck and plant a wet kiss on my lips.

Then she smiled, and it made her eyes twinkle like a thousand stars in the sky. The smile sealed the deal. The smile was everything. She was everything. And I wanted to kiss that smile and those lips every day for the rest of my life. Even on days we fought, I wanted to kiss that smile.

We weren't perfect, but we were perfect for each other and better together.

She was everything I'd ever wanted, and she was worth the wait.

"I'm going to love you forever, Dr. Cutie."

"Not if I love you forever first, Officer Handsome."

The End

EPILOGUE

Jenna

"Come on, babe. Do we have to do this?" Mark asked, squaring his stance and crossing his corded forearms across his chest. His tattoos danced as he flexed, and I bit my lip, watching his muscles ripple, a tingle building in my core. His eyes turned molten as they focused on my lips, and he spread his legs further apart.

God, he knew what seeing him standing there like that did to me—all alpha and unyielding. I loved his voice, his hands, his jaw muscles. I even loved the crease he got in the middle of his forehead when he concentrated. It all turned me into a puddle of desperate need. I padded forward on bare feet and dragged my nails up his bare chest and over his caramel-colored nipples before threading them through him his hair.

A low rumble started in his chest as he leaned into my touch and ran his nose along my collarbone. My back hit the cool granite island in our kitchen, but it did nothing to squelch the heat of my skin as his fingers ran down my arms and lovingly caressed my swelling stomach.

"Please, baby. Let me take you upstairs and erase that needy look in your eyes with my tongue."

My body hummed with desire as I trailed my hand back down his chest and to the waistband of his briefs, running my fingers over his rapidly hardening cock.

"You know we can't. Hmm…but we are the guests of honor." The rumble in his throat turned to a full-throated growl as he bit down on the sensitive spot where my neck met my shoulder, then soothed the sting with his tongue. "And I wouldn't be opposed to arriving fashionably late."

Achy, desperate moans escaped my lips, and he took over, knowing exactly what my body craved.

"Good. Where would you like to come first?" he asked, pulling off my T-shirt and leaning down to take one nipple in his mouth. He sucked hard, knowing how sensitive they were, and rested one hand protectively on my enormous baby bump. His tongue licked and nibbled over my trembling flesh, and I fisted his hair, holding him to me and arching my chest, so there wasn't a millimeter of space between us.

"Shower." I sighed, grinding my hips to the enormous bulge protruding from his gray sweatpants. Seeing water droplets cling to his thick, blonde hair as he wrung pleasure from my body while we stood under the hot shower spray had become my new favorite place to come.

He tilted his head and let go of my nipple, licking up between my breasts to take my lips in a possessive kiss. When he pulled away, and I was breathless and panting, his lips pulled up in the corners, and he grinned, scooping me up and carrying me to the bathroom.

സ

"We're only thirty minutes late," he said, pulling into the large parking lot on the far side of my mother-in-law's townhouse. "How are you feeling? And what do you think they have planned?"

He unbuttoned the second button on his green shirt and rubbed his clean-shaved neck before threading his fingers with mine.

"Ugh, my hands are swollen. And I have no idea how I feel, to be honest. I'm still trying to wrap my head around the idea that your brothers

304

are throwing us a gender reveal party."

"Yeah, me to babe," he said, locking the Tahoe and glancing around the open space.

A breeze lifted my hair, and I smelled the chlorine from the pool and the flowering bushes along the walkway leading toward the clubhouse. It reminded me of summers spent lounging in the sun without a care in the world. I rubbed my belly, smiling at all the ways my life had changed. My wedding ring hung from a long chain around my neck because my fingers had swollen to the size of Vienna sausages, but it didn't matter. The man beside me unconditionally loved my swollen fingers and toes, and I loved him right back.

We walked past the clubhouse on stilts surrounded by palm trees with comfy tables and chairs underneath and headed toward the Olympic-sized pool. Why this party had to be outside instead of in the cool air conditioning was beyond me, but the girls assured me Mark's brothers went all out. I knew it was too much to hope for that there'd be a relaxing recliner and two burly men standing by to feed me grapes and fan me with palm fronds, but a girl could dream.

"What are you thinking about, Dr. Cutie?" Mark asked, squeezing my hand as he led me through a wrought-iron fence with Hawaiian garland strung through it. I touched the flowers and smiled, wondering if his brothers had decided on a Luau theme. Maybe the palm fronds weren't as far off as I had hoped.

The hard concrete of the pool entrance made my feet throb, so I stopped, looked up at Mark, then glanced down, barely able to see my toes.

"Getting out of these shoes and a mocktail."

"Say no more."

Mark tugged me to him then scooped me up like I didn't have a watermelon-sized belly, striding through the covered patio and back into the bright sun where we were greeted by a sea of our friends, family, and every flower within a ten-mile radius. There were catcalls and clapping, whistles and cheers, but I buried my face into Mark's shirt, embarrassed that he picked me up without so much as breaking a sweat.

He nudged me with his shoulder, then leaned down so I could feel his breath on my neck. "Just think, Dr. Cutie. In a few short minutes, we'll know if our baby is a boy or a girl."

"Tell me the truth. What are you hoping for?" I asked as he carried me to the center of the group next to our parents and placed me gently on my feet. He winked but didn't answer, leaning down to kiss his mother on the cheek before reaching out to shake hands with one of his friends on the force.

"Oh, honey! You look beautiful," my mother said, swooping in to grasp both my hands in hers. I glanced down at my yellow maxi dress with spaghetti straps and shrugged my shoulders as she led me to a cushy chair and put a fruity drink with a bendy-straw and pink umbrella in my hand.

"I'll get you something to snack on."

I looked to my left to see Olivia nursing her new baby, Hope. "You do. You're glowing." I leaned over, peeking at her full head of dark hair and adorable button nose. It was hard to believe in a few short months that would be me.

"Do you have any idea what the guys planned?"

"Wait till you see," Annaleigh said, walking around to pull up a chair beside me. "I mean, I know we're all in relationships, but there is a lot of eye candy heading our way."

"Tell me about it," Addison said, looking over at Simon and giving him a sly wink. "Good thing I'm with the best-looking guy here."

Simon shook his head and sat down, pulling Addison on his lap with a grin. It was surreal as I looked around, taking in all my friends and family here to celebrate with us. My eyes were getting misty, and my hand trembled as my mom pushed a plate of fruit in my hands. Looking up, I saw Mark making a beeline for me. He knew my emotions were all over the place, but before he made it to my side, cheers and whistling echoed around the pool.

I braced myself on the chair, and Mark made it over to help me up, pulling me tightly against him.

"Wait till you see them. Come on," he said, leading me to the pool. The girls followed as I saw what was causing the ruckus. I laughed so hard I had to cross my legs and put my hands on my side.

Mark's brothers were standing by the pool in bright swim trunks. Miller wore hot pink, Magnum electric blue, and Maverick purple. They were stretching, flexing, and showing off miles of tan muscles. Addison was right. All kinds of yummy man candy definitely surrounded us.

"Will the guests of honor please step to the finish line as we prepare to race?"

We walked to one end of the pool and underneath pink and blue flags, and the brothers lined up on the other side.

"Okay. I get the boy and the girl colors, but what's with the purple?"

"Twins," Bev said, stepping up beside me.

"What? Twins don't run in our family!"

"They do in ours," Bev said with a grin, patting my arm before turning to her neighbor.

"Twins? There could be two in here?" I said, yanking on Mark's shirt until he looked down at me. I pressed a hand to my stomach, my abnormally large stomach. As my dad held up his hands, the cheers died down.

It couldn't be twins. The doctor would have for sure said something, right? There was no way an entire baby could be kept secret.

But I was huge, I thought, rubbing my stomach.

"Easy, baby. The doctor would have told us if there were twins."

I looked at Mark, focusing on the soft laugh-lines around his eyes and the hard plains of muscles pressed to my side. "Three brothers, three options."

He shrugged his shoulders, and I tried to take comfort in his confidence and not let my mind unravel in a million different directions. A particularly clear image of me holding triplets flashed before my eyes, and my mouth was opened in a half-strangled cry when my dad's voice cut through the panic.

"When I blow the whistle, the race begins. The winner will reveal the baby's gender, and the celebration can begin!"

Whoops and cries filled the air, and my heart rate sped up as the brothers stepped to the edge of the pool. Mark put his hand over mine on my belly and chuckled. I felt the rumble in his chest, and he pulled me closer, leaning down to whisper. "Don't worry. There is one perfectly healthy baby in your belly. Relax and watch the idiots make a fool of themselves."

He pressed his lips to my temple as the shrill whistle filled the air. Maverick dove in the pool like an Olympian, his arms cutting through the water as he took an early lead. Not to be outdone, Miller cannon-balled and swam after him, catching up easily to match him stroke for stroke. Magnum belly-flopped in the water, flailing around before getting his bearings and darting after them.

I saw flashes of blue, pink, and purple as I followed them across the pool. As Miller took the lead, Magnum wrapped his arms around his shoulders and pushed him under, earning him the smallest advantage. But it didn't last long because Maverick grabbed his leg and pulled him back, taking the lead.

The purple trunks moved closer to the finish line, and my mind went in a million different directions. Dark eyes and blonde hair. Cupid-bow lips and dimples. I hardly heard the cheers as a flash of neon darted past the finish line and pulled himself out of the water, proudly displaying his swim trunks.

It wasn't purple!

Eyes glistening, I shook my head, clearing the ridiculous idea of twins or triplets as streamers released and confetti rained down, sticking to our clothes, hair, and anyone standing within a five-foot radius.

I looked at Mark, and his eyes were misty as he swiped his finger across my cheek to catch the stray tear.

"It's a girl. We're having a girl."

I put my hand over my mouth and watched the last of the confetti fall to the ground.

"This is it, Dr. Cutie. You, me, and a baby girl make three."

The party shrank down to the two of us as he brushed his lips to mine, rubbing slow circles on my belly.

"You know it, Officer Handsome. But from now on, I think a new name is in order."

"Oh, and what's that?" he asked, rubbing his nose along my neck.

I tugged on his collar and brought his lips down to mine one more time as our friends and family surrounded us, shouting congratulations.

"Daddy."

BY YOUR SIDE

DID YOU LOVE THIS BOOK?

Thank you for reading *By Your Side*!

I hope you loved Mark and Jenna's story as much as I loved writing it.

Did you know there are so many ways you can support an author without spending a penny?

One of the best ways to support an author is to leave a review. So, if you enjoyed this book, please consider leaving a review on Amazon, Goodreads, and any other book-related sites like BookBub and BookSprout. Your feedback is essential to Indie Authors like me and will help other readers decide whether or not to read this book. You can also follow your favorite authors on social media, post about their books online, and tell your friends.

If you'd like to get notifications of new releases and special offers, please join my email list by going to https://www.katlongromance.com.

BY YOUR SIDE

ACKNOWLEDGEMENTS

Gosh, what a ride! (No pun intended) There are several people I'd like to thank for helping Mark and Jenna find their Happily Ever After.

For my amazing, beautiful, unicorn, essential Crit Chick: It's hard to find words to express my gratitude. Scratch that. There aren't enough words to tell you how much you've helped me on my writing journey, from critiquing to venting and everything in between. I couldn't have done this without you, and I am so incredibly grateful to have each one of you in my life. Thank you, Amy, Jamie, Jenni, Kimberly, Monique, Raliegh, and Sofia. You ladies are badass authors, and I can't wait to see what 2022 holds for us.

For Becky: Thank you for laughing with me, supporting me, and crying with me. As always, your edits are on point. Thank you for helping me make this book the best it could be. You are my person, and I am so grateful we found each other.

For Arielle: My GIF talking editor, who knows the art of crafting one heck of a scene. I truly appreciate the time you spent with me.

For Kris: A million thanks you for creating another perfect cover and for being patient with my million questions, thousand edits, and quick timeline. I promise to get my life together for Addison's book.

For Tante Steph: Thank you for taking the time to check over my work. Your attention to detail is fantastic. I love you!

For my husband, sister, aunt, parents, and every other family and friend that supported me throughout this book, thank you. Sending all the love your way!

BY YOUR SIDE

ABOUT THE AUTHOR

Kat lives at the beach with her Happily Ever After, a daughter, and two irritating but lovable cats.

Before she started writing contemporary romance, she graduated with a Master's Degree in School Psychology. By day, she works in finance, and by night she writes.

Books have always made her heart beat faster, and she started writing her first book after dreaming up an Alpha-Marshmallow.

Her characters are sexy and fearless, but in real life, Kat's the ultimate over-thinker. Let's face it, her inner monologues would not make good reading.

She flips for a good romance and gets giddy anytime there's HEAT!

When she's not reading or writing sexy stories, she's probably watching Animal Planet in yoga pants, trying not to over-water her succulents, drinking too much coffee, and wondering if the real meaning of life is forty-two.

Readers make her world go round!
Keep in touch with Kat Via the Web:

https://linktr.ee/KatLongRomance

HAD TO MAKE YOU MINE

NEED MORE MAX & ANNA?

Read on for a sneak-peek from Book One in the Southern Charms Series:
<u>Had To Make You Mine</u>

I snapped my eyes open with a start, not realizing I had dozed while on the beach. *Rush* softly played in the background as I dug my toes into the gritty sand and hummed along. The weather was a balmy eighty degrees, and the reason I fell asleep in the first place. The sun had reminded me of the stage lights from six; no, seven years ago.

Lyrics drifted around my mind, something about blue skies, bright lights, and memories. But before I had time to jot them down, they flew away, like the seagulls screeching by. That was my new norm. The lyrics that came like second nature were now almost nonexistent. Maybe time didn't heal everything.

Baxter, my boxer, hogged more space underneath the umbrella than me and was doing his best to stay far away from Jenna, who had been my friend since middle school. We had braces at the same time, sang in the same choir, and lived in the same neighborhood.

We spent at least one Saturday a month with our other two friends, and the beach was the perfect choice for today. I smiled at the cover of my romance book before grabbing a beer from the cooler behind me and looking at the four of us. We affectionately called ourselves the *Southern Charms*. I voted for *Bourbon Babes*, but the girls vetoed it, and *Southern*

Charms stuck. The beach, my girls, a book, and a beer, nothing could be better.

"Your crazy dog still hasn't forgiven me, Annaleigh," Jenna said, while tentatively sticking out her hand for him to sniff. Baxter looked up with his big brown eyes and scooted closer to me before laying his head back on his blue beach towel.

"You know, Jenna, you wouldn't be my favorite person either if the last time I saw you, I got two shots, and something stuck up my butt," I said with a smirk.

Jenna smiled and stood up to stretch before she motioned for us to do the same. "Let's go cool off before we all turn into lobsters. The sun is killer today."

I gave a half shrug and stood, stretching my legs and bookmarking my page. The sand wasn't scorching like it would have been in the middle of summer, but we still took our time heading to the shoreline and splashing in.

The water felt amazing as I swam up to my waist before laying back and looking at the clouds drifting across the sky. Jenna and Olivia floated beside me while Addison dragged her chair behind us and sat in one inch of water, keeping an eye out for an elusive shark she was sure was lurking just beneath the surface. I mean, we were more likely to get struck by lightning than attacked by a shark, but to each her own. I believed in signs from the Universe, and Addison believed *Jaws* would attack her in four feet of water.

"I have a new recipe I want y'all to try," Olivia said, dunking her head under the water and coming up with a grin. "It's a lavender scone with tart, lemon glaze."

"Um. That sounds…" I said, trying to find a friendly way to say that sounded gross.

"Weird? I know, but I think it works."

"Hmm. Lemons are toxic to animals," Jenna said. "But I wonder if it would help remove the stick from Dr. Duvall's ass. I'll bring a dozen to my clinic to see. If not, it's his loss, and the pet parents will love them. And I'm sure Addison will take a dozen since she has three open houses this week."

"And I'll bring a dozen to the bank. The new Senior Vice President starts Monday, so all the board members will be there."

"Oh! That's right, Annaleigh. You're getting a new boss," Olivia said, floating closer.

"Yeah. He nailed the interviews and impressed Jake. He should be a good fit. I'm working to get him up and running by the time we have the conference in Tennessee and the Whiskey Gala next weekend."

We let the tide carry us a little longer, then settled back underneath the large umbrellas. I closed my eyes for a second before I dove back into my book and allowed my mind to drift, trying not to think about the fifty things I still needed to get done this weekend.

Opening my eyes with a sigh, I popped an orange slice in my mouth. It should help to keep my exhaustion away. Thank goodness no one had mentioned relationships. Even though Olivia was the only one married, Addison was in a relationship, and Jenna was at least dating. The girls always harped on my lack of a dating life. It's not that I wasn't interested in dating, but I hadn't felt a connection with anyone, and the dating scene was a joke. With the new social media meetups and the men who didn't match their perfect profiles, I was ready for a break.

"Hey, Annaleigh, how was your date the other week?" Addison said, opening another beer.

Oh, Universe, you saucy bitch.

"Nothing worth talking about. The guy was a pervert."

"What happened?" Addison said, peering over her sunglasses and looking concerned. "Did you give him a chance?"

"Uh, yes. We met at the restaurant, and before the drinks even came, he showed me one of his body-mods and asked if I was ready to leave for a private demonstration."

I tried to give him a chance, I did. After going on dates with corporate types, I thought the fun guy with all the tattoos I met at the grocery store would be a nice change. *Nope.* Maybe I had a sign on my back that said, "Desperate."

"His what now?" Olivia closed her book and leaned forward, listening.

"Body-Modification. The guy had a forked tongue and told me he had a Prince Albert before asking if I wanted a private showing."

"Oh my god, I remember him now—Body-Mod Todd!" Olivia said, wagging her tongue at us.

"Damn, props to him for being bold. I wonder how that tongue would have felt between your legs. And I'll bet his cock piercing would have hit all kinds of special spots," Addison said, wiggling her eyebrows and making Olivia almost spit out her drink.

"I just can't believe I didn't notice the tongue sooner," I said, shaking my head.

"But seriously, babe," Addison said. "I know you've had some doozies, but the right guy is out there. I just know it. One day, he is going to walk into your life, take one look at your big green eyes and banging body, and fall head-over-heels in love with you. He'll wonder how his life was ever complete without you in it, and he'll spend his nights giving you orgasms and his days making you smile. And when you find him, you'll know, you'll let him in, let him love you."

Addison held her drink up, and we all clinked the cans together. "To Happily Ever After, and guys with big dicks."

We all took a sip and laughed at Addison's crass comment.

"I'm taking a break from dating. I'm going to focus on work, the bar, and self-care."

"Whatever you say, lady. We should all take a trip downtown to the self-care store."

"You finally going to buy that sex-swing?" I poked at Addison, tossing her the sunscreen with a wink.

"Doubt it. Poor Tommy is so strait-laced, I'd send the poor man running for the hills!" Addison shook her head with a smile, rubbing more sunscreen on.

Opening my book back up, I knew I'd made the right decision. I needed to take a break and put dating on the backburner. It would be enough. It had to be enough.

After I reapplied sunscreen and opened a second beer, I'd started a sexy-time chapter in my romance book when Olivia whispered, "Holy wow, ladies, look what's headed our way."

I peeked over my sunglasses and watched a gorgeous male specimen jog towards us on the shoreline. With the way he was running, he could star on *Baywatch*, just without the trademark red shorts. I must be delirious with heat-stroke because I swear the shoreline shimmered around him like he was nothing but a mirage, and there to remind me that my life was severely lacking in the love department.

This guy was easily two hundred and some odd pounds of drool-worthy muscles, and I swiped my hand over my mouth for said drool, just in case. He was one of the sexiest men I'd ever seen, and I shamelessly watched as he stopped in front of us and took deep breaths. Each time his chest expanded, it showcased his broad shoulders. His dark hair and sharp jawline did all kinds of things to my under-used nether regions. As if he knew I had borderline pornographic thoughts about his chest, he looked at the four of us and waved one hand in greeting.

"Need a bottle of water?" Olivia called as she reached into the cooler behind us.

He nodded, and Olivia tossed the bottle to me with a wink before she sat back down. A normal person would have caught the bottle and handed it to him with a sexy hello, but I caught the bottle with both hands and a squeak and held it to my chest like a football. I hope he didn't mind water with a side of boob sweat and sunscreen.

Smooth move, Annaleigh.

He stalked closer like a man with a purpose and pushed his sunglasses up to reveal his eyes. They were the color of a smooth glass of bourbon. I stood up with more confidence than I felt, and those eyes stayed on me. When he reached out for the water bottle, not fazed by the possible exposure to boob sweat, his large hand engulfed mine, and he didn't let go.

Neither did I.

Lightning sizzled past my fingertips and lit up my body like a Christmas tree. Never have I had that kind of reaction to a touch. The way his hand fit over mine had to be a sign from the Universe saying it was time to go on a date or renew my membership to the toy of the month club.

As if it was no big deal, I wanted to climb him like a spider monkey, he let go of my hand, cracked the seal on the bottle, and drank. He finished the entire bottle and let the last few swallows spill out of his mouth and down his chest. I nervously shifted from foot to foot, mesmerized by the beads of water.

Seriously, now was the time to use words, any words. I opened my mouth to say something that would make him see me as the saucy vixen I was, but Baxter hip-checked me, and I stumbled forward and face-planted into his rock-hard chest covered with a light dusting of dark hair.

Gah, I freaking loved chest hair!

He dropped the water bottle and steadied me, putting those large hands on my shoulders. I felt it again, the spark when he touched me, and those bourbon eyes flashed as if he felt it too.

"Easy there, Blue," he said with a deep voice and a hint of an accent before stepping back to take in my blue bikini and sunglasses.

"Come on, Baxter," Addison said as she stood up and grabbed his leash. "Let's take a walk and let these two get to know each other."

She winked and walked away. Baxter was already partially dragging her toward several sandpipers hopping through the seafoam.

I bent down and grabbed the empty water bottle, tossing it on my beach chair with a smile. He smiled back, revealing straight white teeth, honest to god dimples, and small laugh lines.

"I'm Annaleigh."

There was no way to redeem myself for having a two-word vocabulary, so I went with it, pretending that running into beautiful strangers on the beach was my norm. We still stood close, close enough for me to see the flecks of gold in his eyes. He dialed the smile back to a smirk and reached out to shake my hand.

"Nice to meet you, Annaleigh. I'm new to the area."

The way my name rolled off his tongue, with his midwestern accent, made me think of the other seductive, tantalizing things he could do with that appendage. It also reminded me that I was going home to an empty townhouse with a judgmental boxer.

"What brought you to Charleston? New job? Parents? Girlfriend?"

So much for my two-word vocabulary.

Why did I say, girlfriend? I could have said, what brought you to the beach or offered to lick the sweat off his six-pack, or even offered him a freaking orange slice. It was like desperation oozed off me. Usually, I was calmer and much more collected, but orbiting around that level of manliness had me tongue-tied.

"You ask a lot of questions, Blue."

Blue? He said that before, and it sounded even sexier than my name.

"And you avoid answers like it's your job." I bit my lip and reached down for my beer, taking a long pull, hoping it would break the tension.

"Yeah, it's my only redeeming quality." He rubbed the back of his neck and stepped closer. "I accepted a job and moved here last week." His eyes dropped to my mouth while I struggled to keep the calm and collected facade going.

"You should join us tonight," Jenna said, glancing up from her book. "We're heading to *B's Bar* later on this evening to listen to some local bands and do karaoke."

"Do you sing karaoke, Blue," he said, without a glance to Jenna.

"Sometimes, but it involves copious amounts of liquor and bad decisions."

"Hmm." His smile was back, showing one glorious dimple that was so deep I could've moved into it and lived there happily ever after. "Do I look like a bad decision to you?"

I sighed, "Yes," and took another drink, praying he didn't hear.

I was suddenly aware of the uncomfortable amount of sticky, under-boob sweat my body was producing. Ugh, to be one of those girls that looked dewy when they sweat. I looked straight up like a half-melted popsicle on a hot cement sidewalk.

"Thought so, Blue. Thanks for the offer, ladies, but I have plans later." He lowered his eyes to mine and dropped them down. I felt exposed, as if he could see straight through me.

"Plus," he added in a whisper only meant for me, "I'm not looking for a casual fuck."

What the hell?

He put his sunglasses back on and jogged away, leaving me open-mouthed and staring.

I dropped to my chair to get my heart rate under control while Olivia handed me a fresh beer, ice-cold and already opened.

"What just happened?" I took a drink and looked down at Baxter. He looked back as if to say, "what do you expect when you get too close to that amount of sexiness wrapped up in trainers and board shorts?"

Baxter was *a boss* at silently judging my life choices.

"Tell us again, Annaleigh, how you want to take a break from dating?" Olivia said with a smile. "One minute, you were eye-fucking each other, and the next, your cheeks turned purple, and he jogged away."

Jenna shook her head and filled up Baxter's water dish, then stood up and looked up at the clouds that were getting darker.

"See, you just need to meet a guy like him, one that leaves you speechless. Minus the asshole personality."

Baxter took a tentative sniff of the water before lapping some and adjusting his position to keep Jenna in his line of sight.

"No thanks, Jenna. I'm pretty sure I just solidified why I'm done with casual dating, no matter how tongue-tied I was around that man. We can't just invite a guy to a bar without him thinking I was looking for a hook-up. All Sexy McGrumpy did was remind me that not only has it been way too long since I got some, but my flirting skills are about as under-used as my lady parts."

Addison snorted and shook her head before standing up and grabbing her pullover. "Sexy McGrumpy? No, that's not right. He's more like Grumpy McHotness. I mean, those shorts left little to the imagination. Even though he had the personality of a wet cat, my bikini bottoms got a little damp watching him move."

"Nope. Both of you are wrong. Clearly, tall, tan, and muscles should be known henceforth as Muscles McTightass. With the way you bounced off his chest, Annaleigh, that man is all kinds of sexy."

"Wait! I amend my response!" Addison said, jumping up and pointing her finger in the air in typical, dramatic Addison fashion.

"Amend? Really, Addison."

"Shut up, Olivia. Yes, amend. He was giving off all kinds of BDE."

"BDE?" I said, standing up and brushing myself off. I gave up after a minute, knowing I'd be washing sand out of all my lady-bits for days.

"Yeah, you know, BDE. Big-Dick Energy. My vote is for Broody Big-Dick."

"Ugh, Ladies. As we rehash and analyze this thirty-second conversation over the next few weeks, the obvious choice is Broody McAsshole, but the second runner-up is Broody Big-Dick," Jenna said as she finished her water and packed up.

"Okay, motion passed," Addison said. "Henceforth, the *Southern Charms* will only refer to big-dick beach guy as Broody McAsshole. But, either way, his loss, Annaleigh. Let's head out before those clouds get darker. I want to shower and change before we head to *B's*. And I want to try Tommy again. He hasn't picked up the last few times I've called."

"Everything okay with you two?" I dumped out the rest of Baxter's water and stuffed it in my bag. Addison avoided my eyes and focused on folding her towel. I could see how tense she looked and had a feeling she and Tommy were not on the same page anymore.

"I think so. He's been hot and cold lately, but his new job is causing him all kinds of stress."

"Okay babe," Olivia said. "Keep us updated. Let's get back and ready for *B's*."

We packed our beach gear and piled into Jenna's soft top jeep.

The wind whipped through my hair, loosening the braid, and I tried to stop my thoughts from going back to those bourbon eyes.

Made in United States
North Haven, CT
28 December 2021

13794788R00195